Reaching for September

- Stories -

Paul Newlin

Reaching for September

Copyright © 2013 Paul Newlin

ISBN: 978-1-940244-02-0

A version of Brownie Fine and the Thrashing Ring appeared in *North Atlantic Review, No. 2, Summer 1990*

cover design by
JOSH NEWLIN

Printed in the United States of America

For Sue
Partner in life, love, and the pursuit of the perfect sunset.

CONTENTS

NO HARM NO FOUL

Ralph arrived home in Maine when he came back with Linda from Manhattan that January. Ralph is a standard-bred poodle whose pedigreed name is Ralph Vonderbrink II, and Linda said Ralph was to be pronounced Rafe, the way Ralph Vaughan Williams, the composer, and Ralph Fiennes, the actor, are called Rafe. He arrived with a pom-pom poodle cut, and Linda's husband Larry said he would never call a dog Rafe whose name is spelled r-a-l-p-h and "who looked like an overgrown goddamned freak circus animal."

Ralph had belonged to Linda's old college roommate Joyce Pollard, thrice divorced and perpetually in some kind of litigation, and who now lived off the remains of three different divorce settlements and a meager salary as an editorial assistant for a textbook publisher. For thirty years she had maintained an Upper-West-Side address, and by shopping husbands and discount stores, and maxing credit cards, she affected the chic lifestyle she imagined was validated by stylish though moderately priced apartment furnishings and overbred dogs.

Ralph was Joyce's fourth dog of this decade. His immediate predecessor was Claude, a whippet that Joyce shipped to the North Shore Animal Shelter because she said she couldn't give him the exercise his breed demanded; but the real reason was that people's comments about the dog looking anorexic scraped nerves made sensitive to sly comments about her own thread-like body. The excuse for getting rid of Ralph was that the demands of her job kept her from spending the time with him that his sensitive personality required. The truth was she couldn't afford the cost of keeping him trimmed and she was tired of walking him even though she judged the smiling glances cast their way to be those of admiration rather than ridicule for the poor beast's humiliating haircut. So, Linda brought him home to Maine where he could get all the attention and exercise Joyce and Linda claimed he needed

Of course the reasoning of both women was self-serving: Joyce wanted to get rid of the dog, and Linda wanted to give Larry a companion while she went off to the Peace Corps, announcing her intention of doing just that with her presentation of Ralph.

Larry was surprised by getting an unsolicited dog, but he long ago had ceased to be surprised by Linda's search for, as she always put it, "meaning for my life," with the Peace Corps being but the latest manifestation of her quest. Their marriage had been filled with projects she managed to pursue around two boy babies, now adults, and a sullen tolerance for the confining nature of Larry's teaching career—a career that was undistinguished, underpaid, and unexciting but had some saving grace in Linda's eyes in that it allowed them summers in her inherited summer cottage in Maine. When Larry took an early retirement buyout, it sparked Linda's enthusiasm for yet another new life. They winterized the Maine cottage and moved full time to familiar coastal summer surroundings.

They both always had loved the place, and the move gave them a fresh view of the future. Larry embraced the change and soon fell in love with genealogical software and endless computer searches backward into both of their families' lineages. But for Linda, her new life in Maine was no happier than her earlier "lives" had been. After short bursts of enthusiasm for identifying forest plants, organic farming, shamanic drumming, and political-action work for the Green Party, she began having trouble sleeping. She spent whole days in her pajamas and bathrobe and often voiced such strident disappointment in the impersonal nature of their paltry email that Larry, in exasperation, said, "For God's sake, get a pen pal or start a chain letter or surf the net."

"Surf the net? Terrific idea!" was her disgusted response, which she followed with, "Search the net? How could I? You're forever tracing some bricklayer back to Wales or some absurd place." Larry's suggestion that they should get her a computer of her own was dismissed with a wave of her hand.

She would call Joyce late at night, but from what Larry could overhear, Joyce was irritated by the late calls and Linda had little but boredom to justify her phoning. In an apparent effort to stop the calls, Joyce had invited Linda to Manhattan, making it clear that she could not expect to be entertained or even fed. Linda started buying the Sunday *Times* and spending hours pouring over the Entertainment section. One Sunday she read a profile of a woman filmmaker who had done a documentary on clitoral circumcision in Africa, and she used Larry's computer for email correspondence with the filmmaker. Hoping to meet her, Linda left right after New Year's for a week's stay with Joyce in New York.

She never did meet the filmmaker, but she did return to Maine committed to the Peace Corps and left in late April for training to teach English as a second language in Southeast Asia.

Linda's time with Larry before she left for language training was tense for them both, but especially for Larry. Linda was solicitous of Larry, which added to the strangeness of their relationship since she never had been particularly sensitive to his needs in the past. She gave the impression that she assumed he was in agreement with her decision to go off for two years when in fact she never had mentioned the idea until she announced that she'd signed up. And she spoke in terms of "When I get back we'll do this," or "We'll make plans to visit there"—all abstractions for a vague future but one that nevertheless emphasized his inclusion.

She further had the good sense not once to couch her Peace Corps enlistment as the means for fulfilling her life. The last time she used that expression, Larry had said in mock surprise, "But I thought I fulfilled your life!" She had been startled by his response and, running her fingers through her hair, which she did whenever searching for something to say, she coquettishly had answered, "Well of course you do," and then added "but…you know what I mean—fulfilled in the sense of making my very own contribution to the world."

As a concession to Larry, Linda gave up calling Ralph Rafe. Larry never had called him Rafe, and after a day or two the dog responded to either name. She made much of the closeness that Larry and Ralph quickly established and never missed the opportunity to say, "Oh, will you two guys have a great time when you have the place to yourselves. You can do just as you please—be big slobs—whatever." This brought no response from Larry until, when she said something to that effect the day before she left, he turned on her and said, "Right. Ralph can hump my leg. What do I hump?"

Linda had looked away and replied, "Oh for God's sake. You're an adult. I'm sure you'll work that out."

"Do I take that as license to fuck whoever will have me?" asked Larry. But Linda turned and left the room without answering, and that was as close as they came to having a fight.

The leave-taking the next day was an admirable display of quelled emotions—very civilized, calm, noncommittal. An observer, ignorant of the circumstances, would have thought Linda was leaving for the weekend.

She was sent to the Philippines, a half-day's distance from Manila, and settled in with a missionary zeal. Living conditions were at best basic, but she did have electricity most of the time and access to email in their headquarters. At first she wrote long emails about the country, her cultural shock (which she made great self-deprecating fun of), her work, and her fellow workers, but these soon disappeared and were replaced by emails that in time became perfunctory comments on the weather and news about specific Filipino children and adults whose names became familiar to Larry.

She said she was keeping a journal that took up much of her correspondence time and everyone at home would want to read it when she returned. She might even try to publish it, she said. She called Larry and the boys on their birthdays and at Christmas, and though she had written personalized letters to each of them when she first began using email, she soon started sending the same letter to all—another time-saving device. Time saved for what, other than her journal, was not clear.

Linda had been gone a little over a year when they all received an identical email that obviously had been intended for someone else. It was addressed to letlive@uspcorps.com, and the subject was "More, more, I want more." The letter read: *"Quick note before bed—my bed this time. To think I had to come half way around the world to experience such bliss! Corny? Perhaps, but at my age a woman doesn't expect or even dream such lovely moments will occur. I'm giddy! I'm blessed! Love you, Fuzzy Wuzzy."*

Before the letter came, Larry had taken a vow to quit having more than one drink before dinner; two generous Scotches had been leaving him groggy by 8 pm, besides which he was going through a bottle twice as fast as his budget would allow. But the vow was forgotten when he read the letter, and he just had poured this third drink and was planning a reply filled with moral outrage and self-pity when his youngest son Mark phoned from Albany.

"Hey Dad, did you get that weird email from Mom signed Fuzzy Wuzzy? What the hell is that all about?"

"I don't have a clue, Mark. One thing is pretty clear, don't you think, that it wasn't meant for our eyes. I suppose Tim got the same letter."

"Yeah. I just got off the phone with him and he's all for emailing this Let-Live character and demanding to know what's going on, but I told him to hold off until I talked to you. Are you and Mom having problems or something?"

"What you see is what you get, Marco," answered Larry, immediately alarmed at how glib he sounded. But he went ahead, not knowing where his next statement would lead. "She brings me a poodle dog I didn't want for companionship and goes off to the jungle for two years. There may be a problem or two in that, wouldn't you agree?"

Mark's silence conveyed more of his distress to Larry than Larry wanted to confront, and before Mark could reply he said, "There's probably a reasonable answer to all of this. You know your mother marches to a different drummer, and of course there's the Mr. Kurtz factor, her being out there in the jungle and all that. So let me see what she's up to. I'll call Tim and let him know I'm looking into the thing. Everything okay there with you?"

"Oh sure, we're fine," said Mark, his voice still anxious. "You don't like Ralph? I thought you liked Ralph. He's a great dog. And who's this Mr. Kurtz?"

Larry sighed. "I forget that your generation is illiterate. Mr. Kurtz is a character in Joseph Conrad's *Heart of Darkness* who goes to hell in the Congo. And of course I like Ralph. I love Ralph! He's a wonderful dog. But when your mother dumped him on me I did have a lot of reservations about him." He was going to say "and about her motives in giving him to me," but even in his semidrunk condition he thought better of it. "Ralph's my buddy, and right now he keeps looking up at me from across the room every time I say his name. I guess he's wondering why I'm talking about him."

Larry assured Mark again he should not worry and that he would call Tim. After he hung up he stood looking out into the night, the alcohol-induced buzz humming just behind his eyes while a cold ball of fear lay inert beneath his sternum. Scotch on an empty stomach had left him operating under the influence well beyond Maine's legal limit, but he was in his own kitchen, so not to worry. Right now he needed to rethink his conversation with Mark and try to order his thoughts before calling his other son.

Tim had his mother's personality. He was an activist, a doer, a dedicated social worker who constantly was at odds with his supervisor over bureaucratic restraints—"procedural bull shit" he called it, and there was plenty of that in Columbus where he lived with Judy and baby Emma. "I say one of us should go out there and kick this 'Let-Live's ass," ranted Tim when Larry got him on the phone. "I mean, Mom's a grandmother for Christ sake."

Larry always had been good a calming Tim down, and by telling him essentially what he had told Mark (excluding Mr. Kurtz, which he realized Tim wouldn't get either) he blunted Tim's anger. He assured Tim he should do nothing until what lay behind the cryptic message of the misdirected email had been resolved. "You know the old basketball maxim, Timmy, 'no harm no foul' when it looks like a foul but the contact was unintentional and didn't disrupt the flow of play. We'll just let this thing play out."

Once off the phone with his sons, Larry let his depressed senses range freely. Earlier he had begun to drink to deaden his own anxieties, but Mark's phone call had forced him to try to think straight; now his slowed responses carried him along with no compulsion to make coherent decisions for someone else's benefit. He wasn't drunk, but he wasn't sober either. What he was was sad.

Larry called Ralph and they walked to the laundry room where Larry put Ralph's collar and leash on him. This always excited Ralph because Larry never leashed him unless they were doing something special, like walking along the highway or being someplace where there were other dogs. Ralph leaped around so much that Larry had difficulty getting his collar on; had the circumstances been different, Larry would have yelled at Ralph to calm down, but this night he patiently fastened the collar and restrained Ralph as he leaped into the night.

It was a cold, clear March night with no moon and no hint of spring. The Milky Way was so close that Larry reached up as if to grab some stars and inhaled deeply, infusing himself with the trillions of miles and timeless history between him and whatever it was those lights represented. He took no comfort in the knowledge that whenever it was night there, those same lights shone down on the Philippines. He tried to calculate the time difference, but his muddled mind was content just to assure him that it probably was daylight sometime the next day and Linda would be up saving the world—all except her own family, of course.

As Ralph rooted through the weeds, pulling Larry along at a steady gait, a speed he must have learned traversing the crowded sidewalks of the Upper West Side, Larry composed several bitter, accusatory letters in his mind; but by the time he and Ralph had hiked fire roads for an hour, he was legally sober and quite cold, and they returned home where Larry sent this email: "Tim, Judy, baby Emma, Mark, Rachel and I all got your email addressed to 'Let Live.' Have decided on mass suicide and are stirring up the Koolade now. Have a good day. Love, Larry."

He fixed a four-egg cheese omelet, ate it with great pleasure, and finished the last bite by shouting aloud, "Take that, fucking cholesterol!" His mind wandered the rest of the evening as he sat through a hockey game he cared nothing about and he fell asleep in his chair before the Weather Channel got around to showing the weather in Southeast Asia.

The next morning dawned overcast with low, chunky, gray clouds more common in November than in March. It was cold with little wind, and though the calendar said the first day of spring was only six days away, the reality that winter was still the dominant season struck Larry with the depressing truth. He was still full from the ridiculous omelet of the night before, so he fixed only toast and coffee. His head was clear, but his cheerless mood made his body movements slow and calculated; there was no need to do anything but brood, so he cupped a giant mug of coffee with both hands, sipped, and sat waiting for life to take a turn.

Ralph was not so composed, however, and began to agitate to go out. "What's with you? You just were out!" exclaimed Larry with no anger. "Go lie down and we'll go for a w-a-l-k when I finish my coffee." Ralph began to whine and he raced to the door, looking back to see if Larry was following, but Larry remained at the table, laughing. He loved it when Ralph responded to walk being spelled out. When Ralph first came to stay he would become so hyper at the mention of the word walk that Larry began spelling it out; it took only a week before Ralph knew the spelling meant he would get to go on an adventure, and he responded accordingly.

Ralph's antics distracted Larry from his gloom for merely a minute or two, and he went back to rethinking Linda's letter, his sons' reactions to it, and the sardonic email he had sent in response. He hoped she halfway believed in the mass suicide threat, but his feelings for vengeance went no further.

He put on his parka and headed into the woods with Ralph. Their property was nearly half a mile from the highway and was abutted by woods that stretched for two or three miles in opposite directions, so Ralph always ran free on their daytime walks. This time he ran so far ahead that Larry called him back. He returned with an unusual reluctance and impatiently hopped and pranced sideways until Larry caught up.

"What are you up to?" asked Larry, but at the sound of Larry's voice Ralph turned away and raced out of sight along their usual forest pathway as if he were chasing life's salvation itself. Larry was at first more surprised than alarmed, but as he continued several hundred yards into the woods and Ralph was nowhere to be seen or heard, he called out his name. There was no response.

"Damn it, Ralph," Larry said aloud, and he followed that with a series of shouted calls of Ralph's name. He stopped and listened, hoping to hear Ralph rustling through underbrush, but the only sound was that of a truck grinding up a distant highway hill. Ralph never had run away before, so Larry continued walking, expecting him to appear. But the longer he walked the more angry Larry became, and once in a series of shouted calls of Ralph's name he called out "Ralph, you're acting like a Rafe…Here Rafe, you stupid, dumb dog!"

Larry decided to stop. Maybe Ralph thought he was playing a game with him. But after five minutes, which seemed much longer, Ralph had not appeared and Larry continued walking.

As he came near the end of a fire road that ran perpendicular to the path he was on and intersected a large tract of wooded land that had been for sale for years, Larry picked up the faint residue odor of automobile exhaust fumes, and as he got to the cleared space where the fire road ended, he saw a small black pickup truck, its engine turned off, parked facing into the trees that marked the end of the road. Larry recognized the truck as Sandy Tobin's Nissan, the finish of which was so polished that it shone even in the woods on such a dark day as this one. Sandy sat in the cab, staring straight ahead.

Larry and Sandy disliked each other even though they barely knew one another and never socialized except in instances when they were thrown together in large, impersonal gatherings. Their mutual dislike had no basis in anything that either man could have explained. Sandy was a retired policeman from Bridgeport, Connecticut, who, like Larry, was living in a house inherited by his wife. They had moved to the community two years before when Sandy was granted a disability retirement following a serious heart attack. Rumor had it that the heart attack had occurred during a trial in which Sandy and two others were charged with manslaughter in the death of a derelict who pulled a knife while being arrested. Since moving to Maine he had had a second attack and a bypass operation, and though he looked trim and reasonably healthy, his eyes showed no sparkle and his demeanor was defensive, as if he were expecting to be bushwhacked.

Their unspoken but clear animosity toward one another was visceral, not cerebral. They were like two males of any species contending for space or a breeding female, except that they were in competition for nothing; yet, had their spines been hairy, each would have bristled when the other came into view.

When Larry saw it was Sandy in the truck, he immediately assumed that Sandy somehow had intercepted or injured Ralph, and Larry approached the cab set to do battle. But when he got to the driver's side of the cab he saw that Sandy's face was the shade of weeks-old snow and his eyes were dull and frightened, void of the glowing contempt that was their usual projection when turned on Larry. Larry instantly was disarmed.

"Jesus, Sandy! You all right?"

Sandy's head rolled back against the headrest, and his neck stretched upwards in pain, lifting his vision away from Larry, as he half-shouted, "Get out! Get away, damn it! Leave me alone."

"Hey, come on! You need help," said Larry as he reached for the door handle; but as the door came open, Sandy raised a police service revolver from the seat beside him, causing Larry to leap back. Sandy, his hand twitching unsteadily, lowered the gun back onto the seat. Their eyes met and Sandy, his expression more pleading than hateful, said, "Just let me do this. Go away. Please."

Larry stared at him as Sandy again began to writhe, nearly convulsed. Through gritted teeth he gasped, "Life is shit—I'm through with it."

"Hey, no. Come on, man," said Larry. "Just hang on. Scoot over and we'll go get help."

"No, no! Damn!" moaned Sandy, reaching again for the revolver. "I want it over."

Larry backed away, shielding himself behind the open door. He tried to make sense of the scene and suddenly felt fear rising from his confusion as to what he should do. "I'm going for help," he shouted to Sandy and began running back toward his house, a mile and a half away.

"Asshole!" screeched Sandy. "Don't!" But Larry never looked back.

Larry jogged a quarter of the way back to his house before he was forced to slow to a walk. His haste had been caused by a paradoxical mix of fear of being shot and the natural desire to aid a suffering fellow human, with the former tipping the balance. But now, forced to slow his retreat and with the knowledge that he was in no danger of being shot, he began to put the scene into perspective. It was certain that Sandy was intent on dying. He looked like Hell! Was he having a heart attack or had he poisoned himself or what? Or the gun. What about the gun? Was he going to shoot himself? Larry again slowed to catch his breath. What had Sandy said? "Life is shit...I want it over"? If he weren't in such physical misery, one could figure that those were comments born out of depression and maybe Prozac could save the day. But he already looked dead and was suffering hellish pain. Maybe the gun was a fail-safe thing? If the pain got unbearable he'd go the pistol route?

Larry again picked up his pace, his mind gripping the vision of Sandy's neck arched back in an attempt to ease whatever tortured him, his dead-man's pallor, and, most telling of all, his pleading with Larry—actually using the word "please" in a tone void of pride: defeated, pitiable. Any man who had read Hemingway and imagined himself as the solitary Nick Adams, cloistered, loving, and yet defying Michigan's woods, could imagine Hemingway saying to the night, "I can't write, I can't fuck, I can't drink, I can't remember," and then sucking both barrels of his shotgun into his mouth and blowing off the top of his head.

Larry slowed his walk. He resolved to let Sandy Tobin die whatever way Sandy chose, and he suppressed an edge of fear that in so doing he might be aiding a suicide. His mind was far from at ease, however, and once back in his kitchen, drinking coffee warmed in the microwave, he took stock as best he could. His wife is probably having an affair with someone and his kids know about it, and a guy he can't stand is out there in the woods dying or maybe is already dead and he was doing nothing to prevent the man's death. And, oh yes—his dog has run off.

After finishing his coffee, and more from a need for closure than compassion, Larry returned to the woods. Walking slowly to the spot where the pickup truck stood, Larry saw that the driver's-side door was still ajar. But Sandy was not visible, so Larry moved from tree to tree, circling the truck until he got a vantage point from which he could see into the cab. There he saw Sandy lying across the seat with his head toward the passenger's side and his left foot barely poking out of the open door. As Larry eased up to the door, a foul odor struck him. Whatever Sandy's condition was, his bowels had let loose.

Repulsed by the odor and what it signaled, Larry nevertheless continued toward the truck and called out Sandy's name. There was no answer, so he moved around to the other side of the truck, opened the door, and looked down on Larry's head. It was face down with only a small portion of its left side showing, gray and unmoving. There was no doubt in Larry's mind that Sandy was dead.

Larry closed the passenger-side door and returned home and called the volunteer ambulance number. He told the man who answered that he didn't think there was any hurry, that he was certain Sandy was dead. He had some difficulty telling him where Sandy was because Larry didn't know the fire road number or the name of the property owner, but after he gave the dispatcher various landmarks and names of people he knew who lived near the fire road, the latter said he knew where it was and asked Larry if he would meet them there. Larry hated the thought of returning to the truck, but his voice showed no sign of that as he said he of course would be there.

He set out at once and soon heard the wail of the ambulance up on the highway. Larry broke into a trot, cursing the ambulance driver for using the siren. "He's dead, he's dead, he's dead, you idiots," he said out loud. He got there just moments after the ambulance pulled into the clearing.

Larry didn't know the driver, but the other man in the ambulance was Clay Otten, a hot-tar roofer whose business had died out years ago and who was a fixture as an attendant in the local Mobil station. The two men nodded to Larry and walked to the open truck door where Larry joined them.

"You find him like this—door open and everything?" asked Clay, who made no move to examine Sandy.

"Right," answered Larry. "I was out here hunting for my dog who ran off this morning, and I came on the truck. I recognized it as Sandy's—he must have spit-polished it to keep it as shiny as he did."

"He's shit himself," said the driver, turning to Clay in hopes that Clay would give him instructions that somehow would make the odor go away.

Clay nodded his head. "Yeah. That's a bad sign. A lot of folks do that when they go sudden like. They put diapers on them when they execute murderers. I guess there's no doubt he's dead, but let's make sure."

The driver stepped aside and Clay climbed into the cab, resting his right hand on the back of the seat above Sandy while he tried to turn the body over with his left. He backed out, wrinkling up his nose. "We gotta turn him the other way. Go around to the other side, Bobby," he said with no urgency.

Bobby went around, opened the door and took hold of Sandy under the arms while Clay grasped his feet. Anxious to get away from the odor, Bobby tried to flip Sandy before Clay was ready. Clay lost his grip on the feet and Sandy's body slid onto the floor and wedged under the dash, causing his service 38 to slip from under his body and clatter out the door on Bobby's side.

"Holy shit," screeched Bobby, leaping away from the gun. "Did he shoot himself?"

"Damn, Bobby! Could you wait 'til I got a grip on him?" shouted Clay. "I don't see no blood—just pants full of shit. Let's get the stretcher. Leave him lay."

Assuring Larry they didn't need his help, Clay and Bobby tugged the stretcher over the rough ground to the passenger side of the truck and wrenched Sandy's body out from under the dashboard and onto the litter. "Dead, dead, dead," said Clay. "But I don't see no wound."

While they put Sandy in the ambulance, Larry picked up the revolver and placed it on the seat of the truck. Then he asked Clay, "Is there anything I should do?"

"Well, there's nothin' anybody can do for old Sandy now, that's for sure," said Clay, looking back at the truck. "This is his third ride in this ambulance, and I didn't think he was gonna make it the second time. I guess his heart just gave out and he couldn't get help this time bein' back in here. Lucky you came on him—his family might have hunted for him for God knows how long."

Larry felt a need to explain. "Well, I walk my dog back in here sometimes and he ran off this morning. You didn't see a black poodle comin' back in here, did you?"

"Didn't see a thing," answered Clay. "No, there's no reason for you to hang around here. I'll call the sheriff and I guess he knows what to do with the truck and pistol. He may come by to ask you about finding him. To tell you the truth, I don't know how he works stuff like this."

After the ambulance drove off, Larry circled the truck, opened the passenger-side door and looked in. The faint odor of excrement drifted out, causing him to quickly glance around as he backed away. There was nothing there except the gun, cruelly indifferent in the middle of the seat, and a green pine-tree shaped deodorant device, its air-cleansing properties long dead, dangling from the rear-view mirror. Tears oozed out and turned cold on Larry's cheeks, and he walked home, not certain for whom he mourned.

No one ever questioned him about Sandy, and Larry never told anyone about first finding Sandy alive. Apparently Clay's account to any interested party satisfied their curiosity. There also was no response from Linda to his email until three days after he'd sent it. She called at 6 in the morning, 7 pm in the Philippines, and her angry first words to a barely awake Larry were, "Larry, don't you ever kid around about suicide!"

Larry said nothing, his mind shocked into confusion by her unexpected voice.

"Larry? Larry? Are you there?"—her voice less censorious than her opening command.

"Yes, I am," Larry answered, sounding like he was responding to an intrusive request from a telephone solicitor. And again there was a long pause, both parties waiting for the other to initiate conversation.

"Well, are you all right? Can you hear me?" she asked, phrasing each word distinctly.

"Yes, I'm fine. Still mostly asleep, but so far as I can tell I'm fine" was Larry's calm response. But in fact he was not fine; his pulse was pumping through his left temple and his mouth suddenly was dry. Again there was a long pause as Larry edged onto a stool along the kitchen counter.

Linda finally said, "I'm calling about the letter, the email. Your email. I guess you were just being flip, but it scared the hell out of me."

"Really?" replied Larry, his tone heavy with mock surprise. "Well your email filled us all here with raptures of delight. It isn't often a husband and two sons get a chance to read their wife's and mother's tawdry letters to her lover, or whatever the hell he is. Or maybe he is actually a she? By God, now there's an intriguing thought!"

These last words were spun out in a dry, constricted gasp, done not for dramatic effect but because Larry's mouth was void of saliva and his breathing uneven. Yet another long pause followed. His hands quivered in anger, and he was on the verge of hanging up the phone when Linda said, "That letter was a mistake and something that can't…." She didn't finish the sentence but quickly started anew, her voice businesslike. "The thing to do is not to overreact. A glitch. It was a glitch. So we should dismiss it, forget it happened. It's folly to…."

She trailed off again, and Larry shouted, "A glitch? You call a day-after love letter sent to the wrong lover a mere glitch?"

Linda immediately cried, "No! Wait Larry! Oh Larry, you

and the boys know I love you. It's just that I can't go into this letter thing. It won't...it won't compute!"

"Ah, but it did compute, Linda. It did compute." Larry had regained control over his breathing and swallowed several times as he let this last statement, one which conveyed the tone of a reasoned plea, sink in. But then his voice turned bitter as he continued, "It is really ironic that here you are, supposedly in a third-world setting, being hoisted on your high-tech petard. And, no, I don't know that you love me—at least not out of the context of loving Tim and Mark. I just kind of go with the territory.

There was more silence, and then Larry heard what he at first thought was some muted, aspirated speech, but which he soon took to be sounds coming from Linda. "Are you crying? Linda, are you crying?" he asked, more in disbelief than alarm.

"Yes," she gasped in a high-pitched whine, which immediately became loud, uncontrolled sobbing. It was an entirely new sound to Larry. Linda's tears in the past had slipped out silently in sentimental movies or in rare moments of grief over a dead relative, friend, or pet. But this was new—a great uninhibited wailing, frightening in its suddenness and intensity of despair.

"Hey...oh, look Linda...," his voice suddenly apologetic and self-conscious. "You never cry. Not like this. Are you all right? Is anyone with you?"

At this her crying became even more convulsed, and Larry imagined she thought he was accusing her of being with the person addressed in her email. "I mean, is there anyone there to help you?"

She couldn't immediately answer; but no one physically could continue for long to wail and sob with such intensity, and as the sound finally slackened, Larry, who was by then genuinely alarmed, asked, "Are you okay? Linda, do you hear me? Are you okay?"

The sounds became gasps, then sniffles, and then a wet sigh.

"No, I'm not all right. I'm coming apart," she said amid tears that started anew but now seemed to be in sync with her breathing.

"Coming apart? What does that mean? Are you physically ill? Having a nervous breakdown over the phone? What?" asked Larry, unable to keep an accusatory tone out of his questioning.

"Oh God, I don't know," groaned Linda; and then, her crying having stopped, she cleared her throat and took control of her voice. "I don't know. I don't know what to do." But before Larry could respond, she said, "Hold on a minute, please," and he heard noises of her repeatedly blowing her nose.

"Are you still there?" asked Larry. And after more nose blowings she said, "Yes, I think I am having a nervous breakdown. I've never been like this before. What do I do?"

Her question was matter-of-fact and very nasal. "Do? You're asking me what to do? You never ask anyone what to do—you just do it."

"I know, I know," she said, "but this is different," and she gave a big air-sucking sigh, followed by "Boy oh boy, I've never cried like that in my whole life. Whew!"

"Are you all right now?" asked Larry.

"I'm shaky, Larry. I'm shaky, but, yes, I'm all right. I'm shaky, but I'm not crying."

"Good," said Larry, his voice strong with relief. "Now, what's this all about? Do you want to come home? What's going on?"

"Yes, I want to come home, but I can't. I've got nearly a year to go. It isn't an option. I gave my word."

"Oh, fuck the Filipinos! Don't you think people have bailed out on the Peace Corps before?"

"Well, certainly it happens, but it isn't an option for me. I've got to stick it out."

Even though seconds before he was in a near panic of concern for Linda's well-being, he wanted to say, "Stick it out? According to your recent correspondence you were experiencing bliss there in somebody's bed halfway around the world," but instead he said, "So what's this call all about? What's going on?"

"Well, of course it's about my email mistake and your email back." She sounded as if she were about to cry again.

"And?" asked Larry.

"I love you and the boys, Larry. You know that. There's no explanation for the stupid letter. I mean, we can't talk about it over the phone—it's a face-to-face thing. You've just got to trust me and deal with it somehow until I get home. It will be all right when I get home."

Concentrating every atom of skepticism into his voice that he could, Larry exclaimed, "Really!" and after a long pause asked, "Am I to pass that onto the boys as well?"

"Yes. I see clearly now that it will be all right when I get home. You'll have to trust my love."

Larry was so filled with conflicting emotions of anger, compassion, distrust and yearning that he could not immediately reply. Then, after many seconds of silence that hummed with tension, he said, "Ralph ran away."

"What?"

"Ralph, the dog. Your Rafe. He ran away."

"That's your answer? Ralph, the dog, ran away?" asked Linda, her voice unsteady.

Ignoring her question, Larry said, "It was the call of the wild, I guess. I don't think he's ever recovered from those dumb poodle cuts Joyce gave him. He's trying to find his true self is all I can figure out."

"Oh Larry, please don't punish me like this," she pleaded as her voice cracked into quiet tears, "I'm trying to do the best I can for us both."

He could hear her weeping—soft, pathetic sounds of despair,

unlike her earlier unfettered howls, and he was moved to say, "I'm sure you are." And then he added, "Why don't we just leave it like that? No more questions. Just do the best you can. We'll both do our best."

She continued to cry for some time before she could speak. "Oh, this is so awful, Larry."

"Yeah, well you're right. Maybe we should just hang up now and let things sort out a little."

"I think so," she answered, now calm and resigned. "Besides, this call is eating up all my piddly stipend."

"I'll send you some money," said Larry quickly.

"No, no. You know this is still my show, sink or swim. No money from home."

"How about some cookies then? Some chocolate chippers and some oatmeal butterscotchers?" he asked in a voice filled with sudden good humor.

"Oh Larry, I should have stayed home. I should have had more sense," she moaned, and then quickly added, "But I didn't." There was a heavy sigh before she continued, "So let me hang up and I'll email soon something more coherent than this silly phoned nervous breakdown. I loved hearing your voice, and I love you." She hung up before Larry could say a thing.

Larry spent the rest of the day repeatedly thinking back over the bizarre phone conversation. Linda had told him she loved him more in that five-minute span than she had in the past twenty years, and the hysterical weeping and expressions of love he took to be some sort of a confession—for what he now hoped he would never know.

He called the boys, told them he had talked with their mother and that she was going through some kind of late mid-life crisis, that she missed and loved them, and that they should assume the notorious email never existed. "You all right with that?"

asked Tim. Larry assured him he was and they didn't talk about it again. As for Ralph: Larry put up signs in town and ran ads in the weekly paper, but Ralph was gone forever.

That spring, summer, and fall were Maine's finest in years, and Linda wrote long, newsy emails to Larry alone and shorter ones to Tim and Mark. They phoned back and forth once a month, and though Linda had said she would write a coherent letter about her phoned nervous breakdown, she never did. Larry debated cashing in an IRA and flying to Manila for Christmas, but his instincts warned him off. He grew a beard, which everyone admired, he spent hours online tracing his family lineage, and he took long walks in the woods.

He returned again and again to the clearing where Sandy Tobin had died, and each time he placed a rock on a cairn that he impulsively had started soon after Sandy's death. He did it spontaneously, with no conscious purpose or meaning. He had built it to a height of nearly four feet by the time he and Linda came on it on their first walk after she returned home the next spring.

"What is that?" asked Linda as they walked into the clearing.

"A cairn of some kind, I guess," said Larry.

"What's it for?" asked Linda. "Who would pile those rocks up out here?"

"That's hard to say," said Larry.

Linda went up to the cairn and touched the top rock, gently jostling it to see if it would stay. Then she took his hand and they headed home.

BROWNIE FINE AND THE
THRASHING RING

My first thrashers' dinner (farmers always call the noon meal dinner) came pretty early—I couldn't have been more than seven. Donnie Burkett was twelve and had a mixed-breed Shetland pony, and since Donnie's dad Dewayne was a member of the thrashing ring, Donnie had gotten to be its water boy when he was only ten, his job being to ride around in the fields and supply the men with drinking water. He had a battered gallon thermos that he filled with water and a little lemon juice. The lemon juice was supposed to help quench thirst and lessen the risk of getting sick to your stomach from drinking too much at one time, but I think all it did was ruin the good natural mineral taste of the well water—and that business about drinking too much and getting sick as the result is a lot of horse feathers, too. Once in basic training, we went on a forced march down at Fort Knox, and it was so hot that salt crystals formed on our fatigue shirts when the sweat in them dried out. Halfway through the march they gave us a break and I drained my canteen in about four gulps; my platoon sergeant went nuts when he saw that and shouted an incoherent lecture on the evils of drinking too much water too quickly when one is over-heated. (He also believed that clap turned to syphilis, which in time turned to cancer, and then, as he put it, you'd "have to piss through a sieve.") I stood my ground as best as a basic trainee could and told him I'd bet my monthly piddly-assed pay that I could drink his canteen as well and not get sick, but he wouldn't take me up on it and made me pick up cigarette butts. But back to the thrashing ring.

Donnie and I rode barebacked with me behind him carrying the jug with one hand and hanging onto Donnie with the other. I did it for the fun of it, but Donnie got thirty-five cents a day, and, of course, we both got to eat dinner with the men. I remember only two dishes I ate at the dinner when I was Donnie's so-called helper. Well, actually I don't remember them at the time I ate them, but I remember being told what I ate that day. It was at the Pitts'. Ethel Pitts, a tiny sparrow of a woman who years later would take her own life rather than move into a nursing home, called Grandma the evening of my dinner at her house to tell her with some alarm that all I had eaten that noon was sliced cucumbers and onions in oil and vinegar and gooseberry pie (a delicacy now nearly extinct); she hoped I hadn't gotten sick from it. The dozen or so times Grandma told that story in my presence she always stressed how Ethel Pitts had anguished over whether she should have let me eat such a meal, and how she didn't want to embarrass me. Grandma always laughed when she told that story because it was her belief that I had some good taste to go along with my gluttony since Ethel Pitts' cukes in oil and vinegar and her gooseberry pie were the best she'd ever tasted.

By the time I was in high school I was a regular field hand, and the thrashing dinners took on a new perspective. When you're a little kid you load up on just the things that catch your fancy, and you usually stop when you get full. But when you start looking like an adult and are growing three inches a year, you stoke away food as if each meal were your last. So, imagine working for four hours in sun and heat before eating big helpings of great-tasting fat, starchy food and *then* going back into the sun and pitching sheaves of wheat into a wagon for another four or five hours. It's a wonder we all didn't die by three in the afternoon! The summer of my senior year in high school, one of us did.

For the first ninety minutes we were back in the fields after dinner we would work slowly, soaked in sweat, belching, and light-headed with the chemicals in our bodies foaming and bubbling in their over-stoked vat of membranes and soft tissue. By late afternoon, though, we would move with a lighter step toward ending the job before us, our bodies once again having survived a deadly sin. Brownie Fine was not so fortunate, however, and I never have been able to work out any resolution to the irony of his death on the last afternoon the thrashing ring was in existence.

After the war there no longer was any practicality in a thrashing ring when a harvesting combine in one operation could do the work of ten men in a third of the time and at considerably less cost—especially if one figured man hours of the whole ring into the calculations. Even if combines hadn't taken over, Wink Slaybaugh, who owned and operated the thresher, said it was his last year—he was old and it was hard to get parts for his obsolete machine. We were finishing up at Joe Bitner's, just across the road from our farm, when it happened

Brownie was a short, stocky man, but that wasn't his true body shape. He'd been gored by a bull when he was eleven, and through the combination of serious vertebrae damage and ignorant medical treatment, he grew up a humpback. His head jutted forward and he looked like he was wearing football shoulder pads. Through hard work and an effort to compensate for his injury, Brownie got muscle-bound through the shoulders and chest and, I suppose as compensation for his physical appearance, he overate and had a big belly that bloused out under his enlarged gondola of misshapen bones and ill-conceived muscles. He was tough but kind and could work as hard and long as anybody I knew, and though at first viewing he appeared grotesque, one soon forgot his appearance for the reality of Brownie's good nature and generous spirit.

I felt a special fondness for Brownie because, with the exception of Grandma, he was my most vocal fan at the games I played in high school. He'd come to football and basketball games (he'd ring a cowbell at the latter) and vicariously play the games his childhood injury had denied him; and even when I was awful Brownie would remember the good move I put on somebody just before I dropped a pass, or the clutch rebound I pulled down before overthrowing someone on a fast break that would have led to a cinch basket.

In his own way Brownie liked to compete, and he obliterated me at the church ice-cream social the summer before he died. Every July the "Soul Seekers" adult Sunday school class had an ice-cream social that was a popular event in Hurley. All of the ice cream was homemade, and making the ice cream was a major undertaking. Today ice cream socials get their ice cream at discount from some commercial source, but our ice cream was honest-to-goodness, hand cranked, homemade ice cream made from farm-fresh heavy cream.

The social always was held on a Sunday evening so that the ice cream could be made Saturday and Sunday afternoons. Though the "Soul Seekers" were mostly middle-aged, as a kid I spent many hours cranking an ice-cream freezer while adults added cracked ice and rock salt to the buckets surrounding the ice-cream canisters and kibitzed about the whole process. They made vanilla, strawberry, and chocolate, with the strawberry the best and the chocolate unfailingly the worst because it had a chalky quality, like milk of magnesia. The Saturday ice cream was put in Hobart's frozen food locker and brought out on Sunday to go along with the dozens of pies and cakes and the fresh-frozen ice cream made that afternoon.

I was a big kid and had a gun-fighter's reputation as a big eater from the food I stowed away at thrasher dinners and volunteer fire-department bean suppers. I say gun-fighter's reputation because once in a while somebody would want to go against me to see who could eat the most corn on the cob, hot dogs or watermelon. I had a knack for pacing myself with those foods and could eat corn and melon all day, but sweet, rich things were out of my class; and though once I ate a whole pumpkin pie I was only a journeyman when it came to downing great amounts of dessert. So when Brownie called me out at the ice-cream social, I knew I was not competing in my best event.

The way it worked was that you bought a ticket for fifty cents and then ate as much as you wanted. The pies and cakes, donated by members of the church, were laid out on folding tables beside the men scooping ice cream. The pies were mostly two-crust fruit pies that went well with ice cream, but the cakes were of all varieties, although chocolate predominated. Grandma had made a banana cake with a boiled brown sugar frosting, and I was watching where she put it among the others so I would be sure to get a piece of it when Brownie, carrying a paper plate and spoon came up to me, playfully stuck an elbow in my ribs, and said:

"I understand you're a pretty good eater these days, Jack."

"Aw, I'm just a growin' boy, Brownie—you know how it is," I responded while trying to find some place for my hands, which I finally stuffed in my back pockets—a move that gave me the unintended appearance of being cool if not cocky.

Brownie nudged me again: "Well, get a plate and let's see if you can keep up with an old man like me."

Brownie wasn't old, but he wasn't young either, and somewhere in the back of my mind ran the notion that he was supposed to be a prodigious ice-cream eater—one of many of his generation of men in their fifties who saw a pint as a normal serving. With his humped shoulders, massive chest and hanging belly, he looked plenty formidable, but I had come to eat ice cream and I couldn't brush off his challenge. I got a paper plate and spoon and followed him over to the ice-cream table. Brownie directed the placement of piles of vanilla and strawberry ice cream onto his plate until the amount must have reached a quart and a half, so I said I'd have the same, held out my plate to be filled, and gave a silent prayer for strength and courage.

My plate now held twice the amount of ice cream I had ever consumed in one sitting, and I sensed defeat before I had taken my first bite; then Brownie added more gloom to my prospects, directing us to the cake and pie table for "a couple pieces to fill in the gaps around the cream," as Brownie put it. Brownie chose a piece of nearly black Devil's food and a yellow cake with a coconut frosting while I, loyal to Grandma, took a piece of her cake and a slice of angel food topped with a lemon glaze, which I dumped on top of the ice cream since my plate, as was Brownie's, was full to overflowing.

We sat on the outer fringes at a card table and began to eat. Brownie did the bulk of the talking, which mostly was about our football team's prospects for the fall and the pennant races that were in full swing. I nodded in agreement with what he said and tried to pace my bites; you can't eat ice cream too slowly or it all melts, so I spent many of my bites on spoonfuls that were about to overflow the edge of my plate. I moved pieces of cake to form dams against the melting ice cream, and soon there was room for the angel food cake to slip down among the mounds of ice cream and Grandma's cake and rest on the plate itself.

Brownie showed no sign of weakening or slowing his pace, but I was clearly filling up, and half the ice cream and more than half of the cakes were still uneaten. Sweat formed on my forehead—a new sensation while eating ice cream—and I stretched out my legs to the side of my chair, hoping the movement would shake ice cream and cake already consumed into unfilled internal cavities. Brownie kept eating and talking baseball at the same steady pace.

Maybe I could wash some of this down, I thought. "Brownie, could I get you a glass of water?" I asked in tones more pleading than polite.

"No, no, I'm fine thanks," he answered in a voice that seemed to me to suggest that maybe he thought I was not, and, if so, he was right.

I excused myself and walked the long way around to a table that had water pitchers, filled a paper cup with water, and again took the long way back to my chair. Sipping the water seemed to ease my stuffed feeling, but that was little consolation when I looked at Brownie's plate and saw that he had moved way ahead of me in amount consumed. I broke off some angel food cake and mopped up a puddle of melted ice cream with it. Then I squared off a mound of strawberry, the peak of which loomed over the rest of the plate, and when I had spooned it down to the level of the rest of the ice cream and cake, I felt a psychological boost that I was making headway into the huge amount still remaining.

Brownie ate like a perpetual-motion machine, and I suddenly wondered if I had been set up for this contest. Maybe Brownie hadn't eaten anything since breakfast.

"Man, the way you put that away, Brownie, I bet you haven't eaten all day."

Brownie looked shocked. "Didn't eat? Sure I did. I ate just like always—except I didn't eat dessert. We didn't have dessert for supper." His puzzled look then gave way to a smile of genuine good humor and he asked, "You getting stuck?"

"Well, not stuck, but I'm slowin' down a little—sort of pacin' myself." Then, to make my actions sound reasonable, I added, "I ate a big supper."

"With dessert?"

"No, we didn't have dessert either, but I ate two pieces of left-over chicken and...." I trailed off; I didn't need images of a former meal to add to the burden of what I had yet to eat.

Brownie continued to steadily consume his ice cream, and I began to think that perhaps rhythm was the secret—it seemed to be such an important part of so much of life. I knew that a trotting race horse was finished in a race once it broke its stride, and the same was true with human runners, so I began to eat in a slow, deliberate rhythm a bit behind Brownie's pace. It didn't work. After four or five rhythmic bites I nearly gagged, and I had to stop eating and take some deep breaths. Then I traced some lines and circles in the melted ice cream with my spoon and seriously thought of giving up.

Brownie ate on and talked on, and after I had scrawled out "barf" with my spoon in the melted ice cream on my plate, I tried another bite that I held in my mouth until it had completely melted. Then I sipped a tiny amount of water and washed the ice cream down my throat. Ah, trial and error is a wonderful thing! That worked! And I set up a new rhythm of sorts—admittedly, a very slow rhythm—that permitted me to continue to eat. And I tried to think of something else.

Concentrating on Brownie's sports conversation wasn't much help. He tended to answer all of his questions as soon as he asked them, and I didn't want to bring up new topics that would cause me to carry the brunt of the discussion—I'd reached a point where I couldn't talk and eat too, and I felt sympathy for those who sneeringly are accused of not being able to walk and chew gum at the same time. Besides, I reasoned, one isn't supposed to talk with his mouth full—and, God, was my mouth full!

Bite, melt, sip, bite, melt, sip—on and on. At first I was

afraid to break up the routine to eat my cake, but I admitted to myself that the cake was part of the contest too, and I'd have to try to choke it down. Maybe it was a change in flavors or texture, but the cake was no more difficult to get down than the ice cream— especially if I sipped water before and after each bite—and going back to the rhythm with the ice cream was no jolt. I was in a groove, much like a marathon runner after the first twelve or fifteen miles.

Brownie was finished. He pushed back his empty plate with less an air of finality than a gesture of habit. I had half a pint of strawberry and vanilla, partially blended together, plus several bites of banana cake yet to eat. Brownie leaned back in his folding chair and showed no sign of triumph at all; he simply was waiting for me to finish. Then it became clear to me that it had been no race at all!

I knew from the beginning that it wasn't a contest to see who could eat the fastest, but I immediately had gotten caught up in the calm, workmanlike way in which Brownie put away his enormous amount of ice cream and cake, and I had tried to keep pace; once it had become clear to me that I couldn't eat as rapidly as he, I had worked out my routine to finish second, and now that Brownie had cleaned his plate I realized that if I could just finish we would both win—or rather I would have met his challenge. This gave me new resolve, but my flesh was weakening in a ratio far outstripping any ways I could think of that would strengthen it.

Much earlier I stealthily had unbuttoned the top button on my jeans, and there seemed no possible maneuver left that somehow would give me more space for the rapidly melting ice cream seeping into the chunk of banana cake standing between honor and disgrace. I had to stand up or die! I felt as if the ice cream and cake were pushing my lungs up under my collarbone. My water cup was nearly empty, and a plan was needed before death throes set in.

"I need a little more water, Brownie," I gasped, sounding

like a fat man in undersized briefs pleading for quick death after having ridden a bus for three days and nights. Once on my feet I continued in a voice less constricted: "I always need something to drink with sweet stuff—you know, milk or water."

Walking to the water pitcher took some of the pressure off my lungs, and I gauged my speed so I would get to the pitcher after some little girl I didn't know had carefully poured herself a drink. I again took the long way to and from the pitcher and, though stuffed beyond tolerable limits, my distress was somewhat eased by the time I reached Brownie and our table. By now the ice cream was really runny, so, with the exception of eating the cake, my task now was one of drinking what was left of the ice cream.

Brownie appeared bored and started to kid Cliff Weaver at the next table about the loud sports shirt he was wearing. I tried to get my rhythm going again, but my timing was disrupted by cramps and shortness of breath, and the spoon and cup moved to my mouth in uncertain starts and stops. A sharp pain shot through my rib cage, and I sat up straight in an exaggerated stiffness to ease the pressure I now literally felt everywhere below my ears. Only a couple of spoonfuls of mushy pink ice cream and a large bite of banana cake were left.

I blew my nose and Brownie stopped his bantering with Cliff to look at me with some curiosity. "Cold things always make my nose run," I gasped. "So do hot things." He smiled indulgently but said nothing, and I was able to get one of the remaining spoonfuls into my mouth where it sat several seconds before I could make room for a sip of water to ease its passage downward. Two bites remained—one of ice cream, one of cake.

I cut the smidgen of cake in two, ladled ice cream over it and slid it into my mouth, which, though empty, felt cold and stuffed. A tiny sip of water lubed the bite, and rather than chew I swished it through my teeth and under my upper lip until it disappeared down my throat. One bite of combined ice cream and cake remained on the plate. The finish line was visible—a cliché, so close, yet so far away!

By now force of habit raised the paper cup to my mouth and allowed a trickle of tepid water inside, and as with the previous sip, the miracle recurred and the water disappeared down my gullet. Then, closing my eyes, I forced the final spoonful onto my tongue. There it stayed, even when Brownie, brightening up, asked: "Finished? Okay, we'd better get our seconds before they run out of the good stuff and we have to eat the chocolate."

My glazed eyes confirmed that there was not a grain of irony in Brownie's suggestion, and the shock was so great that the ice cream and cake, which seconds before seemed destined to dribble out the corners of my mouth and signal ignominious defeat, slithered into the obscurest of all spaces somewhere in my body. I had surmounted all of my most reasoned instincts and brutalized my body to survive the battle, only now to lose the war. Competitive spirit, stupidity, call it what you will, gave me the strength to speak in fairly normal tones: "You really goin' to eat some more?"

Brownie already was out of his chair and heading for the ice cream line: "Oh, not as much as that first helpin', but I've got room for a couple scoops and maybe a sliver of pie."

I got up too, because it was less painful than sitting down, but I made no move toward a second helping of anything and leaned over the back of my chair while Brownie made his selections. I breathed quick little wisps through my nose, and my eyeballs felt as if they were being forced out of their sockets. My sensations long ago had ceased to have humorous overtones, and I thought I was dying. But before my life could pass across my blurred vision, Brownie was back, seated, and eating a pint of ice cream and a slice of peach pie. With his first bite my defeat was completed, and all that was left for me was to survive with some kind of dignity—neither would be easy.

While I teetered behind my chair, Brownie started up his baseball talk again, and I took the opportunity to try to learn how to breathe with no lungs. I managed to avoid speaking by nodding my head to Brownie's comments, but finally he put a direct question to me: "Sure you don't want another scoop or so, Jack?"

I risked speaking what I was sure would by my last words: "Couldn't do it, Brownie."

Brownie nodded like he understood and showed no sign of rubbing in his victory. I risked speaking again: "I don't know where you put all of that. I'm about to die."

"About to die?" He laughed a booming laugh and went back to eating after saying, "Nah, you won't die, Jack—ice cream is like the moon shining in your mouth. Why, in ten minutes you'll be back for more."

"I don't think so, Brownie. I don't think I'll ever eat again." And with that I slumped back into my chair, stretched my legs trying to get as prone as possible, and sat unmoving with closed eyes while Brownie finished a second helping that was more than most people could eat in a week.

Brownie was wrong. I wasn't back for more in ten minutes. In fact, and to Grandma's distress, I didn't eat anything until noon the next day. My idiocy in trying to eat ice cream in a contest with Brownie Fine didn't destroy my taste for ice cream, however, but what happened on that last day of the thrashing ring made me reconsider a number of things about one-on-one eating contests—even if only competing against yourself.

Nobody saw Brownie fall. He was just there, face down in the wheat stubble. Joe had hired dim-witted Burdock Simmons to work in the field, and Burdock had been up on the wagon that

Brownie was loading. When he turned around to receive a sheaf from Brownie, Burdock saw him on the ground. "Hey, Brownie's down! He fell over! He's down!" was Burdock's shout to the rest of us, and everything stopped. There was no sound except the muted chugging of the thrashing machine hundreds of yards away, and the flat ticking of the horses' tails batting against their traces as they whipped the flies off their rumps.

"Heat must have got him" were the first words spoken, and they came in tones more expressive of hope than knowledge from Omar Blanton, who ran quickly to Brownie's side. We all moved then and formed a wide circle around Omar and Burdock, who turned Brownie onto his back. The sharp wheat stubble had scratched Brownie's face close to his open eyes and left tiny lines of red across his cheeks.

"Get some water! Where's the water kid?" shouted Omar, and, as short on wits as he was, Burdock had the presence of mind to hold his straw hat as a screen shading Brownie's face from the high, impersonal sun.

Omar knelt beside Brownie, and in a flat voice that showed no urgency said, "Somebody get a car," and after a long pause added, "I don't think it will make a difference—I think he's gone."

I ran for the house with Burdock a step behind me. Omar called Burdock back, fearing, I suppose, that Burdock wouldn't get the message right and would be in the way. When I raced up, Joe was pulling a load of grain away from the thresher, and he just let it sit there in the middle of the barnyard while we ran for his Chevy. Farmers always leave their keys in their cars, so there was no delay in getting the car into the field where Brownie lay. He was lifted onto the back seat and Omar crouched beside him on the floor while Joe drove to the hospital, eighteen miles away.

We stood and watched the car 'til it was out of sight, and no one looked into the face of anyone else or spoke until Burdock said, "He's gonna be okay, ain't he?" The older men looked at their feet while Burdock and I tried to scan their faces for an answer. Brad Williams looked up and shook his head, "It don't look good to me—his eyes open and all."

"But he was all right," protested Burdock, "pitchin' sheaves up all right."

"It don't take much I guess—just some little thing and...." Brad trailed off. He got out his bandana and wiped his forehead, and I noticed that the handkerchief got down into the corner of his eyes. He blew his nose, and with new resolve asked me, "It okay if you work with Burdock, Jack?." I said it was, and we all went back to thrashing wheat.

We were unloading the last wagon into the thresher when Joe and Omar returned. Most of the women who had helped Marj with dinner were still there and had come out to meet the car as soon as Joe drove in, and Wink shut down the tractor as soon as he saw Joe was back. We stood looking across to the yard, and it was clear from the sagging postures and hands raised to their mouths that Brownie was dead—"dead before he hit the ground" had been the verdict of the doctor to Omar and Joe.

It was nearly seven o'clock by the time Joe and I had shoveled the last of his grain into the bins in his granary. Grandma had done all of my chores at home so I could stay and help Joe finish up. We worked silently, trying to behave as if nothing out of the ordinary had happened that day. But a whole lot out of the ordinary had happened—all of it sad.

Once the last head of wheat had been separated from its stalk in Wink Slaybaugh's grand red machine, Wink had closed down his tractor, rolled up the big belt that joined tractor and thrasher in an elongated figure-eight connection, and had gone home for supper, telling Joe he'd be back that evening to tow away his equipment. He came just as Joe and I came out of the barn for the night, and we joined him beside the thrasher.

Wink pulled a stock of wheat from where it had lodged in the conveyer that carried the sheaves into the thrasher and rubbed the grain into his hand. He let the wheat sift through his fingers onto the ground and moved his hands across his body sweeping the chaff from his palms in a gesture of finality. Ignoring my presence he said to Joe, "God damn it, I can't get over Brownie goin' like that."

Joe exhaled the air of a whipped man and nodded in agreement. "Yeah, it's hard to take all right." He slumped down onto one of the heavy steel wheels of the thrasher that was burnished bright from being rolled over the crushed rock of country roads. Then Wink bent down, picked up a couple of pebbles and worried with them as he addressed us both this time: "You know how I take it? I take it as a bad sign, that's how I take it."

He paused to let this soak in, but we didn't know what he meant. "This machine ain't gonna run again—unless it's at the county fair as a curiosity. It's through—its day has passed." Again he paused, tossed the pebbles into the air, and let them fall to the ground. "Ya know, at the end of the day I was gonna mark the event, so to speak. I brought along a fifth, and I was gonna give the fellas a shot or two and sort of kiss this baby goodbye—ya know— have kind of a ceremony. Just a silly thing, but I thought the boys would like it. It's the end of an era, Joe. The thrashin' ring's dead. No more. It don't seem important and it probably ain't—not when you put it against Brownie dyin' in the field like that. A shame, a *God...damned...shame!*" He said each of those last words separately and with anger, and then went about hauling away his outmoded, wooden-sided, weathered old farm implement for the last time.

When I got home, Grandma set out some cold ham and cole slaw and started to warm up some string beans, but I told her to hold off on the beans. It was a hot evening and somehow eating hot food would formalize my meal and I didn't want to be formal. Grandma went over to the Fines to see if she could help Brownie's family, so I fixed two ham and rat cheese sandwiches, spooned out a large helping of slaw, poured a glass of milk and carried it all out to the porch swing. Once again I was hungry at a time when I suppose I shouldn't have been, but the casual pick-up meal was just right for my appetite and mood.

A few lightning bugs began to blink even though it was still fairly light, and the air had the clean odor of hot, freshly ironed bed sheets. I thought about Wink and his premonition of bad signs. Bad signs of what? I wondered what Wink's bad signs were supposed to be applied to? Death? Brownie was dead and so was the thrashing ring, and did the fact that the two came at the same time mean we were all going to die—or the world was coming to an end? No, that was just plain silly, but I supposed Wink saw signs of bad times ahead in Brownie's and the thrashing ring's passing, whatever that meant for any of us.

It was a quiet evening. No sounds of machinery could be heard, and the only man-made noise was the slight asthmatic screech of the porch-swing's chains grating against the giant screw eye bolts from which they hung. A few crickets had begun their rhythm band, and the twilight was black enough to make it difficult to distinguish barn swallows from bats as those speeding dark shapes erratically canvassed the barnyard sky.

The sandwiches and slaw were a wondrous combination of complementary tastes. I savored the goodness of each bite—there was substance there, material delight, the transience of which was part of its real worth. For some minutes after I had cleaned my plate I rocked in the swing and reveled in the solitude and suspended animation of my fatigue. The sinews from my jaw down had been stretched and tested and now were justly at rest with no trace of discomfort; but my head felt too large for my neck and heavy with inert matter, inorganic and alien.

My strength had stood up to the day with ease but now relished the clean calm of earned rest. My mind was swollen and ached from unwanted loads: Brownie lying face down in the wheat stubble, his humped back highlighted by the dark blue his sweat gave to the lighter-hued chambray shirt protruding between stained canvas suspenders; Brownie ringing his cowbell and shouting, "Lookin' good Jack, Jack. Lookin' good," as I came to the bench; Brownie eating ice cream and watching with kind amusement as I played with my spoon and stalled for time; Brownie, wide-eyed, staring sightless into the sun that glistened off the thread-thin scratches gouged by indifferent nature into his cheeks; great platters of fried chicken moving from thick hand to thick hand and being reduced two pieces at a time on their journey around the thrashers' table; Wink cursing the end of…of what—being commander of a 1926 model McCormick-Deering grain separator, the hub around which a circle of peers revolved for three weeks every summer? In and out of my consciousness ran these visions and half-thoughts while the immediate scene grew dark and now blinked with the mysterious yellow-green glow of hundreds of lightning bugs' abdomens. It was more than I could absorb, so I willed a state of stupidity and closed my eyes.

I suddenly was too tired to move and sat many stupefied minutes, swinging effortlessly—a willing captive of the law of gravity. Heat lightning lit up the northern sky in a sudden swift streak, and tree toads came to life as if that had been their cue. I liked their croaks, though they made me feel lonely, so I decided to run a tub of water in the hope that a bath would rid me of some of the day's weight. But once on my feet and back in the kitchen, a new source of energy emerged, and I carried a slice of apple pie and another glass of milk back to the porch swing. Cinnamon, nutmeg, and tart green apples greeted my tongue the way old friends upon their arrival suspend time and banish sad cares.

The headlights from Grandma's car were a welcome sight. She joined me on the swing and talked about how well Brownie's family was holding up and about all of the food the neighbors had brought in. "They could have thrashin' dinners for a week over there with all the food that's been brought in..." said Grandma, whose voice began to trail off, questioning the appropriateness of her observation.

"There won't be any more thrashin' dinners, Grandma. Today was the last one—the ring and Brownie died together, and Wink says it's a God-damned shame."

Nothing was heard for many minutes but the porch swing's screech, the tree toads, and an occasional yelp that in the past I had romanticized as a barking fox until Grandma claimed it was Brubakers' blind milk-eyed terrier. Finally, Grandma sighed a long, heavy, breast-raising sigh and said, "Wink's language isn't always the best, but this time I think he said it about right."

ADULTERY

I somehow had missed the news account of Sheila's death. Her obituary a week later was short of drama except for the latent tragedy in the death of a mother and daughter.

Katy had her own obituary, which was as barren as the one for Sheila, but shorter because she had lived only eighteen years and had acquired fewer statistics than her mother: full names, birth dates, survivors, academic degrees, and in Sheila's case a work history that in its sparse retelling made her co-ownership of a day-care center sound insignificant. The obituaries were stoical, frugal, and starkly sad. I sat alone at my desk and quietly wept.

Ten years ago, almost to the day of her death, there had been a fund-raising wine and cheese gathering for Will Fleming, our first-term state legislator who was running for re-election and being challenged by a right-wing lawyer who was land-deal rich and wholly in the pocket of wily, unprincipled, strip-mall developers. It was save the shore vs. economic development will lower taxes.

I'd seen Sheila at concert intermissions at the nearby university with people I knew I wouldn't like, but we had never met. That evening at the political rally she came up to me and introduced herself. "I'm Sheila. I see you don't have one of Will's badges and it's important that everyone make his or her commitment visible."

"His or her?" I replied. "Even if we're not politically correct?"

"Oh you're politically correct or you wouldn't be here. How about helping with mailings?" she asked, pinning a badge on the lapel of my blazer.

"Mailings? How do you know I'm not a mole—a raving right-wing lunatic? You don't even know my name," I answered, surprising myself with my smartassed attitude.

"You're no mole—you're hands are too sensitive," she said. "So, what's your name?"

Along with her plastic bag of pins, she held a pen and a small spiral notebook that she flipped open. She looked up, expecting me to tell her my name.

"Sensitive hands? These are sensitive hands? These are just... well, hands—your everyday garden-variety hands," I said, turning them over palms to back.

She smiled, a pleasant, confident smile as if there were no doubt that she was correct, and looked hard into my eyes. "No. They're much nicer than most. So give me your name and phone number."

"What if I won't?" I asked, smiling all the time.

"Look! You're wasting my time. Do you want to help Will get re-elected or are you just here for the free wine and to hit on some unhappy housewife?"

This last was said with just enough heat and indifference to cause me to give a little nervous laugh and say, "Okay. Sorry. I have a bad habit of not taking things seriously." I gave her my name and phone number, which she wrote in her notebook and then smiled and said, "Thanks. I'll call you."

She walked away to a group of four new arrivals who had just picked up glasses of wine, and I heard her say, "I'm Sheila and I'm looking for help with mailings for Will." My mood darkened a shade, and I shrugged and thought, "So, nice hands or not, I guess I'm not so special after all."

I watched her for the next forty-five minutes while I milled around talking politics with several like-minded friends and drinking more of the very ordinary red wine than I would have had I not been intrigued by Sheila. She moved from group to group, writing in her notebook, handing out badges, brushing quick kisses on cheeks of those who were obvious friends (some of whom I recognized as people I didn't like).

What made me follow her with my eyes yet kept me from talking to her again? It was more than her body, which was that of a ripe teenager, athletic and defiant; or her face of anonymous features, at once beautiful and plain. Somehow she spoke to every male's condition of being perpetually in heat and in search of someone with whom to mate, if only in his mind's eye.

Not that I didn't already have a mate who fulfilled those demands of nature, and I had two children to prove it. And, though saturated with fantasy conquests, I was monogamous and loved my wife. But Sheila, who epitomized common sense and conventional decency, simply seduced me by being alive and in my presence.

The day after Will Fleming's fundraiser, Sheila called. Because I appraise property for banks and individuals—usually rich ones—and am out of the house, which also is my office, during most of what the business world calls normal work hours, I got Sheila's message on my voice mail: "Hi, Dennis. This is Sheila. We are checking voter registration lists tomorrow night at Barb and Brad Whitehead's, 17 Copper Oak Lane. Seven thirty. See you then." No "hope you can make it," just the assumption that I would be there. And I still didn't know her last name.

Of course I went. When I told Annie where I was going, she looked skeptical and asked, "Why the good citizen bit all of a sudden?"

"Hey, I'm always a good citizen. Besides, the asshole running against Will probably would never use me to assess the property he's hoping to destroy. You want to come along?"

"Better things to do," she said, and I went alone. Had she gone, things might have played out differently, but I doubt it; Sheila had become my secret love the moment she pinned me with "Will Fleming, State Legislator."

That night, while cross checking names, I learned Sheila's married name was Byrne, that her husband was Ray Byrne, the lacrosse coach at the community college, that they had two daughters, Katy 8 and Sarah 5, and that she wore no bra. The last was revealed when she leaned over the card table to hand me a stack of forms, and it made a lasting impression, validating my infatuation and far surpassing in importance my knowledge of who made up her family.

Through the summer and fall leading up to the election, Sheila and I were tireless workers for "the cause"—a cause that for me became Sheila. The week before Election Day, Will's core campaign workers stuffed and addressed envelopes for the last time and went to the lounge of the Sandpiper Inn for a drink amid sighs of relief and self-congratulatory smiles for a job well done. Sheila ordered a careful white wine, as did nearly everyone but Will and me, who drank our usual carefree Scotch.

I maneuvered a spot next to Sheila on the banquette surrounding the piano. Eight of us were jammed onto the banquette, welding thigh and hip of each to the next person. I was on the end with Sheila pressed against me with a physical closeness we had not had before. Ginny Crane, a political junkie, was on the other side of Sheila holding forth to everyone else about unfair apportionment of school taxes, thus freeing Sheila to talk to me exclusively.

The piano player's uninspired doodlings provided more cover for our conversation. Sheila wanted to talk about her girls and spoke of them with such affection that tears soon tinged her smile—an incongruous sight to anyone not hearing her homage to motherhood. She daubed at the tears with a cocktail napkin and still smiling turned her face to me and said, "Really, you should kiss me now, but, please, don't you dare."

"I can't think of anything I'd rather do," I said, which was oh so true. I looked into her face, her eyes still glistening with tears and glee, and added, "But why don't I dare?"

Still smiling, she shook her head and said, "We'd die," and tears again slid down her cheeks.

"We'd die?" I asked, not sure myself whether to laugh or cry, and she immediately pushed against me and in desperate tones said, "Please, I need to get out."

"Your marriage?" I asked, sounding at once alarmed and hopeful.

Her look was one of somber surprise that instantly became a good-natured giggle. "No, the ladies' room, you idiot."

I rose and Sheila moved with a calm deliberateness that betrayed nothing of her emotional state just seconds before.

Ginny turned toward me, her raised eyebrows a silent question. "Ladies' room," I said, and Ginny, satisfied, turned back to the others. I was not as easily reassured, however, that Sheila's hasty "I need to get out" had been in response to her bladder. *Kiss me but don't kiss me. I love my kids so much that it makes me cry.* What was that all about?

Sheila returned looking gorgeous and happy. I stood to let her back into the booth, but with force she said, "Don't get up. Stay and revel. I've got to get home—a big day tomorrow."

I said, "Let me walk you to..." but she stopped me with a stern, "Stay!" which she followed with a "Goodnight, everyone. Win with Will!" She left me standing there, my silence unnoticed amid everyone else's "See ya, Sheila—take care."

I drove home wondering if I had just been made a fool of, or if a glimmer of love and lust had slipped through Sheila Byrne's marriage vows. Such confusion became even greater as my own marriage vows received a major spike of guilt when I got home to find Annie, the mother of my children, and up until then the sole love of my life, weeping silently as Elizabeth Taylor shone her great violet eyes of longing into Montgomery Clift's hopeless eyes staring out from his death-house cell in a television rerun of *A Place in the Sun.* Without a word I sat and snuggled her against my side.

Will won the election, and after the votes were tallied that night, dozens of his supporters drank champagne in the empty rental space of a defunct vacuum-cleaner repair shop that served as his campaign headquarters. I hadn't seen Sheila since the evening at the Sandpiper, and she was with Ray at the victory celebration. I had never met him and decided that then was not the time to introduce myself. Sheila must have had the same thought and made no move to introduce him to me, so I steered clear and swilled champagne as if it were beer.

Someone had brought a boom box, and, after Will had told us in two disjointed speeches how much he loved us all, his teenage son fed CDs of unidentifiable soft rock into the player, and the crowd, which was soon overflowing into the parking lot, got more and more raucous. A champagne cork ricocheted off the ceiling.

"Great! That's all we need," groused Brad Whitehead, shouting into my ear. "Will wins the election and gets sued by somebody losing an eye from a champagne cork—not to mention getting busted for serving booze to teenagers."

"Hey, lighten up, Bradley. It's the American way—doing stupid things to celebrate," I shouted back. "Such as," I continued, lowering my voice so only I could hear it, "thinking of introducing myself to Ray Byrne."

It took me several minutes to spot Sheila in the crowd, and I was beginning to fear that she'd left when I saw her smiling at me from near the rear entrance. I waved and pushed towards her while looking for Ray.

Sheila was holding a bottle of champagne and raised it in a salute as I approached her. "Happy whatever," I said. "Where's the hubby?"

Taking my wrist holding the glass and grinning with self-satisfaction, she splashed in champagne to the top. "Gone to pick up the girls. Like a good parent," she yelled over the yowl of squeals, laughter, and body-jarring bass notes.

"And you stayed. Like a bad parent," I shouted.

She reached up, pulled my head down, and carefully enunciated into my ear, "Exactly!" Then, grasping my free hand, she led me out into the parking lot.

People were arriving and leaving, and no one I knew was in sight or paying attention to us. "I'm drunk," said Sheila, sounding surprised and pleased. "I don't get drunk, you know."

"Well, no, I didn't know that," I said. "But I'm sure you're right, and I'm sure you're not drunk—just a bit loosened up, tipsy...and actually pretty funny."

She let go of my wrist, took my hand, and still holding the champagne bottle led me a short distance across the end of the parking lot and out of the light from the building entrance. "Where's your glass," I asked. "You been drinking out of the bottle?"

"Oh, God. I hope not. Did you see me drink out of the bottle?" she asked, more amused than alarmed. "That would really be tacky—but I have no idea what happened to my glass. You want some more?"

Still holding my hand, she held the bottle out to me. I placed my glass on the ground, then the bottle, and asked, "You know you're holding my hand in a public parking lot?"

"Yes I do. But nobody can see us, can they?" she asked while squeezing my hand and looking around.

"Who cares, who cares, who cares," I replied, each repetition softer than the preceding one, and pulled her against me. Champagne or no champagne, I clearly knew what I was doing.

Taking her head in both hands I kissed her gently and then more forcefully as my hands moved down, pulling her against my pelvis. She returned my kiss and, nearly falling, we reeled against the side of an SUV whose theft alarm began to blast deafening, shrill, wails.

Sheila, terrified and spastic, clung to me with the panicked grip of a drowning child as we leapt back from the car. I grabbed her hand and ran for the shadows of some trees bordering the lot a few yards away. We stopped in the darkness and looked back. Several people with hands over their ears stood looking toward the car. Sheila was weeping quiet sobs which I tried to calm by holding her face against my chest and stroking the back of her head. "It's okay, it's okay. Nobody can see us," I whispered and immediately began to laugh a soft embarrassed laugh.

"Whoa, that thing scared the bejesus out of me," I said still chuckling and trying to calm Sheila, whose body relaxed enough for her to look back toward the lot. Her sobs became little head-bobs, then sniffles, but she continued to cling to me until I again said, "It's okay—just a stupid car alarm."

Sheila grasped my shirtfront and pulled me through the narrow patch of trees to a low embankment topped by a hurricane fence running its length. I took her hand from my shirt and held firm. The car alarm stopped at precisely the same time leaving a momentary uncanny silence, as if our world had died for an instant, only to be revived by the surrounding muffled racket of strip-mall air conditioners, the crackling buzz of neon signs, stop-

and-go traffic, and occasional undefined muted human speech.

"We can't go back, can we?" whispered Sheila, her tone hopeless.

"Of course we can," I said, stroking her head. "We'll just wait until things clear out down there. Nobody saw anything." Then, suddenly concerned myself, I added, "When is Ray coming to pick you up?"

"He's not. I told him I'd get a ride." She pulled away and looked up at me. "But, I mean, we're adulterers now, aren't we? That siren...."

I began to laugh, but looking into her eyes I saw that she was serious in what I took to be contrition over being tipsy, so I stifled my inclination to tease and replied kindly and with no trace of irony, "I don't think so, Sheila. My understanding of adultery is that two people have to have sexual intercourse and at least one of them has to be married—we qualify only on the latter requirement. Right?"

Though I had tried not to be, my reply sounded mocking and condescending, but Sheila's response gave no indication that she was offended. "No. We're adulterers. Intent is the same as the act...and we wanted to."

"Hey, I still do," I crowed, but as soon as I'd spoken it was clear that for Sheila her concern was real and my flip response only had made it worse.

She pushed her hands toward me in a gesture meant to silence more than reject and sat down where she stood. "No, it's the same," she said. "We're adulterers now. We did it in our minds—our souls."

There was nothing about her that suggested she was anything other than deadly serious. It had to be the champagne...or Sheila was delusional. The fact was I hardly knew her, and much of what I knew had been reinforced by what in my midlife folly I wanted to be true.

Blaming the champagne, I dredged my memory for episodes of drunkenness—my own and others—that might help explain her bizarre behavior. I tend to become quiet (for fear of spilling the beans?) and thoughtful after drinking too much, and am a threat to no one, physically or philosophically. And, of course, there are the mean drunks. But Sheila appeared to be in my camp of the quiet and thoughtful, except she was wholly out of character in being adamant about the truth of a clear fantasy.

The first time my college roommate Greg got drunk, he came in and flopped down on his bed, only to immediately sit up again with the whirlies. I pulled off his shoes and stuffed his socks into them, but dizzy as he was he staggered up, retrieved his socks and said, "I always hang up my socks, Dennis." Actually, he never hung up any of his clothes, but this time he carefully draped his out-of-fashion argyles over two pants hangers before collapsing and barfing into his waste basket. I thus concluded that, as with Greg, alcohol and inexperience were the cause of Sheila's sudden madness; I hoped that she would not begin to vomit.

She sat and rocked back and forth, clutching her knees against her chest.

"So, maybe we should see about getting you home. Or do you feel up to going back to the party?" I asked, hoping she would say, "No, no, let's finish where we left off in the parking lot."

She looked up at me, smiled, and continued to rock, but now more slowly and deliberately than before. "No. We can't go back. The party's over," she said, her words sounding clichéd and rehearsed. Then looking around she added, "Where is your car? Can we get to it without going back to the parking lot?"

"Sure. I parked on the street, so if we walk along the fence I should be able to get the car and pick you up—or you can walk along with me to the car if you want."

"Okay," she said, reaching for my hand to be helped up. Still holding hands we walked along the fence, blocked from view of the parking lot by the scraggly oaks left when the strip mall area had been bulldozed years before. Neither of us spoke, but when we reached the cross street, Sheila stopped and said, "You get the car and I'll wait here—please."

On the way to the car I met no one, and when I pulled up to where I had left Sheila, she quickly got in, buckled up, leaned her head against the head rest, and sighed a long swoosh while reaching to pat my right thigh. Her touch, a complimentary gesture signaling a job well done, was maternal in its affection.

"So. What's your pleasure—the moon? The south of France? Home?" I asked before pulling away from the curb.

"Pleasure? What's my pleasure? Oh, God," she moaned. "Pleasure doesn't count"…and after a pause of several seconds she commanded, "You have to take me home." Before I could remind her that I had never been to her house and had only the vaguest notion of where she lived, she added. "I'm drunk, and an adulteress, you know."

"Yes, I believe you are drunk, and no, I don't believe you are an adulteress. Or if you are, who's the lucky guy?"

She didn't reply, but this time she gripped my thigh tightly and held on until I looked over to see tears again oozing onto her cheeks.

She remained silent until I asked how to get to her street. She gave me directions and resumed her silence.

As we neared her street I began to fear she actually might be having hallucinations and could go in and confess imaginary adultery to her husband. "So what are you going to say to Ray when he asks who brought you home?"

"He won't. He doesn't ask things like that."

"But what if this time he does?" I asked, sounding like

someone prompting lines.

"I'll tell him the truth, of course."

"Which is?" I persisted.

She cocked her head at me as if puzzled. "That I was afraid I'd drunk too much champagne and that you were kind enough to drive me home. What did you think...that I'd confess we'd committed adultery? Don't be foolish." And in the pause that followed while I tried to think of something that did not indeed sound foolish, she added, "Even though we did."

I'd turned onto her street by then and decided that we had to come to some kind of understanding about this notion of hers. "It's number twelve...where the light is," she directed, but barely slowing I drove past her house and said, "Look, let's go around the block and you tell me what's going on with this business of your saying we committed adultery, Sheila. We had one kiss—one perfunctory little kiss. That's all."

"Perfunctory? You call it perfunctory? That's a very strange, stuffy word. Not at all what I would call it," she protested, her tone a mixture of surprise and hurt feelings.

"Well, yes. I guess perfunctory is a little stuffy, but what would you call it?" I asked, trying to sound more amused than alarmed.

"I'd call it adultery," she replied at once and with an unmistakable finality.

I stopped the car and asked, "What would Ray call it...or more to the point, what *will* Ray call it?"

She reached for my arm and gripped it. "Ray won't know unless you tell him...or unless someone saw us. It's our secret. Our...I thought...love."

I moved the car to the curb and asked, "You go to church?"

"Sometimes. Do you?"

"Only to weddings and funerals. But my point is," I

continued, "does your understanding of what adultery is come from your religious beliefs...some scriptural passage? I mean, you're not like Jimmy Carter, are you....with that idea that if you lust after someone it's the same as having sex with him?"

She thought for such a long period of silence that I began to think she was trying to control anger or was about to cry, but then she said, "My understanding is spiritual—I wouldn't say religious, necessarily. But spiritual, intuitive. I know it. I feel it. And we committed it. We're committed."

"And the kiss did it?" I asked, as earnest as I'd ever been.

"Yes. The kiss and our spirits. Don't you feel that?" she asked.

She spoke with such innocence and ardor that my common-sense suspicions gave way to resignation. "Not exactly," I replied, sounding more skeptical than I intended, "but maybe it's a male thing...maybe I just lack sensitivity."

She continued to grip my arm with soft slow squeezes and said, "You know, it may be a male thing. Men so hide their feelings. But you are very sensitive. You'll see." She withdrew her hand and added, "But you have to get me home now—I really have to pee."

I pulled into her driveway and barely had stopped the car before Sheila said while opening the door, "I really do have to pee. We'll get together," and ran inside.

"Hail the conquering hero," shouted Annie when I got home. "Your man actually did win?"

"Of course he won. I don't back losers. You popped some corn? God that smells good. Do you think it will go good on top of Will's barely drinkable champagne?" I leaned over the couch and kissed the top of her head while reaching for the popcorn in the bowl on her lap. She slapped at my hand and asked in mock petulant tones, "Why don't you ever take me to your victory celebrations? After all, you so seldom pick a winner I'd think you'd want to show off."

"You may recall that I asked you if you wanted to go, and you said wild horses couldn't drag you."

"Well I didn't know there was going to be champagne. Did they spray it all over people?"

"Come on, Annie. These were mature liberal, environmental Democrats. We're very responsible people, as you know. Besides, it wasn't the Super Bowl or we would have."

I snuggled beside her and she handed me the nearly empty popcorn bowl and asked, "Nobody got drunk, huh?"

I let that sink in for so long that Annie looked to see why I hadn't replied. "Drunk? That's hard to say. Nobody was slobbery or falling down, but some were acting a bit whacked."

"How so?"

"Oh, you know...wearing ball caps backwards like they were teenagers, drinking straight out of the bottle, that sort of thing. Some butt pinching, giggling...run-of-the-mill tipsy nonsense."

"Whose butt did you pinch?"

I shook my head and looked quizzical. "Never got her name, but she was a real beauty. But I didn't push it—she looked like she might really fall for me."

"You wish." She wiped the butter and salt off her hands onto my shirtsleeve and asked, "You want to hit on me?"

"I'd love to," I said, and I meant it. And off to bed we went.

Usually after lovemaking sleep overtakes me like a steady, slow, wickedly pleasant drug, but that night I lay awake for hours trying to sort my tangled emotions into some sort of sensible pattern. What in the world was I doing? I'd come within the yowl of some yuppie's car alarm of God knows what: serious sexual groping? flat-out juvenile back seat screwing—with another man's wife yet—a woman I hardly know except in a kind of infatuation fantasy? Was I in some pathetic midlife testosterone crisis?

Annie slept in her usual curled serene position backed against me and untroubled by my constant fidgets and repositioning. It was madness to think of endangering our loving relationship, our family harmony and fun, by involving myself with Sheila Byrne and by meddling in her family's life. Looking at Annie asleep and content in our bed I felt less guilt than an immense foolishness. How could I be such an idiot?

I cringed in my bed covers, fearing disgrace and ridicule from some hidden observer there in the dark. Yet I still drifted back to scenes with Sheila. With the exception of the traumatic parking lot setting, we'd never been alone. And even though I felt humiliation and guilt because of my sexual feelings for Sheila, and fear of the possibility that they could be revealed to sneers and smarmy comments, the attraction was still there. And as the night tediously prolonged my anxieties, I was able to arrive at nothing more tangible than hope that no more would come of the idiocy I'd set in motion.

The next day was unseasonably cold. I was slow getting around but did manage to plod into the kitchen, pour coffee, and stare at the front page of the *Times* before Annie and the kids got off to school. An ugly drizzle was threatening to transform itself into spits of snow, and the *Times* was chronicling the Democrats' latest statewide internecine election fiasco. Well, at least Will Fleming had won—small consolation for my somehow having been tagged the male half of an adulterous sex act that not only was not consummated but had progressed no further that an abortive kiss on the lips. The day ahead lay dreary, indeed.

The dreariness faded when, just as I was leaving to drop off an appraisal at the bank, Sheila called, sounding bright and in her exuberant mode of setting agendas, be they stuffing envelopes for political candidates or telling me the time and place to meet her for "tea."

"Tea? Nobody has tea, Sheila," I replied, sounding both

grouchy and teasing. "Are you all right? Last night...was everything all right?"

"Everything is fine, more or less. So, we're having tea at Brookside Diner at 3:30. You know where it is? You can come, can't you?"

"No and yes," I answered, still grouchy. "No, I haven't a clue where the Brookside Diner is, and yes, I guess I can be there."

"Nobody knows where that diner is—that's why I chose it." She was still exuberant. "It's about 500 yards south of the Cedar Place bypass. When they put in the bypass, the diner was left on what's really an access road that no one uses. Where's your memory? It was a big deal about eight years ago. The owner threatened the Planning Board chair and got some kind of suspended sentence. What kind of an assessor are you not to remember that? Anyway, the owner...Greek name...keeps the place open out of spite—he can't be making a living out of it. But it's a good place—quiet, obscure. I never get anything but tea and sometimes a bagel. We'll talk."

I agreed to meet her there, and her "we'll talk" was as close as either of us came to mentioning what had happened the night before.

When I got there I remembered the place before increased traffic flow and corrupt politics had made it an instant isolated derelict. Frost-blighted ragweed and crab grass poked through cracks in the parking lot's asphalt, and a pile of cigarette butts some angry apprentice vandal had dumped out was being nibbled away by wind and drizzle.

The diner was empty except for Sheila and a pudgy waitress, somewhere between 40 and 65, nicely made up, who was knitting a deep-maroon sweater. Sheila, pale but otherwise full of health and outwardly pleased with her considerable charm—no tension, no self-consciousness—smiled and waved; nothing remained of the hysterics and mood changes of just 18 hours before.

"You rent this place by the hour or day?" I asked while sliding into the booth so I could face her.

"No cover, no minimum. Can you believe it? But you are expected to buy something," she said, still smiling and nodding in the direction of Madame Defarge who had put down her knitting and, menu in hand, moved toward us.

I waved off the menu and asked, "What do you suggest to go with coffee at 4 in the afternoon?"

"I like the blondies," she said. "They're my favorite here."

Nodding toward Sheila I said, "I prefer brunettes myself but..." and feigning sudden enlightenment added, "Oh, you mean blondie as opposed to brownie? Okay, sure. Black coffee and a blondie will be fine."

Sheila and the waitress rolled their eyes and set their lips in grim acknowledgment of how pathetic my joke had been, and the latter went off, no doubt wondering what a fine-looking woman like Sheila was doing with an aging smartass. "Not funny?" I asked, and before Sheila could respond I said, "Right...so where were we?"

"You've read *The Scarlet Letter,* haven't you?" she asked.

"Probably. I'm not sure. It's one of those books that everybody thinks they read in junior high or someplace—everyone knows the plot."

"Which is?"

"Okay, what is this?" I asked, trying to sound tired of the game before it started. "If I pass do we get to go out for recess, or what?"

"Don't get huffy," she said patting my arm. "I need to know what you remember."

"Need to know what I remember about *The Scarlet Letter*?" I asked. "Why?"

"Because I think there's something in that story that you

may have forgotten or never learned. It has to do with us."

Sheila's eyes and the soft set of her mouth conveyed self assurance, but I was beginning to feel the unease of one set up to be the butt of a joke. The coffee and blondie arrived then, and I used its arrival to remain silent as I stirred the coffee to cool it. Stalling for I wasn't sure what, I sipped at the coffee, burned my tongue and mouth, and gulped down a tear-raising swallow that cauterized my esophagus and left me gasping and fanning my mouth. "Dumb, dumb, dumb," I croaked. "I won't be able to taste anything for a week."

"I'll eat your blondie," said Sheila with not nearly as much sympathetic irony as I thought my folly called for, and she added, "When you recover, tell me about *The Scarlet Letter.*"

"I'm dying here, lady," I whimpered. "Is my memory of the damned book really that important?"

"It is indeed...and I'm sorry you burned your tongue."

"Tongue? Tongue? Everything down to my knees is toast," I lamented, but there was no putting her off. "Okay, this woman... Hester, I believe...has a baby who's not her husband's because he is old and ugly, she is disgraced, and has to wear a scarlet letter A on her forehead or someplace for the rest of her life. The father of the baby is a wuss preacher, they never have sex again, everybody dies. The end. Happy now?"

Sheila ignored my question. "You didn't read it in junior high. They don't teach it in junior high—it's too important." Her tone had become conspiratorial, as if she were giving instructions that must be absorbed and acted upon. "You very well know what the book is about. Admit it or we're lost."

I wanted to drink some coffee in the worst way but knew it was still too hot. Any playfulness that had been in our conversation was gone, and I was genuinely alarmed by the way Sheila's comments continued to include me in what more and more was becoming a situation that I couldn't get a grasp of—a fantasy world solely of her making.

"Look, Sheila, I don't understand what's going on, and I don't like all this fatalistic talk—it's unhealthy. We like each other, we've had a flirtation—a very nice one, and we love our kids and spouses. We aren't lost, for God's sake!"

"We've committed adultery, Dennis," she responded in a calm voice of explanation. "There's no way of getting around it."

I looked away and went for my coffee, holding the mug in both hands and blowing on it so hard that hot drops splashed out on my hands, warning me off from trying to sip. I returned the mug to the table, took a deep breath, turned to her and said, "We did not commit fucking adultery!"

Sheila, embarrassed, looked away. "I'm sorry. No pun intended," I said. "I wasn't trying to be funny or crude—I used that word as a cuss word. For emphasis."

She continued to look past my shoulder, so, enunciating each word, I continued, "We did not have sex. I did not touch your breasts or genitals. We did *not* commit adultery—or even come close to it."

"It's an old story, Dennis," she replied, looking at me again with those deep earnest eyes. "Hester said it to Arthur Dimmesdale. She said, *'What we did had a consecration of its own. We felt it so.'*"

I tried once again. "What I remember was fright. You had too much to drink. We've been attracted to each other all fall and showed it to each other in unspoken ways. We started to kiss and fell against a car whose alarm went off, scaring us and causing us to panic and run away—and you got a little hysterical. If we felt a bond of anything it was thwarted affection and, I say it again, we did not commit adultery!"

She said nothing, but stared down at her fingers, which she spread out on the place mat as if examining them for stains.

After a long silence she moved her hands onto her lap and, looking straight into my eyes, said, "It pains me to hear that. It really does pain me."

The words, the delivery, sounded so dramatically hackneyed that I snorted a scoffing laugh before I could catch myself, and, if I had not seen pain before, there was no mistaking its appearance now in Sheila's eyes. I looked away and into the damning glare of our waitress judging me a soulless brute even though she could have heard nothing of our conversation; a sympathetic resonance, an invisible female connection, had crossed the room and marked me a cad, seducer, scoundrel, rat, in all of the melodramatic Victorian connotations those outdated, silly-sounding slurs conjure up. Now it was I in pain. Whatever was going on, I was in it up to my ears.

I took Sheila's hands and fumbled to lace our fingers. Her fingers slid eagerly between mine, and she ignored the tears now coasting toward the corners of her mouth. "Look, Sheila, I didn't mean to appear insensitive, and God knows I don't want to cause you pain. It's just that we seem to be operating on different...I don't know what to call it...levels of awareness...of reality."

She freed her right hand and swiped at her cheeks while her left hand squeezed my fingers in heartbeat rhythm. "Awareness! It *is* an awareness, Dennis. You just have to admit it into your consciousness, your reality. We're joined. You just have to accept it...and it's good, a good thing."

She released my hand, blotted her tears with a paper napkin and smiled a spontaneous grin that broke my heart. Looking at the waitress, now concentrating on her knitting, I blurted in her direction, "It's not what you think." She responded by dropping her knitting and raising both hands, palms outward, in a gesture of surrender and ignorance, and a frown formed signaling her sense of having been unjustly accused.Simultaneously I had become the object of the waitress' stare of disgust and Sheila's grin of adoration, and I immediately saw there was no way I could prove to either woman that I was not what they thought. Barely able to keep from running for my car, I asked, "Could we leave now?"

In an instant Sheila's grin became opened-mouth surprise and her head actually jerked backward. "But...your blondie" she said, meekly pointing toward the uneaten pastry.

"Fuck the blondie," I said in loud defiance of the waitress, and dropped a ten dollar bill on the table. No one spoke as I helped Sheila into her jacket and, steering her by holding her elbow, directed her out into the parking lot where she stepped away and turned her trembling hurt face toward me. I walked toward her car. She trailed behind.

That was ten years ago, and I'll never rid my memory of her standing there wholly vulnerable, her entire being a metaphor of betrayal and stoic pain. Her eyes never left mine and her head bobbed up and down, not in agreement with what I was saying, but in recognition that what I was saying fulfilled a prophecy she'd hoped to avoid.

"Look, Sheila, I don't know what's going on here. I feel trapped in some kind of sad, dangerous farce that I don't feel responsible for. I mean...okay, I admit that I probably would have had sex with you...I wanted to have sex with you. But we didn't. Sheila, we did not have sex...a three-second kiss is not adultery! It's a kiss. A very short, impetuous kiss...and you were...you'd had too much to drink. It was not adultery. It was not a commitment."

She continued to nod as I spoke, her eyes unwavering until, no longer able to sustain her pain, she began to cry. All I could do was get out of there. Had I stayed a moment longer I would have wrapped her into my heart with God knows what results. "I have to go," I said, walked to my car and drove away.

For the next several days, my emotions gripped me in random spasms of fear and guilt, although the guilt was tempered by feeling that I had escaped an irremediable entanglement. The more I thought about Sheila the more I became convinced that she was at best merely eccentric, and at worst was living out a bizarre romantic identification with Hester Prynne—a heroine of a nineteenth century novel, for God's sake! A letter from Sheila soon proved the latter to be more truth than speculation and turned my fear and guilt to anger.

The envelope was typed and there was no return address. The letter was written in flawless calligraphy of simple beauty and read:

Dear Dennis,

I forgive you for the hurt you have caused me with your hateful words, because I realize that your inability to honor your commitment, a commitment I now see was too easily made, and will continue to blight your relationships with all women. It takes strength to be true to one's commitment, and for that I forgive your lack of moral courage, for I have faith that as with Hester Prynne I too have a "firm belief, that, at some brighter period, when the world should have grown ripe for it, in Heaven's own time, a new world would be revealed, in order to establish the whole relation between man and woman on a surer ground of mutual happiness."

Your devoted,
Sheila Byrne

"I lack courage of commitment? What commitment?" I protested to the wall opposite my desk, adding "And speaking of commitment—commitment is what you need all right, lady, but it should be in a mental hospital!" I was still fuming the next day when, while appraising a five-shop building in a dying strip-mall, I had the proprietor of a going-out-of-business tee-shirt shop silk-screen an ornate scarlet letter **A** onto a white tee-shirt nightie. Though it was the logo **A** for the Arizona Diamondbacks baseball team, its contemporary design still looked baroque enough to have served as the first letter of a seventeenth-century Puritan alphabet book, as in "**A** is for Adam. In Adam's fall we sinned all."

I mailed Sheila the nightie with a post-it on which I had written, "Enjoy! Yours in commitment, Arthur Dimmesdale." I knew it was a foolish, childish thing to do as soon as the box left my hands at the post office; one should know better than to provoke the mentally ill into a possible insane act.

For months after mailing the nightie I looked with caution at all letters addressed to me, and I even worked up several scenarios of explanation to use should Annie answer an insane phone call from Sheila. Ten years is a very long time, depending on its context. People turn gray, get fat, lose weight, lose jobs, give birth, die. The Brookside Diner died a lingering death of neglect, no more letters came, and there were no mad phone calls that needed explanation.

I went into the paper's web site for their account of the accident I had missed. Sheila had been taking Katy back to Binghamton after the spring break. There had been one of those late-March whiteouts in the Catskills, and just north of the Roscoe Diner they hit the big blade of a highway department snowplow head on. Katy had been driving. Both were killed instantly. Both were wearing seat belts. Both were extricated from the wreckage with the aid of the "jaws of life."

They had a joint funeral—closed caskets, of course.

Three weeks after the funeral, a package—one of those large padded envelopes favored by L.L. Bean and Lands' End— came addressed to me. There was no return address, and the block printing was large and careful. Inside was Sheila's scarlet-**A** nightie. The **A** was nearly faded away, and the nightie was threadbare and gray from repeated washings.

OUT-OF-BODY LOVE

It has been three weeks now since I had the dream—July the eleventh, a couple of days after a full moon.

In the dream I was in this large, pleasant room. It was night, but there was enough light so that I could make out the features of the place.

I was naked, lying on the white top sheet of a king-sized bed. A very comfortable bed with a low, polished-wood headboard darker colored than the walls. If there was other furniture in the room, I don't recall it, but there was a simple richness about the place—it smacked of wealth and, ironically, being far from wealthy, I felt as though I belonged there.

So I'm lying on this great bed, feeling really good about everything, when Doris Palmer walked in. And she was naked too. The indirect lighting, wherever it was coming from, lit up her body in segments as she neared the bed, so that I never really saw her entire body uniformly lit; that is, sometimes her head would be in more light than the rest of her, sometimes her midriff or her ankles. Nothing about her was ever in the dark though; it was just that some parts of her always were lighted more than others, and it was a kind of random thing.

But, Doris Palmer? Doris Palmer? I hadn't seen Doris Palmer in more than forty years, and though I knew this was Doris, it didn't look like her at all—not like the Doris Palmer I had last seen in college, nor what I thought she must look like today. At the same time, I knew it was Doris.

Doris. Now, do you know anyone under sixty who is named Doris? Did you ever know of anyone named Doris other than Doris Day? It's an endangered name—nearly extinct. Be that as it may, this Doris was a beautiful, beautiful woman, who looked to be in her late twenties and was spectacular in her girlish, athletic womanliness. She was tall, five-nine or ten, with long legs; narrow hips; pubic hair darker than the hair on her head and lying in an even pattern that looked cropped but you knew wasn't; small breasts that offered little cleavage and turned up slightly at their nipples; and a strong neck that was a bit too short for her head—a tiny imperfection that made her beauty believable.

Her face *was* perfect! Her ears, her eyes, her nose and mouth—each caught and held your eye, the way one's attention is drawn to features of a landscape painting that then blend back into a perfect symmetry of the whole scene. Yet I could not look at her eyes without somehow being aware of her mouth, as the two combined to produce a warmth and an intimacy of attention directed at me.

I never had been the object of such intense—what would you call it? Attention? Scrutiny? No. Those words don't work—they're too clinical, too probing. What she was doing was *admiring* me. What she was doing was *loving* me. *Loving* me! Flat out *loving* me!

I knew it! I felt it! It was an honest-to-God physical sensation that—and I hesitate to tell you this because it sounds so hokey—I felt it in my chest! Not my heart, thank goodness, but, just the same, in my chest—behind and just above my sternum. It was love. This Doris Palmer, who I knew wasn't really Doris Palmer, was loving me.

Sex. You're going to say it was sex. Well, perhaps. But it didn't seem like sex at the time, nor does it now. At least I've never experienced anything sexually that approached this dream of Doris Palmer's love.

Doris was a girl I dated when I was eighteen years old. She was, as far as I ever was privileged to determine, a natural blond, complete with blue eyes and a short, chubby cheerleader's body. And though we dated for a whole winter and did some fairly serious groping, I never got inside her underwear. I suppose because she was chubby she wore a damned panty girdle that gripped her essentials with such determination that she literally must have swathed herself with talcum powder to get the thing on; and once her body got heated up a little she was vulcanized to it. The girdle, in effect, was a chastity belt, and it must have been hell for her to wrench out of at the end of the evening. When warm spring weather came, it would have been intolerable for her to wear the girdle, so in May she dumped me.

But why would I now have a dream about her (only it was a different her) and have her love me with an intensity that has disturbed my waking hours ever since? I'm telling you the feeling of love was intense! It was a pleasure/pain thing, kind of like the way a bruise feels when it is nearly healed and you keep poking at it; but it was a cerebral feeling, too, that comes with accomplishing something great—not that I ever have, but I imagine it feels like that when they hang an Olympic gold medal around your neck and the National Anthem's playing and thousands are cheering you. Only it was better than that—more personal, more private. And she never actually touched me—she just looked at me!

And no, I wasn't on some kind of drug trip. I've never taken any drugs—never even smoked pot. I don't think I've taken so much as an aspirin in the last six months. Anyway, I woke up in a strange way too. I knew I was waking up, and moving from my dream to consciousness was a slow, steady progression that left me stone cold awake. Well, no. Stone cold is not really a good description because, even though I was completely awake, I also was warm from this intense love feeling. There was nothing cold about the dream or its aftereffect at all.

Very alert, I looked across the bed at Marty, my wife, my one and only wife of thirty-five years, and she slept wholly at ease, making soft little exhaling sounds that only the most insensitive husband would have labeled snores. Clearly she had done nothing to influence my dream, unless, of course, she had been dreaming, too, and had projected her love onto me. But that was absurd: she would have had to take on the shape of this Doris Palmer, a woman she had never seen, to love me like I'd never been loved before. Ridiculous!

Ridiculous is the operative word here, I guess, because I remember saying out loud, "Ridiculous! This is ridiculous." But it wasn't ridiculous, because the love sensation remained as strong as it had been in my dream, and I lay back, wide awake, reveling in being loved by...whatever, whoever this Doris Palmer apparition was.

I lay awake, unmoving, the rest of the night—it must have been two or three hours—feeling wonderful. I've never felt so good about myself. As I watched daylight seep around our drapes, I began to wonder in earnest what was going on. Had I died and gone to a heaven I didn't believe in? Marty woke up in her usual slow, stretching, reluctant manner and saw me lying there wide-eyed and smiling.

"What's the matter?" she asked a bit defensively, as if she had been left out of a joke. "Why are you smiling at me like that?"

"Damned if I know," is all I could think to say. "I've had this very, very nice dream that left me feeling great."

"Money or woman?" she asked.

"Old girl friend," I said.

"Pathetic," she said, smiling and grabbing me a little too vigorously in the crotch. "You're pretty droopy down there," she added. "She must not have been all that great."

"Come on," I said, grabbing her wrist. "This was not a sex dream. She was loving me and I never laid a finger on her."

"Or anything else, apparently," she said, glancing down at my hand protecting my crotch and then moving off to take her shower.

At breakfast I told her in detail about my dream, and I told her that I still felt this sensation of love. She seemed a little hurt when I kept emphasizing the strength of the feeling and asked if I had ever felt anything like that in response to her.

"I never felt this in response to anything," I exclaimed. "I feel like I should be exorcised or something."

"Exorcised? This Doris Palmer is some kind of a witch?"

"I'd be very surprised," I said. "The last I saw of her she was...come to think of it, I have no idea the last time I saw her. I was eighteen, for God's sake, and I never even got into her pants."

"No doubt not for lack of trying," she chortled. "Well, there's your answer—unrequited sex. Your frustration built up for forty years and it finally comes out in this dry wet dream that you think was love. You're a real piece of work, honey." She kissed me on top of my head and went off to teach junior-high English.

I haven't dared to bring it up with her again, although I would like to. She's a wonderful person, but talking to her about what I think is love, some ethereal thing generated by an apparition that may or may not have been an old girl friend, seems clearly out of the question, and I don't want her to feel hurt or slighted. She's my confidante, my buddy, as well as my lover, and she's always been the one I shared good, bad and indifferent happenings with. But this time I'm afraid I'm on my own.

I've gone back over everything I can remember that happened the day prior to the dream. I even made a list of the food I ate. Nothing remarkable there. It was a routine day, maybe a little cooler than normal, and I ate stuff I've been eating my entire life. I didn't have a drink, no wine with dinner, no late evening snack. Nothing.

Earlier in the summer there had been some kind of a convention in New Mexico, or some place in the southwest, about UFO sightings over the years, and some baloney about a government conspiracy or cover-up, but I didn't pay any attention to that. And there's a lot of New-Age nonsense around here about shamans and so-called out-of-body death where people claim to have died and come back to tell about what it was like. And then there are those sitting around beating on drums to release the body's noxious vapors. But I laugh at those people, and I wouldn't mention it at all except that the love I feel, this sensation, seems out-of-body, too—like I have no input into it—and God knows I have no control over it.

So, after finding nothing that I thought could have triggered my dream, I was afraid to start reading Freud or Jung on dream interpretations for fear it would reveal that I was a closet Buddhist, or that my regular bowel habits really were disguising a foot fetish. I'm kidding, of course, but I did get concerned enough to do some reading into Freud's notions of the uncanny, and the thing that stuck with me was the idea of omnipotence of thought—you know, Norman Vincent Peale's "power of positive thinking" run amok? It's the idea that if you think about something long enough and hard enough, it comes true or can be conveyed to someone else without any kind of physical communication.

I don't really believe that's possible, but how else to explain Doris Palmer's love for me? Could she have been thinking about me with such intensity that it carried into my dream? I brooded on this for a couple of days and took a desperate step: I hired a detective to check out Doris Palmer for me.

I was amazed by the number of "Investigators" there are in the yellow pages, but I chose the name that sounded the least macho—Joel Phelps, "Private Investigator. Member: U.S. Process Servers' Assoc. Licensed and Bonded"—and went to see him. He works out of a winterized sun porch in his home, and when I told him I wanted him to check out Doris, he was amused and gave me the impression that he thought I was lying.

"Look," I said. "I don't even know if this woman is alive or not. I just want to know if she has a job of any kind, if people think she's normal, and what she was doing the week leading up to July 11th, but especially the day of July 11th."

I told him I had moved away from Iowa right after college, but I seemed to remember that she'd married a pharmacist, and she might still live in Clinton.

"You hope to use this information for any legal action?" he asked, a knowing smile at the corners of his mouth.

"I'm not planning any action of any kind. I'm just curious, that's all."

He lit a cigarette, and after a couple of puffs asked, "Mind if I smoke?" Before I could reply he said, "Chances are good that I can give you her date of birth, social security number, height, weight, hair color, driver's license, names and phone numbers of her current and past neighbors, her past addresses, plus other property that she may own; the same for a spouse and any kids, and a complete financial and medical history for a thousand dollars. What she was doing during a specific week? Well, that's tougher and could run into another grand or two because somebody would have to be on the scene to check that out. And for another hundred and fifty the same investigator probably could get a current picture of her—you know, like coming out of her house or in some public place."

I was stunned—and embarrassed that I had been so naïve; and I also would have felt less foolish if he had quoted the price all in dollars instead of saying it could cost "another grand or two," which sounded like a clichéd line from a 1940s film noir.

"I had no idea that it would be so expensive," I said, trying to sound more apologetic than surprised. "There's no way I can afford your services—not that I think your price is unreasonable. It's just that I don't have that kind of money, and satisfying my curiosity isn't that big a deal."

He nodded and said, "I understand," in a voice that was flat and not condescending, and before an embarrassing silence could set in he continued. "Now of course if you don't need all of those data the cost would be less. I could give you her address, phone number, husband's name, if she has one, kids' names and addresses, place of employment—that sort of thing for, say...five hundred. I also take credit cards. Where does she live?"

Those data? The guy actually used proper grammar and said those data? I was impressed. Nobody but some pretentious PhD, or a guy who was a total science wonk would say "those data."

"Well," I said, "the last I knew, she lived in Clinton, Iowa."

"Right," he said, remembering that I had told him that before. "You see, I can get the stuff I mentioned without ever leaving this room, but to find out what somebody did during a specific week takes leg work and somebody on the scene, and that runs into money. I might be able to get her on the phone, though, and fake some kind of market survey, or some such scam, to get her to tell me something about the week you're interested in. It's amazing what people will tell you over the phone. Why that particular week?"

"Well, something happened to me that week and I think she may have been involved in it." The expression on his face never changed, but I felt compelled to add, "It was something good.

Nothing bad or criminal."

He just sat there, his expression softening into a slight quizzical look, waiting for me to make a decision.

"Five hundred?" I asked.

"Tops," he said. "Less if we're lucky." Then he added: "You know, there are some guys who have these websites who claim they can tell you how you can get this kind of information by using their software or something, but I'd stay away from them. Who's to say they wouldn't set up a file on you, and paying these guys might be a little iffy, too. And I'm here, man, face-to-face. You gotta problem, don't like how I work, I'm here—a living body."

I had no idea how I would conceal from Marty a five hundred dollar fee to Joel Phelps, Private Investigator, but I told him to go ahead, and I left his sunporch office feeling the first twinges of anxiety since I'd had the love dream.

He called the next afternoon and said that Doris Charlene Palmer had died of lymphoma in Clinton, Iowa, April 29th, 1997. Her married name was Spencer, and her husband, Duane William, an insurance agent, was still living; she had a married daughter, April Susan Spencer Cartwright, born in 1970, and another daughter, Jennifer Ann, born in 1972 with Downs Syndrome, who receives a social security supplement. Doris had no work record outside the home. "Frankly," said Phelps, "I hope I'm not out of bounds saying this, but Doris Palmer's life may have been one of the dullest I've ever investigated." The fee would be two hundred seventy five dollars, and he would send me a printed report. He assured me that the report would come in a plain envelope with no return address.

So there I was. And so much for Freud's omnipotence of thought—unless Doris was loving me from the grave. Before I would even allow myself to think twice about where that kind of nonsense could lead, I dismissed the notion, but I did think about

Doris more soberly for the next couple of days. I felt bad that she'd had what surely must have been a sad life, and Phelps' observation about its dullness didn't help.

So if Doris Palmer didn't influence my dream, who did? It still bothered me, and on top of that my feelings of being loved seemed to be ebbing—the glow was going.

I half seriously thought about calling Phelps again and asking him if for another fifty he'd let me tell him my dream and then tell me what he thought my dream meant. But I was afraid he would have some kind of dream-interpretation software and would just run me through his computer. Nonetheless, I really needed to tell my dream to another human being. I hadn't told the dream to anyone but Marty, and I suddenly felt a compulsion to do so. But I didn't call Phelps. I went to a bar instead.

Okay, so maybe it's a generational thing; but isn't there some popular belief or cliché that says bartenders are supposed to be sympathetic, nonjudgmental listeners? And what did I have to lose? I'd pick a bar where it was unlikely anyone would know who I was, tell him my dream, and see what kind of response I got. I mean, it's no more crazy than ancient Greeks hunting up blind oracles who were born with club feet or something and were supposed to have all the answers to anybody's questions.

So the next afternoon just before happy-hour time, I entered the lounge bar of the Timberfield Lake Steak House—a restaurant I'd never been in, but one whose well-kept parking area and antiqued wooden sign painted with gold leaf letters gave the place a superficial aura of leathery comfort and discreet self-indulgence— the perfect place to woo someone else's wife, get quietly drunk, or, as in my case, confide an out-of-body love experience.

The lounge was spacious, heavily carpeted, and furnished with knee-high dark glass-topped tables and wine-colored leather chairs on ball casters. Apparently the bar did a big business at dinner time with plenty of room for patrons waiting for their tables, but now a couple (expensively dressed, he fortyish, she younger, and both nervous), the bartender, and I were the only people in the room.

I chose a stool a foot or two away from where the bartender stood carefully peeling strips from a stack of lemons. He was younger than I expected my confidant would be—late twenties, probably. He also was slightly built, wore glasses, and pared the lemons with a deftness that suggested he knew what he was doing—a small thing but something that gave me confidence. His smile was sincere as he asked me what I would like. I ordered a draft Bass Ale and let him return to his preparations for the evening's martini crowd before engaging him in conversation. Tapes of wonderfully romantic cocktail piano, classic Cole Porter, Rodgers and Hart, came from speakers in the ceiling.

"First time I've been in here," I said. "Pleasant place."

Looking up he nodded and thanked me. "We try to do it right," he said.

"Given the number of lemons you're stripping bare, you must do a good cocktail business," I said, sounding too much like I was prying into the restaurant's business affairs.

"We do okay," he responded. "I like to keep ahead so I don't have to do this when we get busy."

It was all very innocuous prattle, friendly enough, but it gave me no opening for my dream, not that I could imagine any normal conversation that would. After a couple of sips of my ale, I decided to hit things straight on and asked, "People confide their troubles with you in a classy place like this?"

He chuckled. "All the time." Then he asked, "You think this is a classy place?"

"Well, it's not Bemelman's Bar at the Carlyle, but, yeah, I think it has a nice classy suburban quality to it. Don't you?"

He didn't answer as he mounded the lemon strips into a stainless steel dish, but then he said, "You're in real estate, right?"

"Good God no!" I answered, as if I had been accused of a crime. "Actually, I'm a retired elementary school principal. Did I sound like I was trying to case the place for a prospective buyer?"

"Something like that," he said, and then diplomatically added, "There's nothing wrong with being in real estate."

Since he'd asked about me, I thought I had an opening to inquire about him, so I asked, "How about you? You bartend full time?"

He began hanging wine glasses from a tray onto the wooden rack above his head. "Pretty much. Five nights a week. It's a good job for what I'm really involved in." He then gave a short, self-deprecating snort and said, "I'm a graduate student in art history."

"No kidding," I said, and, before I thought, added, "Is there any future in that? I mean, jobs? Are there any jobs?"

He snorted again. "Hardly any. But, what the hell? It's what I like. Maybe I'll get lucky and some filthy-rich regional museum patron will like my Irish coffee and give me a job. Stranger things have happened."

I almost leaped off my stool. He'd given me the perfect opening! "Speaking of strange," I said with a laugh, but with an intensity that seemed a bit out of place. "Let me tell you about the bizarre, and I mean bizarre, dream I had."

He glanced over at me with a look of curiosity and no hint of dread, so I began at the beginning of my dream and gave him the entire story, complete with Joel Phelps. When I finished I felt an embarrassing sense of anti-climax. The whole thing was sounding so stupid that, in an attempt to convince him about the effect the dream had on me, I said, "In telling this, I'm afraid I haven't conveyed how profound the feeling was that this woman imparted to me. I'm telling you it was intense."

I nearly shouted out *intense*, but then in a calm, lowered voice I added, "It was a feeling of love. A spiritual thing. Love."

He didn't look at me while he continued with preparations behind the bar, and if I had embarrassed him I didn't give a damn. That was my dream, take it or leave it.

He then looked at me, cocked his head as if he'd been amazed and said, "Some dream," and walked into the kitchen.

I sat there, looking into my beer and feeling defiant and foolish. He came back with another tray of wine glasses that he again started to place above his head.

"So what do you think?" I asked, in a tone more of a challenge than one of curiosity.

As if tired of hanging wine glasses, he left the tray, stood before me while leaning back against the counter behind him, and said, "I don't know what to make of your dream. But it's clear it has really gotten to you, and before I say anything more I want to know that you don't really believe in that stupid myth about bartenders somehow being folk psychiatrists or some damned thing. Do you?"

I began to feel hopeful again. "I'm not sure what I believe anymore, but I don't trust psychiatrists and can't afford them anyway, and I had this compulsion, this need, to tell the dream to somebody, and—well, yeah, I bought into the bartender myth. Not that I thought you would know what the dream was all about, but that you'd at least listen to me. Which you did, and for that I thank you very much."

I drank off the rest of my ale and reached for my wallet. He seemed not to notice and asked, "You say you're retired?"

"Right," I answered. "I'm sixty two, draw social security and my teacher's pension, and can bench press 200 pounds. Well, actually the last is a lie, but I really am sixty two and retired."

He looked at me kindly and said, "Okay. Now you're old

enough to easily be my father. You've probably forgotten more things than I'll ever know, so there's no reason in the world to think that what I make of your dream has any value. But for what it's worth, here's what I think."

He poured himself a wine glass of seltzer and continued. "The dream sounds like some kind of religious experience to me. I don't know anything abut your beliefs, but this whole business about the physical strength of a spiritual thing sounds like a revelation or something. An epiphany. I just think you were lucky a naked Jesus didn't walk into your bedroom and start loving you. That would really have fucked you up."

I cringed, not sure whether it was the image of a naked Jesus or the language of "Jesus" and "fucked up" in the same sentence that bothered me the most.

He paid no attention to my body language and said, "I have no idea why an old girl friend, or whoever she was, got mixed into this if there weren't sexual overtones, but if you say your feelings weren't sexual I believe you. Your description of Doris is esthetic, not lustful—you saw her as a beautiful female figure, the way we're supposed to view sculpted or painted nudes but really don't. But I tell you, the one thing I get out of this dream is your reaction—your sense of being loved! I mean, that is great! Man, I know dozens of people who drop acid and dump unbelievable shit into their bodies, desperate to feel something like that, and here this dream just lays it on you out of the blue."

He smiled and shook his head in wonderment and continued, "But what's sad to me is that you can't just lie back and enjoy being loved by who or whatever it is. Now that's not criticism. I don't know how I'd react to…what did you call it, out-of-body love? But, hey, it would be great if you could just forget about what it's supposed to mean and where it came from and just revel in it. Just dig it. No strings attached. Just let yourself be loved."

Two business types had come in and sat at the end of the bar. One gestured toward the bartender while the other took out a cell phone and punched in some numbers. The bartender waved to me that he would be back and moved down the bar to take their order.

While he was gone I tried to assimilate what he had said. He was of course right. There was a huge block in my sense of proper behavior that denied me the pure pleasure of being loved by whoever was loving me in this dream. But the source was all-important. I was a married man and it was immoral, or at least unseemly, to accept love from another woman even if the love was asexual. Ah, that was it: there is no such thing as asexual love between sexes. Didn't modern psychology make the claim that even love for one's mother has a sexual foundation? Besides, hadn't I tried like the devil to seduce Doris Palmer when I was eighteen years old? It was all becoming muddled, and maybe it was the pint of ale, but suddenly, under my breath, I started to sing, "Jesus loves me this I know...'cause the Bible tells me so."

The bartender came back and began making two Manhattans. He looked up and said, "I wouldn't worry about it. Go with the flow. It was a terrific dream. Would you like another beer?"

"Sure," I said. "Sounds good."

And while he carried the drinks to the end of the bar and drew my second Bass Ale, I tried to follow his advice. The love from my dream was getting mingled with the ale, and I took a deep breath, shook my arms hanging down at my side, and relaxed into a contented slump.

This is a wise young man, I thought. I wonder if he can explain to me why I'm supposed to think Jackson Pollack was a great painter.

DAMAGED GOODS

For as long as he could remember, Everett Charles Holmes had disliked his first name. He was thirty-five years old and never had known anyone his age who was named Everett. Indeed, the only Everett he had heard of was C. Everett Koop, Reagan's Surgeon General, whom E.C. had admired, though he thought Koop's first name must be really horrible if he chose to call himself C. Everett.

Early on Everett Charles had taken to calling himself "Chuckie"; but when in his teens "Chuckie" began to sound to him like a ten-year-old purse snatcher or a horror-movie psychopath, he renamed himself E.C. And if asked what E.C. stood for, he'd lie and say, "Nothing. Just E.C."

Now, E.C. waited on the second level of the *Downtown Cinema's* lobby, feeling fortunate that he had gotten the last ticket for the next showing in the theater's tiny 50-seat auditorium for a British documentary that had been following a group of kids every seven years since their seventh birthday, 35 years ago.

The area where he stood was four steps up from the main lobby and gave him a view of everyone buying tickets or waiting to enter the much larger theater space below where a woman of uncertain middle age caught his eye. She wore an outdated brown down-filled coat stained with dark oily spots. Gray sweat pants and dirty red Chuck Taylor basketball shoes showed beneath the coat, and a plastic white gardenia was pinned above her right breast. The woman climbed two of the four steps to the lobby where E.C. stood watching, folded her hands across her breasts like a diva commencing a song in a recital, and loudly proclaimed, "I am not now, nor ever have been, a member of the Communist Party."

All heads turned to look at her, but the heads returned to their former directions in cool New Yorker disregard of the bizarre when the manager grasped the woman's upper left arm and, without a word, gently but swiftly maneuvered her out onto the sidewalk.

Continuing to watch, E.C. was intrigued by the beatific smile and dignified carriage of the woman as she was hustled out of the lobby. She struck E.C. as someone other than one of the dozens of the certifiably insane who walk Manhattan's streets daily, albeit her clothing and her disclaimer about the Communist Party made her appear nearly as demented as the expensively dressed matron he once had observed pushing an empty grocery cart along East 38th Street while loudly cursing the Army for "hoarding all the God-damned matches."

E.C. went up to the manager, who by now had returned to his post taking tickets, and asked, "That woman you just...Is she...? What's her story?"

Glancing out at the street and then examining E.C. in an instant furtive surveillance, the manager said, "What you see is what you get. She's been coming in here every night for a week."

It was clear that the manager had no intention of making conversation, and as patrons began filing into the little theater where E.C.'s movie was about to be shown, he started for the steps leading up to that room's entrance. But looking once again out onto the street, he saw the woman standing as resolute as before, and in an uncharacteristically impulsive move he pocketed his ticket, exited the lobby, and went up to her.

"Excuse me. I was just in the lobby there, and I was wondering if someone is bothering you or something? I mean, the business about not being a Communist—is the FBI harassing you for some reason? A mistaken identity maybe?"

The woman examined E.C.'s face, squinting as if probing for details, and in a dispassionate clinical tone asked, "You don't have much luck with women, do you?"

"No, no, look! I'm not trying to pick you up. I just thought you sounded so forceful when you spoke—like you wanted everyone to hear what you said. Like you wanted to be exonerated—something like that."

Scowling, she asked, "What are you, some sort of aging transvestite Valley Girl? What's with all of these 'likes' you keep saying?"

E.C. reddened. He wasn't sure whether he had been trying to pick her up or not, but she was right on one count: he had not had much luck with women. And now he was being humiliated by this weird, crypto bag lady who in the lights from the street appeared to be older than he first had thought. He raised his hands, palms outward in the universal gesture of defenselessness, and was about to tell her to forget the whole thing when she again smiled her beatific smile and said, "Yes, you may buy me coffee."

"Coffee? What makes you think I want to buy you coffee? Or anything else?" he asked in a weak defensive tone.

"You want to," she said, taking his arm and turning him up the street with surprising firmness, her smile now exaggerated and mocking.

E.C. fell into the rhythm of her swift pace, and, crowding past others, they went half a block without speaking.

"In here," she said, freeing his arm and standing to the side of the entrance to *Rag's*, a coffee shop that changed owners and names yearly and had nothing to recommend it other than its convenient location. E.C. held the door for her and followed as she passed up three booths in favor of the fourth, which to E.C. seemed identical to those she'd rejected, their menus in clear plastic sleeves wedged behind the sugar canister and the paper-napkin holder. E.C. tried to hand one to the woman, but she waved it away, staring at him with a new, barely perceptible smile that wavered at the corners of her mouth.

To shield his self-consciousness, E.C. studied a menu. Then, while examining the long lists of choices, a simple plan took shape: he would order coffee, make small talk as best he could, and when the check came put a twenty dollar bill on the table with the check, excuse himself for the men's room, and stay in there long enough for the woman to take the money and disappear, which he was certain she would do.

"Find something you want there?" she asked in a voice you might use with a child you had been forced to entertain.

"I think I'll just have coffee, but go ahead. Order whatever you'd like," answered E.C. Then he extended his hand and said, "By the way, my name is E.C. Holmes."

Her hands stayed in her lap, and she said nothing, making him feel increasingly ill at ease. Finally she said, "That's nice, but why did you feel compelled to tell me that?"

Trying to conceal his growing irritation, E.C. explained, "Well, I don't feel compelled. It just seems like the conventional, polite thing to do."

The waitress arrived while E.C. was thinking of something to add, and the woman in a dramatic lilt ordered coffee and two bagels with cream cheese—strawberry jam for one, and grape jelly for the other.

"Just coffee for me, please," said E.C., sounding so uncertain that the waitress asked, "You sure?" to which he responded with a nod of his head.

They sat in silence—E.C. concentrating on hiding his discomfort while the woman seemed unaware of his presence and showed not the least sign of self-consciousness. When the food came, she immediately began to eat her bagels and, chewing rapidly, ignored E.C., not once looking up from her plate except to pour cream into her coffee. The arrival of food had made the absence of conversation less awkward, and E.C. sipped his coffee while taking advantage of her concentration on her bagels to look at her without fear of discovery.

He couldn't determine her age. Barely discernible crow's feet fanned out from the corners of her eyes, but the rest of her face was wrinkle free, and though he would not have described her as pretty, E.C. found her face oddly alluring. Her hair was black and dull, medium length, and, though mussed, showed some part in the middle. Her eyebrows and lashes also were black, but E.C. wondered if her hair were not dyed? It needed a shampoo, that was certain, and though her black hair was alien to her skin tone, her brown eyes seemed natural to both. Suddenly looking up, she said, "Why do you stare at me?" and, in turn, stared at him until he looked away.

"I'm sorry," said E.C. "But would you accept that I was admiring you instead of staring?"

"Accept?" she scoffed. "I accept the obvious, and that, dear friend, is that you don't have much luck with women." She reached across the table, patted his hand, smiled the smile of a very poor winner, and added, "It just *exudes* from everything about you," and resumed eating.

E.C.'s tolerance reached its limit. "Look, I don't know what's the matter with you, but I see no reason why I should stay around and be insulted." He reached for his wallet and added, "I'll leave some money and you can pay the tab—whenever your happy little heart feels like it."

He started to rise and the woman said, "Oh for God's sake sit down. You men are all alike—constantly measuring everything by your shriveled little penises." And then, pointing a jam-smeared knife at him, she added, "When I'm finished here, you are going to take me home."

E.C. settled back onto the edge of his seat and replied, "Oh I am, am I? And where do you live? The Dakota, no doubt."

The woman's laugh was one of genuine pleasure, and still smiling she said, "Oh you're such a petulant little shit! Not my house—*your* house! *I* don't have a house." And before E.C. could protest, she added, "You picked me up, remember? I didn't pick you up."

"I *didn't* pick you up, damn it!"

"Of course you picked me up! Oh you really are hopeless! Here you are—what, thirty years old? twenty eight?—having spent a life of failing with women, and you finally pick one up…namely, me—a gorgeous, cultured, highly intellectual woman in the prime of life, and you want to blow the whole thing." This last was said with mock incredulity while she gestured toward the waitress and pointed to her coffee cup.

"Oh, really," sneered E.C. "Actually, I'm thirty five— and you're either one of those…what do you call them…lesbian performance artists?, or are flat-out crazy."

The woman bunched the collar of her coat so that it was snug against her throat and fixed her eyes on E.C. with the intensity of one guarding against a striking snake. "Why do you say crazy? Are you saying I'm insane?"

E.C. tried to gauge the woman's response and answered in a placating tone, "Just a figure of speech—you know, like when Steve Martin kids around and calls himself a wild and crazy guy? I don't know you—I'm not saying you're insane…Just calm down."

The waitress, a tired robot in a stained tan uniform, arrived just as the woman, still staring at his face, said with whole-hearted contempt, "You're pathetic!"

Pouring the coffee, the waitress gave no indication that she had heard a thing; but as soon as she turned to leave, E.C. asked, "May I have the check please?" Then he rose and stood beside the booth while the waitress went off to tally their bill.

Looking up at E.C., the woman said, "Sit down. You look foolish standing there. As if we'd had a lovers' quarrel—or something equally absurd." E.C. ignored her.

The waitress brought him the check and moved on with her pot of coffee to other customers. E.C. took money from his billfold and started to put a tip on the table, but moved his hand away and turned to leave, when the woman sighed such a loud, aspirated sigh that E.C. turned back to see if she were ill. She smiled the same strange smile he'd seen earlier in the movie house, patted the table in front of where he had been sitting, and in a dramatic wistful cadence said, "Failed again. Another failed attempt to make some meaningful contact with a woman. It's a shame." Then brightening, she added, "But I'll give you one last chance."

"One last chance? For what? To be the butt of your ridiculous...." He couldn't think of a word and blurted out, "Yes! You are insane! Crazy as hell—a total nut case!"

By now his legs were quivering, but instead of leaving he glowered at the woman, hoping to see that his words had caused her pain. But she did not react defensively as she had when earlier he had called her crazy. Exasperated but calm she said, "Why don't you just sit down and drink your coffee. You've got a whole fresh cup, and it would be a shame for it to go to waste. Besides, I'm not ready to leave yet."

Defeated, E.C. shook his head and slumped back into the booth.

"Now, where were we just before you had your tantrum?" asked the woman, now beaming and lifting her cup to her mouth.

E.C. had no retort. He was a house mouse being battered about by a cat prolonging its jungle-bred pleasures of dominance. He had lost the urge to bolt for the door and he stayed, confused, with no new plan of escape.

"Now," said the woman, pushing back her empty plate as if she were beginning to share a secret, "This time I think we are finished dining, wouldn't you agree?" But before E.C. could respond, she continued, "So it's time to go home. Pay the check." And with that she slid out of the booth and stood patiently waiting for E.C. to follow.

He counted out several bills and placed them on the table. He decided he would wait until they were out on the street to make it clear to the woman that the evening was over. But once outside again, her appearance struck him as it had when he first noticed her standing in the movie-house lobby: small, feminine, and vulnerable in her soiled, shabby coat; and it was as much a sudden renewed sense of compassion as his inherent indecisiveness that kept him from speaking until she asked, "Which way?"

Raising his hands to signal stop, he said, "Look, I'm confused about how this all came about, but it's time to call a halt. I'm going to go home, and if you need a place to stay...well, where were you planning to stay? I mean, before you met me?"

"I didn't meet you. You met me. Remember? In front of *Downtown Cinema*? You picked me up. Remember?"

"No. Please! Don't start that again. I asked you if you were all right, and for some reason you made the assumption I was trying to hit on you...and then you forced me to buy you something to eat."

Shaking her head and again bunching her collar tightly around her neck, she asked, "How much do you think I weigh?"

And when E.C. didn't immediately answer, she asked again, loudly enough for people near them to turn and stare, "How much do I weigh?"

"How do I know for God's sake? I'm no good at things like that."

"Or much of anything else, I would say. But I'll tell you how much I weigh. One hundred and fourteen pounds—the last time I weighed. And you're going to tell me that I forced you into buying me coffee and a couple of bagels? I mean, you're not much of a specimen, but, sweet Jesus, I couldn't force you into doing anything you don't want to do. Now, which way do we go?"

Embarrassed by the attention they were drawing, E.C. turned and began walking. Glancing into the store-front windows, he saw that the woman dogged his steps, and before they had gone half a block she again caught his arm and looped one of hers around it, measuring her step in rhythm with his. To anyone on the street they were a couple.

They continued this way for another block, heading uptown on Second Avenue. At 12th Street, E.C. stopped, moved a step away from the woman and said, "Look. Let's get this straight right now. You are not going home with me. I know nothing about you. I'm not interested in any kind of a relationship with you. Nothing!" He looked around to see if they were being observed before continuing. "Apparently you don't have any money, so let me give you some…twenty dollars…and you'll have to go your own way."

E.C. took a bill from his wallet while the woman, exasperated, watched him. Again glancing around, E.C. held the bill out to the woman who stared him into dropping his gaze. They stood motionless until she took the bill, folded it twice and suddenly grabbed E.C.'s belt at the buckle and pulled him toward her with a force that caused him to stagger; but before he could retreat she thrust the bill downward between his waistband and his shirt, pushed him away and asked, "Not interested? Not interested? Don't I recall you coming up to me, uninvited, and asking me if someone was bothering me? Did I imagine all of that—your Good Samaritan intentions?" She pushed her face close to his and continued, "What do you take me for, offering me money like I was some two-bit whore?"

E.C. backed away, fumbling for the bill that was wedged inside his pants. "God! You're impossible!" he shouted. "I was just trying to be nice to you!" And moving further back added, "Christ! Whoever said that no good deed goes unpunished sure as hell got that right."

The woman matched each backward step E.C. took, as if she feared missing a step in her partner's improvised dance until, giving a cry that was half shriek half whimper, E.C. ran across the intersection and sprinted east on 12th Street, running as fast as his unathletic gait would carry him.

Caught off guard, the woman watched E.C.'s flight, his straight-backed, high knee-lifting form causing his open raincoat to flair behind, giving him the ludicrous appearance of an urban, terrorized Ichabod Crane. She jogged a few steps after him, stopped, cupped her hands to her mouth and shouted, "Loser! Pathetic, fucking loser!" as E.C. disappeared around the corner at First Avenue and headed back downtown.

E.C. slowed and wove around pedestrians who made room for him and who looked back up the street to see if he were being chased. He continued running until he came to a still-open fruit stand whose sidewalk displays gave him cover from where he could look back uptown and spot anyone coming from that direction. Fearful of drawing attention to his loitering behind the stand's carefully arranged wares, he bought two bananas with the twenty dollar bill he still gripped in his hand, and after a few minutes stepped out onto the sidewalk. He did not see the woman, but he crossed the street as a further precaution and continued rapidly walking into the East Village, away from where he assumed she might still be.

Fiddling with the change from the twenty he had used for the bananas, E.C. decided he would take the first cab he could hail going back uptown. He felt luck was with him for the first time that night as in a matter of seconds he was able to hail a cab and get back to his apartment.

In the otherwise dark apartment, the phone's answering machine's tiny signal light gave off an unblinking comforting glow, connecting him to a world where life functioned unerringly and whose passionless order he suddenly viewed as a virtue. For a time he felt safe, and he chose to sit in the dark, rubbing the bananas as if they were elongated worry beads. Depression settled over him in nearly palpable folds.

The apartment was an illegal sublet whose legal lessee was onto some oil-field scam in Australia and who had made elaborate arrangements to have rent checks sent in his name each month to the building owners. E.C. in turn sent his monthly rent checks to a box number on Staten Island and hoped he would not be found out—just another of the anxieties that periodically rode into his consciousness and triggered depression.

After a while the answering machine's steady light took on a mocking quality. The machine wasn't even his; indeed, very little in the apartment was, and in the eight months he had lived there, only one phone message had been recorded, and that had been from an insurance salesman making desperate random calls with the hope that someone would be foolish enough to call back.

E.C. reached for the lamp beside him and lit the room with low, soft light. Moving into the kitchen, he dropped the bananas onto the counter before returning to unplug the telephone with its answering machine.

He turned off the lamp, sat for several minutes, then muttered into the darkness, "Loser. Pathetic fucking loser."

FREE LUNCH

Betsy had not returned the phone to its base before regret took hold. She so seldom received calls of any kind that she had agreed to meet him for lunch before her better judgment and innate good manners could cobble together an excuse to reject his invitation.

It had been years since a former student had sought her out ("tracked her down," as one actually had said), and she had felt safe from their cloying attempts to make something out of a past that never had existed except in their undergraduate romantic delusions. And now, "Philip Warner, Class of '58," just had gotten her to pretend she remembered who he was and agree to have lunch with him the next day.

"Betsy, you don't mind if I call you Betsy, do you? After all, I'm sixty-three years old, and calling you Dr. Cochran now seems...well, kind of silly. I mean, we all called you 'Betsy' back then anyway. Of course, not to your face...I mean not in class. But you were always 'Betsy' to us. Still are."

She hadn't responded directly to him, but had said, "Things did begin to become more informal about that time—I think probably for the worst. People just started going by a first name, as if everyone in the world actually knew everyone else. In this year 2000 it still seems presumptuous. Damned silly if you ask me."

"Oh, God, that's wonderful! So like you! So...direct! So... so unflinching. Well, I mean, you always called me Philip—never Phil. Unlike Jon Rasmussen—you remember him—he always called us Mister and Miss. Mister Warner. Never Philip."

Literally hundreds of students had sat in her classes, had come to her office, and had sat in her series of modest apartments, crammed with books and canvas butterfly chairs, drinking strong coffee (never alcohol) and brewed loose tea (never bags). In forty years of teaching, perhaps fifty students stood out. Philip Warner was not one of those. But like many before and after him, he thought he was. Fortunately for Philip, inherited wealth and an immensely romantic lack of self-knowledge had eased his way, happy and clueless, through college.

"Jon Rasmussen was a lovely man. A kind, intelligent man whose manners never got in the way of anything. On the contrary, I should think giving you some formal status would have impressed you. Do you actually see being addressed as 'mister' by a teacher as a flaw in that man's character or intellect? That's astounding!"

Philip scrambled for a defensive position and said, "No, no, I meant no offense to Ras...I mean Professor Rasmussen...it's just that you had the common touch...you know, a way of making us feel on equal footing—not that we ever thought we were your equal in anything, but you put us at ease. You were a friend, not a mentor."

"Really?" queried Betsy. "I'd hoped I was both."

"Oh and you were!" crowed Philip, still scrambling, and becoming more foolish with each increasingly obsequious gaffe.

So the conversation went, with Philip trying to ingratiate himself but sounding the fool, and Betsy, with little tolerance for fools, getting closer and closer to telling Philip, "If the fact were known, Philip, or Phil, or whatever you think I called you, I don't have any idea who you are; I don't remember you at all. And there is absolutely nothing I can imagine that we would have to talk about over lunch, over a drink, over coffee, over tea, over anything, and I would appreciate it, if you do harbor fond memories of me, to never, and I mean never, contact me again. Good-bye!"

She did not, however, say such things. Perhaps beneath the liberating feeling that had come with old age and allowed her license not to suffer fools lay enough vanity in being remembered to overcome her urge to shut Philip up. In any event, by remaining silent to his request she had agreed, by default, to meet him the next noon at *Diane's*, an upscale, trendy Italian wine and open-faced sandwich bar Philip had gotten wind of the moment he checked into his motel.

"I'll be there early to be certain we're given a decent table," enthused Philip. "I've put on more weight than I should have, so you may not recognize me at first, but I'll be on the lookout for you, and I'll be sure the maitre d' knows to expect you...and I'm sure you haven't changed at all."

"Changed? Of course I haven't changed. I'm 82 years old— why would I have changed?" replied Betsy in tones so arch that Philip cringed at how badly his intended compliment had missed its mark. "As for a maitre d'—this is Albany! This wine place... whatever you call it...may have a manager at the door or a hostess, but a maitre d'? Hardly!"

Philip's nervous laugh was grotesque, even to his own ears, and after a long pause he said, "Well, of course...uh...I'm sure it will work out well." Another pause, then, "But...by the way, let me give you my number in case you might need to reach me."

"Oh, yes...an excellent thought," said Betsy with an enthusiasm that left Philip wondering if she might again be chiding him. Philip gave her the number and awkwardly signed off, his "It's been wonderful talking with you after all these years" sounding at once heartfelt and false.

Even as Betsy wrote down Philip's number, a notion had taken vague shape; she would call that evening with an excuse for not meeting him. Now, with the conversation behind her and a sense of having just been duped by a hard-sell telemarketer, she thought that any excuse would do: anything to keep from having to sit through "remember whens" that she was certain she wouldn't remember or would have no desire to recall—things that once may have seemed vital or even profound, but now, with the passage of some forty years, would sound banal or embarrassingly silly. But the more excuses she invented, the more preposterous they became; any excuse she thought up was a transparent lie and would appear so even to someone as dense as she imagined Philip to be.

By nine that evening she had given up the idea of calling and canceling, and, though her first response was one of not giving a damn what Philip Warner would think, she had begun to nurture a growing curiosity as to what, indeed, motivated a sixty-something man to want to flatter and impress her. Was there some genuine sentiment there? Something that might prove interesting?

Lunch with Philip Warner slowly began to take on a sense of adventure. And, after all, how long had it been since she had not paid for her own lunch in the company of someone other than her tiny circle of aged, like-minded women? How long since she had sat across the table alone with a man and enjoyed the experience? Or, "For God's sake," she thought, "since I sat across the table from *anyone* and enjoyed the experience?" Betsy smiled and thought, "I'll do it—what the hell! Maybe it will be a good lunch, and it's free"—not an insignificant consideration for an old woman on a fixed income. But then her smile became more a look of resigned whimsy than an expression of unalloyed pleasure, and she said aloud, "Come on, Betsy, you know there's no such thing as a free lunch."

She walked into her sunroom, a narrow space the

diminutive limits of which were comforting, not cramped, and where Betsy spent her days alternately sitting in two identically shaped overstuffed reclining chairs—the forest-green one for morning reading, the rich chocolate-colored one for afternoons and evenings. From atop a stack of books and magazines piled beside the brown chair, Betsy picked up a library copy of James Branch Cabell's *Jurgen* and settled into the recliner.

The book looked old but unworn. Some days before she had been rereading an anthologized collection of literary put-downs and had again come across Dorothy Parker's caustic, "Whatever happened to James Branch Cabell, I hope." Betsy loved Parker and for most of her adult life had viewed Parker as an alter ego of sorts, albeit a tragic alter ego—but that made her all the more delicious.

Jurgen had been a racy, avant-garde novel of some vogue in the nineteen-twenties, and long had been on Betsy's list of forgotten books to read. Reading Parker again had inspired her to seek out *Jurgen* at the University library, where it had lain on a shelf unread nearly as long as it had been on Betsy's list; so it was with a sense of scholarly adventure that Betsy now turned to its first page. But before she read a word, she thought again of the next-day's lunch, and again spoke aloud, "There's no such thing as a free lunch...Never play poker with a guy named Doc...Never eat in a restaurant called Mom's...."

It was a little after 11 p.m. when *Jurgen* slid from Betsy's lap. Even before the book hit the floor she awoke with a muted feeling of disgust for having fallen asleep while reading, something she had begun doing only in the past several months. Part of her displeasure was reserved for the first three chapters of *Jurgen*, which was as far as she had gotten when she nodded off. "Rubbish," she said, picked the novel from the floor, looked it over to see if it had been damaged, and placed it beside her stack of unread books. Then, having a second thought, she took up the novel again, turned to page 5 and read in a deep, pompous, stage voice, "I am looking for my wife, whom I suspect to have been carried off by the devil, poor fellow." "Rubbish," she said again, returned the book to the floor and added, "Cheap humor of an insecure frat boy! Back to the stacks where you belong."

Betsy had not always dismissed a book after only a few pages. Prior to turning eighty, she always finished a book she had started no matter how much she hated or disagreed with it from its early pages. "Don't forsake a book," she had told her students. "A book is an entity. Someone wrote it to be evaluated as a whole, and it is unfair to do less. So, if you start a book, finish that book. Don't be frivolous." Her brighter students would object, "But doesn't that limit your reading? You could read an awful lot of bad stuff and soon be afraid to try unless one read criticism first. You might never try a new writer," they'd protest.

Betsy would smile and say, "Take a chance. Be willing to suffer a little...for art." Betsy never supposed anyone actually followed her pretentious, rigid credo; but she was convinced that just suggesting such a thing made books take on added value for young people who grew up sampling and throwing away everything unfinished, from breakfast cereals to lovers. Yet she herself followed her rule with the fervor of one having taken holy vows. She had read hundreds of terrible books before she decided life was too short for such a rarefied restriction, and in the past two years the act of abandoning books thrilled her with the high that comes at any age with defiance.

She read no more that night and went to bed with lingering unease about the next day's lunch with Philip Warner.

Diane's was in a strip mall near the airport. It had been a failed sporting-goods store, and Betsy found the large display windows now filled with pots of climbing greenery surprisingly tasteful. The pleasing plants and the ease of parking in the near-empty lot raised her anticipation of what was to follow from a low-level misgiving (the feeling one has when attending the funeral of someone you knew just well enough to make your appearance and signature on the funeral home's registry a social necessity) to that of mild anticipation.

She arrived ten minutes late in hopes that Philip would be there already seated at their table so she could inform the host or hostess that Mr. Warner was expecting her and thus avoid any awkwardness about their not recognizing one another; her only clue as to Philip's appearance was a vague sense of what an obsequious sixty-something man would look like.

The hostess probably was Diane herself, a stylish, carefully prepared woman in her forties, dressed in a lime green sheath that few could have dared wear but which was perfect for her dark features and pliant body. Her smile of greeting was one of practiced pleasure, and when Betsy said, "Mr. Warner is expecting me," the hostess nodded with assurance, said "Of course," and led Betsy to a curved booth discretely set away from the bar in a cove of yet more tall greenery.

Philip, seeing them approaching, rose too soon and remained awkwardly suspended over the table in a half-crouch until Betsy was close enough for him to slide out and nearly collide with her in his haste to greet her. Reaching for her hand he said, "Betsy... Professor Cochran...it's so good to see you...," and Betsy filled in his loss for words with a good-natured "after all of these years?" and added "My, my," which sounded appropriately inane. The hostess with practiced deftness handed out her menus, told them their "wait person" would be with them in a moment, and glided away with an amused, though not unkind, smile.

Perhaps because Betsy was 82 years old, or perhaps because she was Betsy Cochran, she stared at Philip, unabashedly trying to get a sense of who and what he was, while Philip, self-consciously averting his eyes, failed to disguise the shock of confronting the aged face that came nowhere near the image he'd carried with him for forty years. "Well...you can't imagine how good it is to see you," he said in constricted tones that slid into a throat-clearing rasp.

Betsy, feeling a long-absent sense of being in control, tipped her chin and caught his gaze straight on when he looked into her face again. The usual meaningless response would have been to say, "It's nice to see you again, too, Philip," but instead she asked, "How long has it been, actually?" and before he could reply added, "What brings you to Albany?—not exactly a spot much sought out."

Betsy no more recognized Philip Warner than she recognized the bartender, a man near Philip's age but more nattily dressed. Philip was five-foot eight, twenty pounds overweight, and had a full head of graying brown hair that was his best feature. Bushy brows darker than his hair crowded his eyelids, and his eyes looked tired—perhaps from avoiding looking straight on. He wore a tan suit—one of those promoted for their "wrinkle resistance and ease of care"—a color-coordinated maize shirt, and a dark brown tie with small diamond designs in greens, black and muted orange.

His appearance was perfectly acceptable, yet there was something annoying about his bearing. He kept his right arm slightly bent and rhythmically flexed his elbow in a slow cadence as if he were priming his arm to extend it. And though for the most part he avoided looking Betsy in the eyes, he suddenly would lean forward and concentrate on her face for seconds at a time before looking away.

From the time she sat down and first looked at Philip, Betsy had decided that the whole event would best be endured as a game in which she would do her best to keep him from talking about the past. The goal of her game was not clear to her, yet she knew that it somehow was cruel.

"I'm here visiting my daughter—actually my stepdaughter—my children from my first marriage are married with families of their own and live out west. Oregon and Washington," said Philip. "Kim, my stepdaughter, is a junior at Skidmore. I'm combining a business trip with a chance to see her."

"Wonderful," said Betsy in a drawn-out expansive tone, which she followed with an enthusiastic, "Ah, our waitperson cometh."

A young man with polished assurance announced, "Hello, I'm Carl, and I'll be your waitperson this afternoon. May I interest you in one of the wines we're featuring today?"

"Carl? You don't look like a Carl," said Betsy playfully. "Tell your parents you are more of a Kevin. But no, I'm not interested in one of your featured wines. However, I would dearly love a vodka Gibson with two onions."

"And I would dearly love to bring you a vodka Gibson with two onions," said Carl. "And you sir?"

Philip was unsettled by the good-natured interplay between Betsy and their waiter and felt he must have missed something, but, flexing his right arm, he said, "Yes, well, why don't you just bring me a glass of your best featured red wine."

Carl was a pro, and sensing that Betsy would be more than Philip could deal with, he chose to treat him with his sincerest, "Good choice, sir. That would be a 1998 Tramonti Innocento, a lovely wine I'm sure you'll enjoy." Then he added, "I'll tell you about today's special menu offerings when I bring your...." He paused, glanced at Betsy and instead of saying "beverages" said, "Gibson and wine."

The natural awkward pause that followed was quickly broken by Betsy. "And what business would that be, Philip? The one that brings you here?"

Philip looked momentarily alarmed but leaned back in the booth and with an incongruous stage bravado said, "Books. I've been in books since Channing...or almost."

He was no more forthcoming, so Betsy, unable to control herself, asked, "Books? You mean you take bets?"

Philip giggled and squirmed. "No, not bets, but that's very good. You still have your wonderful wit...like, was it Pope who said, *True wit is nature to advantage dress'd. What oft was thought but ne'r so well express'd?*

Betsy clapped, holding her hands high above her head. "Excellent, Philip! Excellent! You win one of my cocktail onions when the drinks come. But what are we talking about here with your books?"

"Well, I wasn't suited for my family's wholesale business, so I started as a text-book salesman with Prentice-Hall, made good contacts, and founded a small publishing house with my brother-in-law. Incidentally, I never did marry Connie Monterro, as you might have thought. I married someone you never knew." His eyes moved away from Betsy as he paused, giving the clear impression that he wished he had never brought his marriage up.

Betsy had no memory of Connie Monterro, though at least her name sounded vaguely familiar. "Connie Monterro? Oh, yes. What became of her?"

"I believe she died recently. Someone told me that, but I had no contact with her after graduation," said Philip, sounding strangely pleased with himself. "But where was I?"

"Taking bets with your brother-in-law?" answered Betsy, sounding so smartassed that she felt an immediate twinge of shame.

"There you go," giggled Philip again. "No. What we did— and this was my idea—we caught the Strunk and White wave. Remember when everyone was buying E.B. White's take on his old comp teacher's rules? *The Elements of Style?* Everybody just called it

"Strunk and White." Well, we brought out a really cheap knock-off called *The Soul of Grammar*—cheap in its production cost, that is. It was smaller, the paper was thin, and so forth. I wrote the whole thing...of course drawing on traditional grammar texts."

"Plagiarism?" asked Betsy, arching one eyebrow.

"Oh, no. Not really. I mean, grammatical rules are there for everyone to use, aren't they? I just checked to see I was always on sound ground." Then, sounding more sad than defensive, Philip added, "No, there was nothing dishonest about it."

At that point Carl arrived with the drinks and recited a list of half a dozen sandwiches, all of which seemed to contain arugula and goat cheese in combination with what sounded to Betsy to be everything from the world's largest antipasto that could possibly be layered on "rustic wheat bread," their "own olive baguettes," or "dense Tuscan white." Betsy and Philip looked equally boggled, and Betsy perversely thought of making Carl recite the list again, but instead said, "I'm tempted to order one just to see what they look like, but they sound absurdly excessive. Do you have something as gauche as a humble *Minestrone*?"

"Indeed we do—a lovely *Minestrone* as well as my favorite, *Zuppa di Fagioli con la Pasta*."

"Bravo, Carl," cried Betsy, again applauding above her head. "After that, how could I resist the *Zuppa di Fagioli*?"

"Excellent. And you, sir?"

Philip appeared confident in not being able to make up his mind, and again asked Carl to make the choice, "so long as there are no anchovies and it's on white bread."

"Today that would be the *Mozzarella in Carrozza*, and hold the anchovy sauce. It is our only sandwich that is not open-faced. Indeed, it is grilled, hearty, and a very popular choice. I'm sure you'll like it. Would you like time to savor your drinks, or should I put your order in right away?"

"By all means let us savor our drinks," said Betsy cheerily. She was beginning to enjoy herself and added, "Yes, I really think you should change your name to Kevin."

Carl, smiling, bowed slightly. "I'll take it under consideration while I bring you some breadsticks."

After he left, Philip scowled and fidgeted and looked past Betsy while asking, "Do you think he is patronizing me?"

"Not at all. Nor me either. He's clever and simply humoring an old woman who is acting silly." Betsy lifted the swizzle stick from her drink and offered an onion to Philip. "Your reward for quoting Pope."

"Oh, no thank you," said Philip, raising a hand in protest. "I don't...I'm not fond of those little onions. And besides, you explicitly ordered two. So, no. Please have them both." Then he raised his wine glass, held it toward Betsy, and said, "To Professor Elizabeth Cochran, my inspiration, my friend."

His toast was so clearly rehearsed that Betsy was slow to respond, thinking there was more to come, but when nothing followed she was touched by the grand, grotesque sentiment that Philip felt, and said with a sincerity that surprised herself, "Why, Philip! Very nice...and I thank you."

Holding the impaled onions aloft, Betsy followed Philip's cue and sipped her Gibson. More silence followed until Betsy popped one of the onions into her mouth and exclaimed while chewing, "Will you look at that? I haven't seen a swizzle stick that wasn't just a plain skewer in years. Look at this thing!"

She held up the stick still holding the second onion and examined it closely, oblivious to the drops of vodka and vermouth puddling on the tablecloth. The stick was white plastic, but the end opposite the point was made into a relief of a gilded chariot, Ben Hur vintage. Philip could not make out what had excited Betsy about the stick, and before Betsy could explain what she was looking at, Carl arrived with a basket of pencil-thin breadsticks.

"You're right," he said, nodding to Betsy. "I'm changing my name to Kevin tomorrow."

"Wonderful!" shouted Betsy, more loudly than she intended. She quickly added, "Now, Kevin, would you please bring my friend a swizzle stick. I want him to see its sculpted motif. But you know, you really should tell Diane that instead of a Roman chariot she should have used a moon. After all, Diana is the moon goddess and it would be much more appropriate given the name of this place."

For a moment it appeared that Carl/Kevin was about to sit down with them, but he merely leaned over close to their heads and said, "Actually, there is no Diane. The owner is an Irishman, and I have no idea where the name came from, but I'll pass along your swizzlestick suggestion. It probably would be cheaper to manufacture, and God knows they're interested in...." He stopped abruptly, then added, "I'll get you another swizzler."

He was back promptly with another swizzlestick, and Betsy and Philip looked over each of theirs carefully, with Betsy marveling at the detail of the molded chariot. The Gibson was a generous drink, and Betsy was beginning to feel its effect—a pleasant nudge toward imprudence. "Books," she said, forcefully. "Back to your books and E.B. White."

"Well, the grammar sold really well. We sold thousands to junior colleges and four-year schools. Never could get places like Berkeley's book stores to stock it, but the less prestigious places made us a lot of money, and we even got some public high schools to buy it." Philip's glances toward Betsy as he spoke were wistful, but there was pride in his voice.

"We published other things, too—manuals...mostly manuals. The manuals weren't really for sale to the public though. They were manuals for Chinese toy manufacturers—and that was my idea, too. Did you ever try to assemble a pedal car or a tricycle from one of their manuals?"

"Not recently," said Betsy, assuming a dour, straight face that led Philip to grin foolishly, shake his head and say, "Of course you haven't, but my point is that those things are so badly written that it's next to impossible to follow them...I mean there are legendary tales of frustrated people trying to assemble something on Christmas Eve from those ridiculous instructions."

He paused to sip his wine and noticed that Betsy was nearly finished with her Gibson and asked if she would like another. The thought was tempting; she was feeling very good but knew that another drink was not wise. "I think not, Philip. Thank you. This one is awfully good, but I think I'll just linger over these last sips and cap them off with onion number two—now nicely marinated."

Philip was delighted by her answer. Not because she declined another drink, but by the way she spoke, and he told her, "I love to hear you talk. I always did. Nobody says things just the way you do...it's hard to explain." He looked away and began his arm-flexing fidgeting.

"Really?" said Betsy, not wholly averse to his flattery but still on guard against some truly maudlin display. "I'm not aware of any special gift of expression. You're too kind."

This last carried an edginess that Philip took to signal Betsy's suspicion that his praise was false, but that was so far from the truth of his feelings that he bumbled ahead. "No, really. It's a gift...a cadence. It's unique. Do you remember Dick Queen?"

Amazed that he had mentioned someone she *did* remember, Betsy replied, "Why, yes, I do. Bright boy. Actually got some Broadway roles later as I recall."

Philip nodded and went on, "Dick Queen was a great mimic. He's dead too, you know. But he would imitate all the faculty. Had everyone down pat...everyone but you. He could never get you right. Did you know that?"

Having no idea where all this was leading, Betsy answered, "No, I didn't. Is that good or bad?"

"It's good," said Philip with enthusiasm. "See, it proves my point. You're unique—like Walter Cronkite. No impersonator has ever been able to get Cronkite's voice down."

Betsy screeched with joy! "Think of that! Just like Walter Cronkite, when all along I thought I was just like Lauren Bacall. Had I known I would have demanded tenure based solely on that instead of writing all those dreary articles on Christina Rosetti's imagined love life—with a priest no less. Did *you* know that?"

"Well, no I didn't," said a somber Philip. "Should I?"

"Of course not, no one should. Ah! Here comes Kevin with our lunches. Good timing, Kevin, good timing," said Betsy continuing her lighthearted mood. "And, you know, I think I'd like a glass of the wine that Philip has."

Philip, with some hesitation, decided to have another glass as well, and they sat admiring their food until the wine arrived. "So Philip, how did you get from printing toy manuals that people actually could make sense of to whatever it is you are doing now?" asked Betsy, playing in her soup with her spoon to cool it.

"Well, over the years the business did very well. We did all kinds of publishing—printing really. Cookbooks with CDs were a big profit maker, for instance. But then Jenny, my wife…well, suffice to say our marriage fell apart and a very big mess followed." He looked down and shook his head. "A very big mess."

"Oh God," thought Betsy. "I don't want to hear this." She sought to divert him and asked, "How's your sandwich?…What did Kevin call it?…It looks quite tasty."

Philip picked up the sandwich and bit into it. It was enormous, and with his first bite a string of cheese pulled away from the bread making an unbroken connection from the sandwich to Philip's lips. He tried to reel the string into his mouth with his tongue and lips while still pulling the sandwich away from his mouth, but the cheese string held fast. The more he tried to break the connection, the more cheese was pulled out from the bread slices until the string broke and fastened itself to his lower lip and chin.

Betsy tried to stifle her laughter, which came out a muted shriek, but she managed to exclaim, "Good God, Philip, that thing is impossible to eat. Kevin should have warned you."

Philip wiped the cheese from his chin and leaned back, looking at his plate as if it held an explosive.

"It's like fried chicken—there's no way one can eat chicken neatly, so just dig in and eat it any way you can. Maybe a knife and fork?" suggested Betsy, sounding more matronly than she intended in her effort to ease Philip's embarrassment.

He pushed the plate away and picked up his wineglass but did not drink from it. His face flushed. Neither spoke, but Betsy, ignoring Philip's discomfort, began to eat her soup with gentle, graceful swipes of her spoon.

After several moments of what would have been uncomfortable silence to Betsy had she not been contentedly sedated with vodka and wine, Philip looked directly into her eyes for the first time that day and asked, "When was the last time you were back at Channing?" He sounded hopeful, like an ill person questioning his doctor on the possibility of a new diagnosis or a wonder drug.

"Channing? Oh, I never went back. There was no reason to go back. Why would I go back?" There was an earnestness—almost a challenge—in her voice. "Students come and go every four years, colleagues—those you can stand—die or get better jobs, as did I, and that awful little Ohio town...well, I had no desire to visit there once I left."

She picked up her wine glass and settled back into the cushions. "As for Albany? Well, let's see. I came here from Channing in 1960. Taught until I was 72. Traveled in the summers...and read books." She laughed a pleasing self-deprecatory chuckle, raised her wine glass and said before sipping, "Not everybody's idea of the good life, but my regrets are few...and I've been lucky." She spread her right arm across the top of the cushions in a luxurious, self-satisfied pose, pausing for effect before leaning toward the table once again and saying with intentional comic fatuousness, "But enough about me."

Philip sat glumly silent, playing with his glass until Betsy, sounding interested, said, "We still haven't heard the rest of your book-making, book-selling, bookie life."

Philip shook his head dismissively. "It's not worth telling, really. Divorced, remarried, now back to selling text books again— full circle, you might say, except I buy books, too." His voice took on an envious tone as he said, "You must have an enormous library by now—and you've read everything." He was unprepared for Betsy's response.

"Philip? Has this lunch been merely a ploy to get a look at my library, perhaps to bilk me out of my now priceless collection of first-edition twenty-five cent paperbacks? Fie, fie, for shame!"

Though Betsy's accusation was meant as obvious, gentle teasing, Philip recoiled and cried, "How could you think such a thing?" His eyes distorted with pain, as if with no reason or warning someone suddenly had slapped him hard across his face, and he stammered, "My God no! I would never do that!" His eyes filled with tears. "Where did you get such an idea?"

Betsy, shocked by Philip's reaction, reached a hand across the table, trying to grasp some part of him, but he sat stiffened against the back of his booth. "A joke, Philip! It was a joke!" And pulling her hand back added, "And a very poor one, I see."

She sighed and took a deep breath, signaling vexation and an acknowledgment of being at once victimizer and victim. Anger quickly replaced her instinct to placate and comfort, and as she sat watching Philip blinking back tears in a pitiable display of childlike confusion, she wished only to be rid of him and whatever it was that led him to think they had some common history. "I was mad to come here," she thought, keeping a rueful eye on Philip as he limply leaned forward and began to move his wine glass around as though it were an oversized chess piece he was reluctant to commit.

Betsy's anger stayed within the bounds of vigilance as she waited for Philip's next move. Staring at his face she drank off her wine, and any sympathy she initially might have felt gave way to hoping her unwavering gaze would increase his discomfort. But he said nothing, played with his glass, and avoided eye contact.

She was about to rise and dismiss the whole sad event with a cold, clear declaration—something to the effect of "Apparently you are not in control of your emotions, Philip, so I'm leaving. Thank you for lunch, and I hope you find the answer to whatever it is that is troubling you. Please don't get up." But before she could speak, Carl/Kevin was suddenly at their table.

He looked at Betsy's half-eaten *Pasta Fagioli* and Philip's nearly whole sandwich, and in exaggerated incredulity asked, "You didn't like your lunch?"

Philip, incapable of speaking, merely waved a hand, the meaning of which could have meant almost anything except a desire to eat what was there. Betsy, hoping at least to save her own face, said sweetly, "Mr. Warner is feeling a bit peckish. The soup was quite good, but I think we're ready for the check."

"Of course," said Carl/Kevin, not wishing to enter into whatever had taken place by continuing the playfulness established earlier between Betsy and him. As he turned to leave, Philip came alive, said "Excuse me" to Betsy, and hurried after Carl/Kevin.

Betsy's eyes followed Philip, curious as to what he had in mind, and she was just able to see him catch Carl/Kevin as they turned out of sight.

Her innate decency and years of engaging in what she would have defined as time-honored ladylike behavior prevented her from following her alcohol-induced urge to just get up and walk out before Philip returned. He was such a wreck! Perhaps she should stay and offer to pay for her lunch? She was in the process of rejecting such a notion when Philip returned and slid into his side of the booth, and, as if he had just paused in the midst of an on-going conversation, said, "I went back—just last week."

Showing no emotion, Betsy asked in flat tones void of curiosity, "Went back where, Philip?"

"To Channing." He looked away, flexing his arm. "I expected it to look the way it was, but it has changed so much—it's just so different. Everything but Pusey Hall. It's still there, of course, but surrounded by so many new buildings—fewer trees. And Pusey seemed smaller than I remember it."

She wanted to say, "Maudlin nonsense!" Instead she said, "All things in the past are smaller...the way things diminish as we move away from them. Do you know that great description Crane gives in *A Bride Comes to Yellow Sky* when Jake Potter's looking out the window of the train as it moves across a Texan plain and has the sensation that all he can see is getting smaller and smaller and is sweeping away over the horizon? You get to my age and that's the way everything appears." She sighed and added, "That's the way it's suppose to be, Philip—you wouldn't want it any other way."

"Yes, I would," answered Philip, sounding not wistful, but nearly belligerent, and without another word he rose and again headed for the lobby.

Several minutes passed and Philip had not returned. Betsy was becoming increasingly impatient and anxious to end their grotesque luncheon. Looking toward the lobby she saw neither Philip nor Carl (she no longer found a reason to call him Kevin—all the play was gone from the luncheon). A glance around the room showed no one paying attention to her, so, making the best out of her predicament, she poured Philip's wine into her glass and sat back to sip it at her leisure.

By the time she finished the wine, Philip still had not returned, and her indignation demanded action. She slid out of the booth and paused to wonder what had happened to the bill. Though she was damned if she was going to pay a cent for her humiliation, the soup and wine had been good and she especially wanted to make certain Carl got a generous tip. He had seen her rise and came quickly toward her, his manner embarrassed and apologetic.

"Before your friend left he asked that when you were ready to leave I should tell you he had taken care of the check and to give you this."

He handed her a plate on which checks normally were placed. It held a twenty-dollar bill, folded twice, and nothing else. "Left? He's gone?" asked Betsy, unsure that she had understood.

"Yes, he is," said Carl, wary of what her reaction might be. "He left some minutes ago, and I was waiting until I thought you were ready to leave also."

"That's it then—no message?"

"No message," said Carl, his embarrassment palpable.

"The money? What's the point of the money? It must be your tip."

"Oh no," said Carl. "He left a very generous tip. Perhaps he thought you had come by taxi and this was your fare home...or wherever it is you want to go."

Carl stood awkwardly holding the plate with the money, and finally acknowledging his embarrassment Betsy smiled and said, "Please keep the money. After all this nonsense you deserve it and more." She shook her head and said, "I can't imagine what you must make of all of this—I have no idea myself. A very, very strange man!"

Instead of going to her car, Betsy, who was feeling the added effects of Philip's glass of wine, chose to walk around in a nearby huge drugstore until her head cleared. The store was virtually empty of customers, and she walked the aisles, focusing on the colorful items in bottles, spray cans, and plastic bags while trying to sort out her encounter with Philip Warner. What was she in the bizarre mix of his hang-ups, lost dreams, failed relationships? His comments and actions were a series of non sequiturs. There was no continuity, no context, yet in many ways he seemed on the edge of today's disjointed, freelance mode of living and was close to what passed for being normal.

A huge pyramid-shaped end-of-season display of windshield-washing liquid caught her eye. The plastic bottles of electric blue solution were gallon size, and Betsy first took them to be huge bottles of mouthwash. They were stacked four deep to prevent them from tipping over, and open boxes of the bottles, four to a box, were stacked in front of the pyramid so that customers could remove jugs from the boxes rather than disrupt the pyramid's shape. The idea of giant plastic bottles of windshield-wiper fluid being sold in a drugstore grated against Betsy's aesthetic sense, and she felt a quixotic urge to pull one of the supporting jugs from a corner of the display and bring down the entire pyramid. "I could get away with it too," she thought. "Eighty-two year old women aren't supposed to have any common sense."

She pulled one of the jugs from a box rather than from the pyramid display and shook it as hard as she could. The blue solution foamed, and a tiny dribble of liquid slid down the outside onto her hands. Betsy smiled, slipped the jug back into its carton, and left the store feeling newly empowered and a bit more sober.

She walked the length of the strip mall, past *Diane's*, and across the large parking lot into a neighborhood of shabby tract houses made virtually unsalable by the advent of the strip mall ten years before.

The April sun shone through the bare trees, making patterns of symmetrical stripes along the sidewalk; it was necessary for Betsy to keep her eyes lowered so as not to confuse a shadow with a raised crack in the concrete, which could cause her to trip. She felt that breaking a hip was the most degrading thing that could happen to one her age—it so equated one with brittle bones, leeched of life and symbolic of decay and helplessness. For years she had been stockpiling pain pills and sleeping tablets carelessly dispensed by her dentists (two of whom she had outlived) and clinic doctors, now nameless and ever changing. The romantic notion of a cyanide capsule appealed to her, but the pills would do if the time came. "I'd hate to end up like Philip Warner," she thought, well aware that she was twenty years older than he.

But Philip was not easily dismissed, and as her head cleared enough for her to feel secure in driving home, she walked back to her car, trying to imagine why he left as he did and where he would have gone. She knew that her smartest response to Philip's intrusion into her set life would be to dismiss him, as she originally had intended, and to make certain she never got involved with him again. But she began to worry about the state of Philip's mind beyond the obvious neuroses, nervous tics, and social awkwardness. Was he a genuinely disturbed man who had called out for help and now had been driven over the edge? And the twenty-dollar bill. A mocking payment for something undelivered? Was he signaling he viewed her as some sort of intellectual whore? Why do you give women money? Was it a gift—an awkward, inappropriate gift? Or perhaps Carl was right—it was cab fare.

When she arrived home, the daylong sun had warmed her house and left cheerful patches brightening her hardwood floors. She was heading for a nap when the blinking light on her answering machine caught her eye. Few people phoned her, and fewer yet found her not at home when they called, so she clicked on the message with heightened curiosity—much like receiving a hand-addressed envelope with no return address. There was no message—just the dull click of a receiver being replaced, then silence until the machine beeped and the tape rewound. Philip Warner calling to explain? To apologize? To announce his intention to do himself in?

The number Philip had given her the night before was still on the pad beside her phone, so she immediately dialed it. "Capital Inn. How may I help you?"

"Yes. Could you please connect me to Philip Warner's room?"

"One moment please," came the practiced, indifferent male voice, followed by rhythmic clicking sounds. Several seconds passed before the voice said, "Mr. Warner is no longer a guest here—he's checked out."

"Checked out? Yes, of course. Thank you," said Betsy. She replaced the receiver and was again angry, feeling that once more she had been made a fool of. Her eye caught the copy of *Jurgen* resting on the floor beside her evening chair and she said to the empty room, "Whatever happened to Philip Warner, I hope?"

Betsy lay down for her nap and didn't awaken until there was just enough sunlight left to be disorienting. Was it dawn or twilight?

AFFECTION

Cold! Cold! Cold! It had gotten to him. Everything about that morning in some way had been involved in combating single-digit temperatures. Turning up the heat, showering, shaving, layering his clothes and driving to Bernie's for breakfast with Junior Harley were overspread with an exaggerated sense of winter as a personal antagonist.

Now, sitting in a booth, his hands encircling a warm coffee mug bearing a Bernie's Bay View logo, Ray saw through Bernie's storefront window piles of curbside, grime-encrusted snow in front of what used to be a Newberry's that long ago had been done in by Walmart. It now was Down East Collectibles, a tourist trap of rusted and broken junk and framed yellowing photographs passed off as antiques run by an overdressed, mysterious, elderly woman purported to be from Boston or Providence or Taos, depending on whichever rumor one was likely to hear on any given day.

Above that building the late February sky was the color of a dead squirrel's belly and thick as decades-old concrete void of even the tiniest hint that calendar spring was a mere three weeks away. It had been the coldest Maine winter in a decade.

Ray's wintry gloom, slightly relieved by the coffee's warmth and caffeine jolt, did not improve with the arrival of Junior Harley who, with no greeting, slid into the booth and griped, "I never knew how the hell this place can call itself 'Bay View.' There's not a bay within six miles," and, while zipping open the neck of his Carhart jumpsuit, added, "And another thing. The woman running that so-called antiques place has to be sellin' dope. There's no way she could be makin' a living in that store—especially in the winter. You ordered?"

"Waiting for you," answered Ray, at which Junior began waving his arms at a waitress already advancing on their booth with coffee pot and mug.

"Don't need a menu," said Junior. "Just pour the coffee and bring me two eggs over, home fries, white toast, and I'm goin' to need more milk for my coffee."

"And I'd like two scrambled eggs, wheat toast," said Ray, and as the waitress drew away he said to Junior, "So what's this all about—as if I didn't know?"

"What's that supposed to mean?" asked Junior, pouring so much half-and-half that his coffee ran over.

Everything Junior Harley said came off as if it were a warning to keep off his property. He and Ray had been classmates in their small high school class of 1967, and this in Junior's mind meant they were friends though they never had so much as gone to a movie together and seldom had been in each other's home. But, if you were the same age, had gone to school together, and still lived in the same town, in Junior's mind you were friends and obligated to act like a friend; and if your sister once had been married to that guy's brother, well, that made you related, didn't it?

"It means," said Ray, "that you want free legal advice after having punched out an eighty-four year old man, breaking his upper plate, detaching a retina, and cracking some ribs because he supposedly sexually abused your mother. My advice? Get yourself a good defense lawyer and do what he tells you—cop a plea, whatever. Because you don't want to go to trial. As stupid as the juries in this county are, they'll cook your goose in a minute. Most of them would love to convict you without even hearing testimony from anybody—especially you."

Junior leaned down to slurp from his overflowing mug. "You mean you won't take my case then?"

"Junior, you have no case. You beat up on one of the most beloved men in town and he's eighty-four years old for God's sake! Besides, you know I'm not a trial lawyer, except once in a while some financial fraud."

Junior leaned toward Ray, and in a lowered voice pleaded, "Aw, come on man. All the same you're a lawyer aren't you? I'll pay you something—I don't expect no free ride. I mean, how much would a defense lawyer cost? I'm not a rich man, you know."

Ray shook his head and smiled for the first time that morning. "Oh please! You want to show me your tax forms for the past eight years? Even before that you were making good money as a finish carpenter, and since then you've shown more good sense than anybody gave you credit for by starting that construction outfit of yours....Come on! How many trucks you got now—six? That poverty whine doesn't wash. Buy yourself a good lawyer."

Junior avoided Ray's eyes, pursed his lips and looked around the restaurant as if hunting for an ally. Then, with more resolve than anger, he said, "This guy tried to rape my mother—a demented old woman in a nursing home! No jury would convict me. I'm the victim here—Mom and me. And why don't that pissy County DA charge Dennis with sexual abuse or something? I just may defend myself."

"Buy a lawyer, Junior. Spend the money. You're in deep shit."

Junior went into a long, profane-laced denunciation of tax laws that "killed" small-business people, which he bolstered with bogus anecdotal tales of ruin, each more implausible than the last. Ray let him vent until their food arrived and Junior fell silent while

salting his eggs and overcoming a brief embarrassing moment
when their hands inadvertently met on the peppershaker.

"So what would you have done?" asked Junior, shaking his
head in frustration. "I go in the room and Dennis has his hand
inside Mom's top rubbin' her tits. I suppose you would have
said, 'You know, Dennis, it isn't polite to feel up old women with
Alzheimer's. I think you should apologize.' You'd have busted the
bastard too."

As if to emphasize the strength of his argument, Junior
jabbed an egg with a corner of toast and directed the runny
yolk into the mound of potatoes. Ray made no reply and both
remained silent, Junior bringing food to his mouth like a man
pumping water, in contrast to Ray's haphazard motions. Halfway
through his plate, Junior semaphored his mug several times to get
the waitress's attention and said, "If I hadn't come in when I did,
Dennis would have been in her pants next."

"Diaper."

"What?"

"Diaper. As I understand it from Jackie Coons, your mother
is incontinent and has to wear a diaper."

"Oh, for Christ sake, Ray," protested Junior, throwing down
his fork so hard that it bounced. "This is my mother you're talkin'
about! And what does Jackie Coons know anyway?—that nosy
bitch!"

"Well, Jackie knows what everyone else in the nursing home
and in town knows about your so-called sexual abuse case, and that
is you don't have one. Jackie's the one who pulled you off Dennis,
right?"

"Nobody pulled me off of Dennis. I was just gettin' him away
from Mom. And what's she doin' talkin' about what goes on in the
home? Isn't that supposed to be confidential? It's against the law for
aides to discuss patients. She's just tryin' to save her own ass."

"From what?"

"From not bein' in the room to protect my mother from that dirty old bastard. Where was she—down the hall drinking coffee or something? What did she tell you anyway? And whose side are you on?"

"Mary Alice's...and all the other residents over there whose children don't visit them."

Junior's eyes widened in disbelief. "Don't visit? Don't visit? What the hell do you think I was doing when I caught Dennis feeling her up?"

"Jackie says it was the first time you'd been over there since before Christmas—two months ago."

Shaking his head, Junior fiddled with the small pile of empty plastic half-and-half containers beside his mug and pleaded, "Well, what's the use of visiting someone who don't even know who you are? I mean, shit! She don't have a clue! I could be Superman for all she cares."

An image of Junior as Superman made Ray smile. "So you think Mary Alice doesn't care about anything now? She just sits in her wheelchair or lies in bed, her mind blank? Does she ever smile? Does she say anything that makes sense?"

Junior, annoyed, frowned, but after some thought said, "She doesn't say much of anything at all. She's just always reachin' out to get hold of you...your hand. And if she gets your hand she smiles sometimes."

"Really?" asked Ray. "She wants to take your hand?"

"So? So what about it? That makes me a bad son because I don't want to hold hands with my senile mother?"

Ray took a deep breath and looked past Junior across the street to the dirty snow piles. Since his divorce three years ago Ray had had a hard time getting through winter. He pushed his plate away, disappointed in how unsatisfying the food, like everything so far that morning, had been. "You know, Junior, in a way I think it does, but I doubt it's your fault."

Junior, who had sat through the meal with his faded blaze-orange ball cap on, raised it, ran his fingers through his hair, replaced the cap, leaned forward and asked in tones quiet and menacing, "What the fuck are you telling me?"

"You know that Dennis visits the home nearly every day and has been doing it for years—all the time June was there, and he's kept it up ever since. After all, he's known half the residents over there all his life. He regularly visits Mary Alice, and he says she always takes his hand and holds it while he tells her things that are going on outside. He knows she doesn't understand what he's saying, but he says talking to her gives her some dignity—it makes her a part of the community. He did the same with June."

Ray could see how vexed Junior was becoming. "And he says sometimes Mary Alice takes his hand and puts it on her breasts and holds it there. Long ago he told Jackie and all the women working there that she did that, and they said she often did that with their hands, too. It's affection, and if Mary Alice gets some satisfaction out of it, who's to know or care? Dennis says it's not sexual, and why shouldn't we believe him?"

"Oh, come on!" protested Junior. "You gonna sit there and tell me that if Dennis was doing that to your mother you wouldn't have acted just like I did? You'd be less of a man if you didn't."

The waitress brought the check and placed it in the middle of the table between them.

"Did Mary Alice ever put your hand on her breast, Junior?"

Barely pausing to consider the question, Junior, scrambling and banging his way out of the booth bellowed, "I'm outta here!" He paused long enough to wrench some bills out of his jumpsuit pocket, dumped the money onto the table and, having difficulty speaking, gasped out, "This ought to about take care of my share."

But as Junior turned to leave, Ray said, "Not so fast," and pushed Junior's money and the check toward him. "My breakfast is on you—take it off your taxes as business legal expenses."

Junior, in a panic to leave, without a word scooped up the money and check and hurried toward the cashier.

Ray watched him leave. He put a two-dollar tip on the table and sat there many minutes staring out on winter's ugly leavings.

He had no answer to what this encounter with Junior Harley meant. There was no satisfaction in it for him.

He dreaded going back out into the cold.

*   *   *   *   *

Winter didn't let up. Ray went through the motions of daily life, inching along, hoarding body warmth, determined to outlast the unseasonable season. A week after his breakfast with Junior, Ray ran into Jackie Coons in the supermarket's liquor aisle. She was putting a half-gallon of coffee brandy into her cart when she saw Ray and greeted him with an embarrassed grin.

"Big bottle of booze, Jackie," said Ray in a tone both mocking and friendly. "I often wondered what people do with coffee brandy—it sounds like gawdawful stuff to me."

"I like it after dinner in my coffee with a lot of milk. It's pretty sweet but....." Her voice trailed off.

"Not my thing," said Ray, lifting the bottle from her cart, examining it, and adding, "Forty proof, huh?"

"It is? I never pay any attention to that proof stuff. I don't even know what that means."

"It means that it is twenty percent alcohol, but hey, I'm not making a judgment about your drinking habits—or am I?" asked Ray, laughing. "I shouldn't—the stuff I drink is eighty proof."

"What would that be?"

"Scotch, mostly—an acquired taste I guess," answered Ray, hoping not to sound condescending, but also lying since he drank vodka, usually with cranberry juice. But this cold dismal day made Scotch sound more masculine, more worldly wise.

"I liked coffee brandy right off," said Jackie. "But that may be a girl thing—you know, like Brandy Alexanders and piña coladas. So, how have you been, Ray?"

"Wintered out, I guess. Depressed, mean-spirited—my usual upbeat emotional state. How about you?"

Jackie looked away, then back. "Depressed, period. Did you know I got fired?"

"Come on! How could you get fired?"

"I've asked that a lot the last couple of days." She glanced at her grocery list before continuing. "Actually, in a way you're partly responsible."

"Me?"

Jackie nodded. "Junior Harley came to complain to Susan that I had revealed confidential medical information about his mother to you, and that you used this information to humiliate him and make light of Mary Alice's condition. When Susan called me in and told me what Junior claimed, I wanted to laugh—in fact I did, which seemed to really piss her off. But that's beside the point. How in the world did you get talking with Junior about Mary Alice being incontinent—the diaper?"

For several seconds Ray could only shake his head in disbelief, and then he told her what he could remember of his conversation with Junior, especially Junior's hyperbolic claim that Dennis would have fondled Mary Alice's genitals if he, Junior, had not come to her defense—that is, by beating Dennis up. "'Get into her pants,' I think is exactly what Junior said, and I corrected him by saying something like 'into her diaper' in an effort, I guess, to jolt him out of his fantasy about Dennis being a potential rapist. But, my God, Jackie! You can't get fired for telling me Mary Alice Harley wears a diaper! Half the residents over there must wear diapers! Anyone who's ever visited there knows that."

"Did Susan call you?"

"Nobody's called me or said anything to me. Gawdamighty, Susan Douglas must be the only one in town who'd pay any attention to what Junior says about anything! What's her problem?"

Jackie nodded and smiled. "I'm her problem. I've taken her on in some staff meetings about some of her dumb rules. I mean, she makes up rules that make no sense just to show she's in charge—like not allowing more than two visitors in a room at a time, no matter what, which, of course, has reduced the number of visitors who come because some of the residents have big families and people are not going to sit out in the hall for half an hour waiting for somebody to leave so they can visit their own mom or dad. She's inflexible and, frankly, a pain in the ass."

Ray again lifted Jackie's bottle of coffee brandy out of her cart and examined the label while saying, "Well listen, I'll go talk to Susan. This whole thing's ridiculous."

Jackie took the bottle from Ray, put it back in the cart and said, "No. Don't bother. I don't want to work there. After a while you just can't take any more."

"What will you do?"

"Oh, there's a big nurse's aid shortage, of course. But I'll have to commute somewhere. Probably do practical nursing—home care—or something like that. But there's no benefits and I guess I'll need a better car."

"Eddie?"

Jackie, who smiles easily but less in pleasure than in mild derision, smiled and continued, "He doesn't want me to work at all, says it makes it look like he can't support me and the kids—

which, of course, he can't. The kids are in high school now and I can continue to do it. There's no choice. We need the money."

"Damn, damn, damn! I really feel bad about this, Jackie. I think I should talk to Susan. This just isn't right."

"Suit yourself," she said, reaching to touch Ray's arm. "But don't plead for my job. There's no way I'll go back. Thanks just the same." She began to push her cart and added, "I've got to finish my list. See you."

"Okay. Take care, Jackie. I'll let you know if anything good comes out of this...which I doubt. But...well, easy on the coffee brandy."

This last was said with a good-natured grin, and Jackie responded without looking back, "Don't worry about me," and as she went down the aisle added, "Don't drink your Scotch alone."

*   *   *   *   *

Ray's law office was in an old two-story furniture store that had been converted to offices decades ago. Adding still more to his sense that winter had chosen him exclusively to torment, the building's ancient boiler died a wheezing death forcing the place to be shut down for three days while overworked plumbers cannibalized parts and jerry-rigged it to get the heat up again.

Ray brooded at home, disregarding Jackie's admonition not to drink alone by pouring vodka and cranberry juice as early as 4:30 instead of his accustomed 5 PM (an arbitrary hour facetiously chosen to insulate him against alcoholism's snare).

He went to see Dennis, who was staying with his son Donald. (Dennis' family was one of those in which the parents' and all five offspring's first names, by design, begin with the same letter.) Dennis was in pitiable shape: his breathing was raspy and painful because of his taped-up ribs; his upper plate was still being repaired, which made speech difficult and eating next to impossible, and his eye was patched; but worst of all, he was demoralized and had aged markedly since Ray had last seen him. Dennis had vowed never to visit the nursing home again and was horrified that anyone would think he had sexually abused Mary Alice. "I was just being kind," he would plead every few minutes, no matter the subject being discussed or the person with whom he was talking. Criminal charges were still pending against Junior, but Donald was pursuing a civil suit against him in an avowed effort to recoup Dennis' medical expenses and "bankrupt the scummy little bastard."

Curiously, the town had become disinterested in the whole sad nursing-home fiasco. Few knew of Jackie's firing, and as far as Ray could tell, no one knew of his own involvement except Junior, Jackie, Dennis and his family, and Susan Douglas. Yet Ray was so unsettled by Dennis' sad shape that he called and made an appointment to talk with Susan the following afternoon at 3:30.

His mood throughout that morning was uncharacteristic; instead of being slow moving and deliberate, he was agitated, quick to anger, impatient. He arrived ten minutes early to find that Susan had left at noon complaining of a migraine. Debbie Burk, her administrative assistant and part-time accountant, had no idea Susan had made an appointment with Ray and was effusively apologetic that Ray had not been called to cancel. "With her headache and all, she must have just forgotten you were coming," she said while doing a charade search through some papers on Susan's desk.

"Or perhaps she correctly figured I would make her headache much worse," replied Ray. "She didn't forget, you can bet on that."

Debbie looked up, and after a few seconds of indecision

said, "Maybe I could help you? Is it about a resident?"

"It's about Jackie Coons being fired for doing her job. It's about Susan trying to scapegoat Jackie. It's about Junior Harley being a horse's ass. It's about...." Ray's voice had been rising with each assertion, but it suddenly dropped off, and after a pause he said, "I'm being unfair. It's not about you—you had nothing to do with it and here I am beating up on you. I'm sorry. I should know better."

Debbie played with her watchband, avoided Ray's eyes and remained silent. Ray moved to the door but then turned back and asked, "Mary Alice Harley... Could I visit her?"

Relieved to be able to say something that would appease Ray, Debbie, sounding too eager to please, answered, "I don't see why not. It's another hour or so until her supper. I'll have one of the girls...no, I'll go myself... and bring her into the Living Room"

"Living Room?"

"Well, that's what we call it. It's that nice room with all the plants just off the main dining room," said Debbie, her voice rising as if she were asking a question. "Susan...the committee... decided that since most of the rooms are shared, it's better if the residents see visitors outside their rooms so as to not disturb their roommates. Of course close relatives can still visit in the rooms if they choose...and there's space." And again brightly, to the point of sounding shrill, Debbie added, "Why don't you just go over there and I'll bring Mary Alice right along?" Then, as an after thought, "It may take a few minutes if she isn't in her wheelchair."

Ray found the room empty. It was a pleasant space, or would have been if its large steamed-up windows didn't look out on the smudged frozen dregs of winter. In the dead light of late afternoon a stand of crowded birches faded into a woods of bedraggled spruce and tangled bare alders that smacked of abandonment and unnatural, fertile chaos; the blacks and greens were dull against the gray aging snow. Ray took a chair whose back was to the windows. The room's furnishings were tasteful: new overstuffed chairs and a couple of love seats, one covered in burgundy and one in a forest green material, velvet-like in texture. As much as winter's cold still plagued him, Ray thought the overheated room, comfortable now, must be oppressively hot in the summer. Large bright paintings of white saltbox houses with colors blending into their shadows hung on the walls, equal distances from the corners, and the room gave a feeling of fanatical orderliness. Living Room? Hardly. Waiting Room? Waiting-to-Die Room? Of course.

Debbie, ever smiling, wheeled Mary Alice into the room directly in front of Ray so Mary Alice could see into the woods. Ray rose and, not knowing quite what to do, stood before his chair, drew back his hand that he'd begun to extend as a handshake toward her, and said, "Hello, Mary Alice. I'm Ray McCutcheon. You may not remember me, but...."

Mary Alice, giving no indication that she had heard Ray, interrupted and asked, "Is it cold outside?"

"Oh my yes!" answered Ray. "You're fortunate to be in such a nice warm place...and what a pretty sweater you have!"

Mary Alice, in her seventies and handsome, who, even with her confinement to a wheelchair and the lost time and space that dulled much of her expression, conveyed the stylish appearance of a younger woman. Her sweater was bright red with a band of navy and pale blue diamonds woven just below the armpits, and she wore black sweat pants and white running shoes—incongruous attire for one who no longer could walk. Her hair was cut short and shaped its fall to her face—a face thinner than Ray remembered.

"Is it cold outside?" she asked again, sounding like a doll whose repeated speech was initiated by pulling a string in its back.

Ray looked at Debbie, who nodded, smiled and said, "It's still winter, Mary Alice. Cold. But spring's on the way." Then to

Ray: "Sit down, Ray, and I'll just wheel Mary Alice around here so we three can have a nice visit."

Ray had imagined Debbie going off and leaving him to talk to Mary Alice on his own, although now that she was there he didn't know what he intended to say. Debbie maneuvered Mary Alice on an angle close to Ray's right side and then pulled over a straight chair and sat directly in front of Ray where Mary Alice had just been. They sat silently for several seconds, Debbie smiling, Mary Alice expressionless, and Ray looking from one to the other in search of some sign of…he knew not what.

"Is it cold outside?" asked Mary Alice. Ray smiled, mirroring Debbie's perpetual expression and thought, "smiles must be the way they communicate here."

"On the way here, Mary Alice, I saw a pileated woodpecker— you know, one of those big woodpeckers with red markings on its head? It can't be very smart though, hanging around here while there's still snow on the ground. But maybe it knows something we don't about spring? Birds and flowers seem to have their own calendars. Crazy crocuses pop right up out of the snow."

Mary Alice's expression changed not a bit, but she did look at Ray with clear, deep, brown eyes which, if they did not show recognition, displayed a sudden concentration.

"I haven't seen a robin yet," continued Ray, uncertain of where his monologue was leading.

Mary Alice reached her right hand toward him in what Ray took to be a belated move to shake his hand, as if his earlier introduction of himself was just now getting through to her. He took her hand, which was surprisingly cold given the overheated room and her heavy sweater; but instead of shaking it she placed his hand against her left breast.

Ray jerked his hand from her grasp and looked to Debbie who, still smiling, said, "Oh, that's just Mary Alice. She likes to hold hands close to her. I think it gives her comfort."

Looking at Mary Alice, who again reached out toward him, her face showing neither distress nor pleasure. Ray took her hand, but this time he held it away from her body in an upright position much as if they were about to arm wrestle, and he kept it there while accusing Debbie, "You knew she'd do that, didn't you?"

"Well, not really. Don't get upset, Ray. It's nothing to get upset about. That's just her way," said Debbie, rising and moving to the wheelchair while continuing, "I'll just back her up a little if holding her hand makes you uncomfortable."

"Oh, come on Deb! Holding her hand doesn't bother me, but holding it against her breast sure as hell does," said Ray letting go of Mary Alice's hand. "Surely you know what happened to Dennis Crimmins, who, unfortunately, shared your view of innocent hand holding?"

"It *is* innocent, Ray. There's nothing sexual happening. There's not even a breast there. It's a prosthesis, a padded bra. Mary Alice had a mastectomy a dozen years ago."

Ray said nothing, and after a long silence Mary Alice again asked, "Is it cold outside?"

Debbie moved from behind the wheelchair so Mary Alice could see her. "It's a cold day, Mary Alice, but it's a late-winter cold. Spring's on the way. Why, Ray saw a woodpecker today and there's probably a robin or two somewhere out there as well."

Ray stepped behind the chair he'd been sitting in and rested his hands on its back. "So, why did you help me see Mary Alice, Debbie? I came here to see Susan about another matter and Mary Alice was an afterthought. I feel like I've been set up to be embarrassed or look foolish or something."

Debbie's smile disappeared with a long sigh. "Ray, you asked to see Mary Alice and why would I refuse you? Set you up? Look. I work here. I try to do the right thing. I try to follow common sense and be nice to people. This is an unhappy place. If you think I could get some kind of kick out of seeing Mary Alice put your hand where her breast used to be, well...that's just too sick for me to know what to say." She began to push Mary Alice toward the door and added, "I'll take her back to her room now."

Ray stood behind the chair long after Debbie and Mary Alice had left, his thoughts a confusion of a desire to flee and a sense of obligation to stay and clarify what had just taken place. He hardly knew Debbie (she was a friend of his ex-wife) and was unsure of her marital status—it seemed more and more of their generation were divorced, and Ray couldn't remember who she had married or if she still lived in town. To him she'd always been pleasant. Looking out on the yard, a crack of dead yellow sunlight broke through above the woods.

After several minutes he realized that Debbie was not going to return, so he put on his parka and walked back to the office. She was at her desk reading a pamphlet and looked up when he entered.

"You know, you could get fired for telling me about Mary Alice's mastectomy...I mean, isn't that some of your privileged medical information, like the stuff that lost Jackie Coons her job?"

"I really don't know," answered Debbie. "But I do know that more has been made out of a really nice old woman's natural gestures than could be imagined by a hundred crackpot lawyers, social workers and friggin' sons. Just what is it you want from me anyway?"

Ray saw that whatever it was he had come for that day, it was gone forever. "Well, I don't want anything from you, Debbie. I just think it is a goddamned shame that an old man has gotten beaten up and a really good woman has lost her job over...over... jeez, I don't even know what it's over any longer." Pausing as he turned to leave, he said, "I'm sorry if I've upset you."

As he reached the office door Debbie called, "By the way, Ray, those woodpeckers don't migrate—they're here all winter." He again turned to face her and she added, "But you don't have to stay. Go to Florida. Get a couple weeks in the sun."

They starred at each other until Ray dropped his gaze. He nodded. "You're right. I don't have to stay, and for sure I could use some warmth, Debbie. But...two weeks? It will take more than two weeks in the sun. Way, way more.

ELEANOR ROOSEVELT'S LOVE LETTERS

Howard's sister Anne had found the box, along with other long-forgotten items, in the crawl space under her first-floor stairway when, after a forty-year residency, she sold her house. "There's some unbelievable stuff of yours in this," she told him when he picked up the box, along with their father's ancient favorite easy chair, some bad paintings and prints, and a pristine set of the *World Book Encyclopedia*, which their father purchased after both of them were out of high school. Their mother had died twenty years ago and, after their father remarried, the things their stepmother wanted removed from the family house had come to Anne's Framingham house for want of a better place to put them.

"I didn't snoop through everything," said Anne, "but there are programs from your senior play, grade-school class pictures, your crossing-guard badge—priceless stuff."

Anne had been divorced for years, her ex was dead, her children and grandchildren lived in Arizona, and she finally had given up the fantasy that her house, the one she'd lived in since her marriage, was the symbolic family home. Icy suburban winter streets had deadened sentiment, and she longed to get the transition over with and move on to year-round sun and freedom from trying to maintain a house that was too big and in constant need of repair.

"You know you're really going to hate Arizona, Annie," said Howard when he came for the box and the other leftovers. "There's not a damned thing out there you like except sunshine."

"We'll see," she responded with confidence. "Right now sunshine sounds like more than enough."

Together they loaded the chair, pictures, lamps, and the box of memorabilia into Howard's pickup truck. "You really need this truck—four-wheel drive?" asked Anne. "You live in Queens, for God's sake."

"Yeah. Well, you never know when we'll get another winter like 1970, or who'll be Mayor. If people had had pickups then, Lindsay probably would have become President instead of being remembered as the guy who couldn't get the snow off the streets. Besides, my lady friends think it's cool." They both laughed.

Their mood was decidedly sober, however, as Howard said good-bye to Anne and her house. "A lot of good times here, Annie," he said as he kissed her on the top of her lowered head. All she could do was nod as tears began. She would see Howard in ten days when she came down to stay over before her flight from Kennedy to Phoenix, so the serious good-bye could wait.

On his drive down through Connecticut, Howard had decided he would keep the chair and the other large items until after Anne had gone so she would think he valued them as links to their past, but his little frame house, circa 1925, which had been his second wife's, was an anachronism among the brick duplexes and post-war apartment buildings that dominated his neighborhood and was way too small for castaway furniture and unopened encyclopedias. The box of personal items of his youth, however, transcended his lack of sentiment for the rest of his truck's load.

The box was an Old Crow bourbon carton, the kind long prized for packing books, and the lid's flaps had been folded alternately under each other so the box would stay closed. Howard pried the flaps apart, revealing the browned, brittle, first section of *The Boston Globe* for Thursday, March 18, 1960, that covered the box's contents. Edges of the paper had broken off when Anne had lifted them days before, and now pieces crumbled and filtered down over stacks of yellowing comic books, score cards from Red Sox games, several invitations to his high school commencement, a photograph with a fake autograph of Ted Williams, five years worth of Street and Smith's baseball yearbooks, and dozens of loose greeting cards from birthdays and Valentine's days as far back as his seventh year.

Wedged against one side of the box were six envelopes of the same uniform size and blue color that had taken on a yellowish green hue around the edges. They had been bound by a rubber band now dried and clinging to the envelopes in sticky, crumbling, broken segments that left black tracks when Howard brushed them away. The letters were love letters to Howard from Eleanor Roosevelt, written during the summer of 1957, between their sophomore and junior years in college.

Eleanor Roosevelt was a black woman who was ambivalent about having the same name as the much admired wife of the thirty-second President of the United States. She admired the President's wife for being a vocal supporter for good causes and especially for her brave championing of the great black singer Marian Anderson against the bigotry of entrenched Washington society. But she also was sensitive to her constant identification with a white namesake, admirable human being though she was.

Elie, as Howard and everyone called her, was the daughter of West Coast black school teachers, who in the late 20s had been prominent undergraduates at Channing, Howard's and Elie's small college. They were a beautiful couple whose physiques and light brown skin bespoke of the best gene pools of their Negro and

Caucasian ancestries, and Elie's beauty had turned admiring eyes from the time of her early infancy. The Roosevelt surname had been a name change made by Elie's grandfather, Frederick Flatter, a native Californian and an early conservationist who was an admirer of Teddy Roosevelt. Elie's name had been chosen in turn by her parents who, survivors of the Great Depression, continued the family's admiration for Roosevelt Presidents, this time for Franklin; and though aware of the irony in the choice, they hoped pride in the Roosevelt name would offset complications such a name might cause Elie as she grew up.

Elie was as beautiful and animated as the President's wife was plain and composed, and men approached her with a barely contained sexual ardor that she relished deflecting. Those most humiliated by her calculated rejections called her a cock teaser, and though Channing College was renowned for its religious and racial tolerance, many of her rejected white male suitors were not above calling her a "nigger bitch" behind her back. Their anger and frustration was heightened because Elie, almost from her first day on campus, had, as if inviting trouble, declared she was there to marry a white man. The few black male students had nothing to do with her and refused to be drawn into late night dorm talk about her with their white friends.

Howard was as attracted to Elie sexually as were the others, but at first he was afraid to do more than fantasize about sex with her; her declaration of whom she was going to marry made him wary of falling in love with her. Yet it happened.

In the spring of their sophomore year, Howard affected a farcical dance, mimicking Ray Bolger dancing and singing "Once in Love with Amy," with which he entertained his buddies by leaping across campus on the way home from illegal beer drinking bouts at a notorious nearby tavern whose existence the college chose to ignore. His Ray Bolger bit got enough praise from his tipsy fellow students to encourage Howard to try out for the chorus of an original college musical. He had been in Psych and English classes, both small, with Elie, so when he discovered she too was auditioning for the chorus, instead of fearing that he would make a fool of himself in front of her, he sensed that this was a great opportunity to impress her. If they both got in the chorus he'd get to know her—sing with her, dance with her.

At the audition, a playful Elie came up to him. "Hey, Howie. You a song and dance man?" she asked in a tone that could have been either mocking or encouraging—he wasn't sure. But he wasn't intimidated, either. His hormones overcame his caution.

"Come on! I was born backstage with a traveling *Student Prince* troupe in Kansas City. I just got my first pair of lederhosen and was gonna be featured at age five when the princes all got drafted into World War II and my folks became sheep herders. What about you—you a song and dance girl?"

Elie looked at him, surprised by but enjoying his nonsense. "Just watch my stuff," she said, matching his bravado.

He almost blurted out, "I've been watching your stuff ever since I first saw you," but knew that would be fatal. He nodded and smiled.

They both were chosen for the chorus of five boys and five girls, and for the next six weeks they sang silly songs, danced as partners, and fell in love—love that dismissed caution and transcended for Howard Elie's announcement of her intention to marry a white man.

Howard took uncommon pride in being identified as Elie's boyfriend. After all, in the nearly two years Elie had been on campus no one had gained such notice, not that Elie was ever without a male companion when she wanted one or when convention called for one—dances, movies in town, after game beer blasts with fake IDs—but she seldom dated the same boy more than twice, and her public attitude toward those she chose was a playfulness of the kind she had shown when she came onto Howard at the audition.

They became a campus couple the way Howard had imagined college lovers were, except this was before the pill, before Roe v. Wade, and when buying condoms meant walking up to a pharmacy counter and stating what you wanted to purchase within clear earshot of any nearby patron. But the factor in their love affair that most inhibited Howard also was the most obvious: she was black and he was white, and the line was drawn, if only in his subconscious.

His spring with Elie was a delight, regardless of Howard's caution. She was beautiful, bright, funny. After the three night run of the musical, which was a great success and made campus celebrities of all connected with the production, Elie and Howard continued to sing and dance their roles under the trees in the seclusion of back campus, and Howard would do his Ray Bolger bit, causing Elie to giggle and protest how awful his routine was. It was a lovely Indiana spring, and Howard and Elie absorbed its warmth, becoming as newly vital as the blossoming sap-filled trees and the extravagantly sprouting greenery. There was an excess of sensual newness everywhere, and Elie dropped her sexual restraint as easily and gently as she might brush away a strand of hair blowing across her eyes. She and Howard touched, rocked, rubbed and clung to each other's bodies in desperate actions that stopped just short of penile penetration and left them mutually orgasmic, exhausted, yet still expectant and wistful.

These bouts invariably concluded with Howard saying some variation on the following as their bodies disengaged: "Jesus, Elie! We're gonna have to be careful." She would remain silent and respond to his warning with only a nod and tight smile; then, after a quiet time, they would gather themselves and hand-in-hand emerge from their hideaway to resume chaste student lives.

Their attraction was heavy with new pleasure yet boggling to Howard with its intensity, and as the school year drew to an end he became uneasy and more and more concerned as to just how his campus world viewed Elie and him. She had, after all, declared her intention to marry a white man, and he wondered was he the one? Was he her trophy, her great white hope?

Their last evening together, before Elie left for Chicago to take the El Capitan back to Los Angeles, peaked in sudden sex play. As Howard worked his hand into her unzipped jeans, she pushed his hand away, pulled from her pocket a foil-wrapped condom, stepped out of her jeans and underpants and without a word handed the condom to Howard.

He had never seen her naked from the waist down. He stared at her exposed body while reaching out to take the condom, not realizing what she was handing him. "What's this? Oh, what the hell, Elie? Where'd you get this?"

She reached for the fly of his jeans and began unzipping him. "Put it on. I want you inside me. We love each other, don't we?"

"Oh, God, Elie. I don't know. I really want to do it, but...I don't know. It's risky, isn't it?"

"I guess," whispered Elie, pulling the waist of his jeans downward. "But...let's do it. Let's do it, Howie. Let's do it. It's our last night."

Neither of them knew how prophetic Elie's statement was. Howard would ejaculate into the condom Elie was trying to force onto his penis, and the rest of the evening would be spent with Howard apologizing and trying to bring Elie to climax with all of their old tried and, up until then, true manipulations that had developed naturally during weeks of maintaining their virginity. Howard would curse himself for years for not being able to fulfill Elie's wants that night—his regrets being wholly self-serving.

When Howard kissed Elie goodbye the next morning on the station platform for the bus to Chicago, he was full of bravado and made no attempt to disguise his passion. He kissed her so long and hard that she finally was forced to break loose, eyeing him with suspicion. A dozen fellow students were there saying goodbyes or waiting for the bus, and Howard wanted to make sure they all saw him kissing this beautiful black woman. "To hell with what they think," said his body language while his wish was that they would think him courageous and, perhaps, a little crazy.

Elie wrote her first letter while still on the train—a cliché-ridden note about how much Howard meant to her. It was signed, "Love always, Elie," but the name on the return address on the envelope was "Eleanor Roosevelt," and though the street and city were foreign to the former First Lady's eastern residence, anyone reading the envelope would have been drawn up short by the name and be left to wonder, "Is it really President Roosevelt's wife?"

Five more letters came that summer in the same blue envelopes with the same name and return address. Howard's letters to her from the first were guarded and cryptic. He always told her how much he missed her and how he couldn't wait to be with her again in the fall, but anyone reading them would have been put off by the self-pitying tone surrounding his vague comments about their last night together, the unspoken subtext being that he was asking her to make things all right, to tell him they could be lovers, real lovers, but without anyone ever knowing it. He wanted to write, "The next time we'll really do it, Elie, I'll really make love to you"; but fearing someone other than Elie might read them, he never could write those words.

Elie's letters varied little. They included lines that she passed off as her own but which he recognized as ones lifted from popular songs. She never once alluded to sex. Her letters began to include more and more about what she and her friends were doing, none of which interested Howard, and he would skim through them, pausing only to reread the plagiarized love lyrics.

There was a break of three weeks between her last two letters, a pause that Howard hardly noticed. It was his practice to promptly answer her letters, but never before receiving one from her; so he didn't fret about the passage of time following his latest response to her and rather enjoyed not writing. He was truthful when he wrote that he was looking forward to renewing their relationship in the fall—one that he viewed now as wholly sexual although he had no more of a notion of how he was going to have sex with Elie while not having sex with her than he had when he kissed her goodbye three months before. Thus her last letter knocked his socks off!

It was such a short letter that he had memorized it without trying.

Dear Howard [she had never called him anything but Howie], *Let's face it, you don't love me—never did. I don't love you—never did. I'm not coming back east to school, so you're off the hook.*

It was mostly fun. Good luck.

Elie

He never responded.

*   *   *   *   *

When Howard took the packet of fading envelopes out of his memorabilia box, he immediately sat down to read through the letters. He had not reread them since the summer they came, and he wondered why he had kept them. Rereading them now brought back memories of Elie's sexuality with such strength that even though there was no specific mention in the letters of their mutual masturbation, he became sexually aroused to a degree that he had not experienced in months—until he came to the final letter, that is, and the sexual fantasies ceased.

"Damn," he blurted; and then he asked himself, "What was she all about? Really. Was I actually the great white hope—the white guy she wanted? Did she marry one I wonder? Was I just being used?" The last thought gave him comfort, however, when he answered himself, "I gave as good as I got, by God. I could have fucked her!" Then he chuckled and said aloud, "I wish I had. I wish the hell I had." He dropped the letters back into the box.

The next day, while watching Sports Center, Howard again went through the box, methodically reading the greeting cards and all other printed matter, sorting out what to keep. He threw away everything but things that had his name printed on them, his miniature crossing guard badge, and Elie's letters. These he held in his hand many minutes, lifting them and lowering them as if weighing their value; then he put a new rubber band around the letters and added them to the "keep" pile.

His Eleanor Roosevelt was much on his mind the rest of the day and that evening. Had she married? The next morning he brought up his college's website and emailed a request to the alumni office asking if they had an address for Eleanor Roosevelt, class of 1959. He knew that the college tried to keep track of anybody who had ever walked across campus in hopes of getting a contribution from them, and Elie's two-year residence would have made her more than eligible for their requests for money. Later that day he got an answer back from someone calling herself Muffie Barlow and identifying herself as "Alumni Relations Director." Her message was astoundingly straight forward, *"Why do you want to know?"*

Intentionally misspelling her name, Howard wrote back. *"Dear Muffin Barlow: Have no fear! I'm not trying to compete with you for a donation from Eleanor. She was a dear friend whom, unfortunately, I've lost track of. I'd like to resume contact with her, so* *if you'll send me her address I promise to contribute $50 to support the girl's field hockey team."*

The reply didn't come until the next morning. *"We must take care not to divulge addresses to telemarketers or others who might abuse the privacy of our alumni. I note that you are indeed a graduate of Channing, class of 1959, and a past contributor to the Alumni Fund. The women's field hockey team does not have a separate account, but we will be glad to accept your contribution to the Athletic General Fund. Thank you. The last address we have for Eleanor Roosevelt, class of 1959, was in 1990, under the name of Eleanor Roosevelt Reddington, c/o Christian Ministries, Mombassa, Kenya."*

Now that he had it, Howard didn't know what to do with this information. Had she disappeared into the jungle? Reddington? What kind of name is Reddington—a white name or a black name? Christian Ministries? Sounded awfully pious for the Eleanor Roosevelt he remembered.

Howard again picked up the packet of her letters, passing them from hand to hand, feeling their heft. He read the return address on the top envelope and smoothed a wrinkle that the old rubber band had created. "Oh, this is ridiculous!" he said aloud and lobbed the letters into his wastebasket. There they rested until after his sister Anne visited on her way west.

He mentioned the letters to her, laughing about the incongruity of Elie's name. Just think," he said. "If I had married her, you could have had fun for years telling people that your brother was married to Eleanor Roosevelt after FDR died—and then playing with their disbelief, even win some bets on it."

"Those letters pretty graphic?" she asked.

"Hardly. Just clichéd stuff—she used to steal song lyrics as if they were her original expressions of love or whatever. They're in my waste basket—you can read them if you want."

Anne waved away his invitation as if she were getting rid

of a bad odor. "No thanks. But somebody might want to read them—you know, letters from Eleanor Roosevelt? Why don't you put them on eBay and see what happens?"

"Get serious," scoffed Howard. "I think there are laws that apply to fraud by internet, sweetie."

"Fraud, shmaud! Who said anything about fraud? You just say you have love letters Eleanor Roosevelt sent you and you want, what...fifty dollars apiece? And if a prospective buyer wants to know more, just truthfully answer his questions."

"Right! Why, of course! There must be hundreds of people out there waiting to pay fifty bucks for letters from a faux Eleanor Roosevelt. You're out of your mind!"

"Laugh, but you can't imagine the junk people buy, or at least want to sell. You just said it yourself: think of all the fun you could have telling people you have love letters from Eleanor Roosevelt. It's a cyberspace joke—an online version of the old fake can of peanuts where you take the lid off the can and a cloth covered spring snake leaps out at you. I bet you'd sell them all— three hundred dollars."

He drove Anne to Kennedy the next morning, but as soon as he was back in the house he retrieved the letters and googled Eleanor Roosevelt Reddington. The search turned up dozens of Reddingtons but no Eleanor Roosevelt Reddington. Then he set about writing a description for eBay: *Six love letters hand written to me by Eleanor Roosevelt in 1957. Perfect condition on blue stationery in matching blue envelopes, the latter slightly faded around the edges. Most signed, "Love always, Elie" but each envelope has "Eleanor Roosevelt" clearly legible in the hand written return address. Will sell individually or all six as a packet. $50 each.*

Howard waited overnight, letting the whole notion of trying to sell the letters soak in. But the next day he went through the unfamiliar rigmarole necessary to place his letters for sale on the internet, and with some misgivings waited a response. Responses were soon to come, all voicing various degrees of skepticism, some accusing him of outright fraud before he had a chance to respond to the questioners' suspicions, and to one threatening to expose him to other potential buyers and to the Roosevelt family,

One respondent was interested enough to make an offer of one hundred dollars for all six letters after being given assurances by Howard that the letters were from an old girl friend whose name actually was Eleanor Roosevelt, and that all but the last letter was signed, "Love always, Elie." Howard held firm on the price, however. *"These letters are not only a unique curiosity but are an authentic glimpse of the mating rituals of an earlier time. They are worth every bit of $50 each. "* He surprised himself with the bit about mating rituals and wondered where he had dredged that up from, but the bidder made no further offer.

Howard felt both relieved and disappointed; then the original bidder came back three days later agreeing to the three-hundred dollar price. The deal was made, a money order arrived, and Eleanor Roosevelt's love letters were mailed to a man in Detroit.

That night Howard went with a complimentary ticket to Alice Tulley Hall for a concert by a string quartet made up of four extraordinarily gifted and attractive young Asian women. In his younger days he never would have considered going to a concert or even a movie by himself; since shortly after college and until Carol had moved out, he had been married or at least "attached" to some woman, so until now going out alone was never an issue.

He and Carol had lived together for three years when she left him for an older man, a retired Air Force colonel whose major attraction for her seemed to be his desire to winter in New Mexico, and the two of them had moved there last fall. Her leaving had left Howard more bemused than bitter, but having been widowed twice and dumped once he felt no compulsion to connect, legally or otherwise, with someone new. But now, sitting and watching these four lovely women, their petite beauty enhanced by the passion they brought to their playing, a loneliness began to intrude, and by the end of the concert, when everyone was leaving the hall, Howard's eyes teared and he felt sorry for himself for the first time in months.

Instead of going directly home, as would have been his usual routine, he walked up Columbus Avenue, which was simmering with late-evening city energy. Every woman, no matter her age or body size, was clothed in black, the decade-old fashion color, and the men appeared determined to be happy in adolescent self-conscious ways that made the women seem all the more dominant. Couples or groups waited for tables in jammed undistinguished restaurants, and even where people walked there was no sense of random movement—everyone but Howard was going some place. He took a cab back to Queens.

The next few days were unseasonably warm and bright in a February false spring. Howard's loneliness began to irritate him—self pity was no fun. He brooded about the past and began to blame Anne for dumping remnants of his childhood and late teenage years on him. And he kept coming back to Elie's letters. Why had he sold them?

He was suddenly embarrassed to think that some guy in Detroit had a piece of his life and was no doubt making fun of it. He wondered who was crazier: he for selling the letters or Mr. Detroit for wanting to buy them? There was virtually nothing erotic in them, no talk about their sex together, no juicy terms of endearment, nothing for some deviate to get off on—except, oh no, the name! Howard shuddered to think that he could even imagine someone being so aberrant as to lust after a homely, celebrated woman who had been dead for forty years; he was beginning to lose perspective and common sense. He'd get the letters back and burn them.

Composing an email letter to Mr. Detroit took most of the afternoon. He would have to make it clear that he didn't want the letters back because he had gotten a better offer, which was sure to be Mr. Detroit's suspicion. If the guy were a deviate or just a practical joker with more money than he knew what to do with, Howard thought it was unlikely he would have any legal expertise. Of course Howard had none himself, but he would wing it just the same: *It has come to my attention that there may be some copyright problems with my sale of Eleanor Roosevelt's letters to you. Since only the author of letters retains the copyright, the recipient of the letters may never publish their contents without permission from the author, and since it is not clear that this Eleanor Roosevelt is still alive, the copyright privilege could be a legal can of worms for anyone other than Ms. Roosevelt's estate (if she is deceased) or the original intended recipient of the letters, and even disclosure of the contents to another reader by the current owner of the letters theoretically could lead to potential defamation of character charges by the original recipient of the letters, not that I have any reason to suspect that such action might be necessary in the future, but prudence in legal matters is always wise. Therefore, I think it fair and reasonable to buy the letters back from you and to compensate you for your time and effort. To ameliorate any disappointment you may feel in giving up the letters, I'll pay you an additional $25 beyond the original purchase price of $300.*

Howard heard nothing for two days, then Mr. Detroit replied: *Ha, ha, very funny! In a pig's eye. The deal was fair and square. So sue me, or whatever.*

Howard wrote back immediately, not even taking time to think up a strategy: *I really believe you should reconsider. My offer is generous in spirit as well as monetary value, and it could save you a good deal of grief down the road."*

There was no reply. Howard considered offering more money, but he guessed Mr. Detroit would be convinced that Howard had a big offer from someone else and would never sell the letters back. He then became suspicious himself and went into eBay to see if Detroit was trying to sell the letters again. But what he discovered was no offer to sell Eleanor Roosevelt's letters; rather, there was a note from Mr. Detroit warning others not to do business with Howard because "*he harasses purchasers of his items.*"

Howard was palsied with rage, but he at once saw the hopelessness of any retaliatory attempt. The letters were gone, and for the second time in his life, so was Elie. How had she ended it? "*You don't love me—never did. I don't love you— never did.*"?

For several days he could find no place to direct his anger other than at himself for falling prey to sentimentality. He had forgotten about the letters for more than forty years, and only on rare occasions during those forty years had he thought about Elie—sighting some beautiful black woman would cause him to wonder how Elie had aged, or someone singing one of the Cole Porter lyrics Elie had passed off as her own would cause him to smile and stir pangs of unrequited sex that would linger briefly. He should have left the letters in the trash basket, or, better yet, burned the damned things.

For a few weeks Howard checked his email and eBay daily, but Mr. Detroit's one day vendetta to defame didn't resurface, nor were Elie's letters being offered for sale.

Spring came on schedule with an occasional lapse into a nasty cold day, and Howard's embarrassment remained private and waned as the weather improved. His loneliness faded as well, even though he had few social contacts, and he resumed his desultory ways: he went to bed when he wanted, arose when he wanted, and spent his days as he pleased. Every day became an adventure of the mildest kind and allowed Howard to fool himself into believing that his destiny lay outside of his control yet somehow favored him. The episode with Elie's letters was a case in point, he decided—an object lesson showing him the folly of being innovative with the past. It was better to give up the past altogether, go with the flow, take no chances.

Nonetheless, early May's warmth, weighty with the odor of plants and sun- drenched old wood, brought Howard memories of his college spring days that he could not dismiss. So, midmorning, midweek, he drove his truck into New Jersey, through the Delaware Water Gap and into Pennsylvania's Poconos, feeling as if he were on a pilgrimage—not to revisit the past but rather to observe primal nature anew.

Nothing remotely suggesting primal nature was evident until he had turned off of Interstate 80 and its endless stream of bullying eighteen-wheel tractor trailers and scowling motorists contemptuous of those obeying the speed limit. Following a two lane state highway, he stopped at a motel that undoubtedly catered to hunters and illicit lovers. His room was pleasant—cleaner than he expected—and smelled only mildly of pine oil disinfectant and years old cigarette smoke. He felt good about his choice and lay down for a nap before the five-to-seven happy hour announced on a nearby restaurant's marquee.

The picture window of his room looked out on woods and flowering ornamental pear trees, their white blossoms framing the edge of the motel's property like a crocheted doily. Howard closed his eyes and said to the empty room, "You're wrong, Elie. I loved you the whole spring semester."

UNBLEST

Amy had seen Josh Wilcox only one time in her life, yet that encounter eleven years before had haunted some part of nearly every day since. Now Matt, her husband of three weeks, was asking her about Josh Wilcox, and she knew that her answer could infect their marriage as surely as a neurological disease ultimately tightens and withers one's body until it becomes an inanimate yet living mummy.

"Here's one I don't know," said Matt, holding out a greeting card to Amy. "Josh Wilcox?—Do we know him?"

"Please, God," she said in a voice so muted that it was unclear to Matt. She took the harmless-looking commercial card, white with royal blue lettering on the outside that merely said "Congratulations!" Opening it with a haste that belied her dread, she read the card's printed quotation:

> "God, the best Maker of Marriages,
> Combine your hearts in one.
> Shakespeare, Henry V"

Amy had difficulty reading the crude handwritten script below the card's message but finally made it out to say: "Hope you have healed. I never will. Josh Wilcox."

She turned her hand outward to return the card to Matt, then let it fall to the floor while her hand continued slowly toward him. "What?" asked Matt taking her hand.

Without withdrawing her hand, Amy said, "No. The envelope. Give me the envelope." Her face had become so pale that her lips were the purplish brown of dried blood, and her movements were the slow, careful actions of one trying not to vomit.

Matt handed her the envelope, which she held close to her face, squinting, trying to read the postmark. In the same measured tones as before, she said, "I can't make it out. Where's it from?" and handed it back to him.

"It's all smudged. Somewhere in Arizona—I think Williams, or maybe it could be Winslow," answered Matt, examining the envelope as he reached down to retrieve the card from the floor. "There's no return address."

Amy leaned forward with Matt, not to pick up the card but to ease herself onto the floor where she rested her back against the front of their new couch and let her head dangle between her legs. "I'm faint." Her voice was barely audible.

Matt dropped down beside her, took her head in both of his hands and began to keen, "It's okay, Amy, it's okay. It's all right, it's okay. Don't faint, don't faint, it's okay. Easy does it, easy, easy. It's okay."

She forced her head backward from between his hands and rested it on the couch cushions. Her eyes were closed but color had returned to her face, and in quiet resignation she said, "Holy Mary mother of God. What rotten luck. What rotten, rotten, unfair luck."

Amy was neither religious nor profane, and Matt, who had known her for two years and had lived with her for the last one of those, had never seen her react in any way remotely close to this. She lay back, limp, her eyes closed, her head resting against the couch cushion so that the full length of her neck was exposed, giving her body a sacrificial vulnerability. "What can I do, Amy? What can I get?" asked Matt, gently pleading.

Without opening her eyes, Amy took his hand and held it against the small breasts he loved so much. "Nothing. There's nothing you can do. It's already been done." Then after a pause, she added, "I'll have to think." Tears traced her cheeks.

They sat in silence. Crumpled against the couch, the only movements she made were rhythmic squeezes of Matt's hand. Cramped by his crouched position, he had to shift his weight, and fearing he was moving away, Amy opened her eyes and tugged his hand back toward her like a child clutching a favorite stuffed toy. Matt assured her, "Let me just resettle. I've got a cramp in my calf," and he eased her torso forward from the couch and positioned his body so she was leaning back against him, his arms and legs surrounding her in a protective embrace.

They did not speak for several minutes. Astonished and unnerved by what just had taken place, Matt held back asking the reasonable questions that could clear his confusion. He wiped away her tears with his fingers, rocked their bodies back and forth in a comforting rhythm and waited for some explanation.

He began to wonder if Amy had fallen asleep when she said, "Oh Matty, Matty. My worst nightmare," and before he could ask what that meant, she asked, "What time is it?"

"I guess a little after three. Why?"

She said, "Let me up," and ignoring his question went to the phone and dialed her mother and left this voice mail message: "Mother. Terrible, terrible, terrible news! Josh Wilcox has surfaced."

Matt had moved onto the couch, and after hanging up the phone Amy came back and again took his hand in both of hers, holding it in her lap as she snuggled up against him. Amy never called her mother "Mother" unless she was angry or impatient with her, but she now seemed neither. "Bad as all that?" asked Matt.

"Worse," was her one word reply. "Well, so what is this guy? A serial murderer or something?" asked Matt. "I don't get it."

She said nothing while she traced the veins along the back of Matt's hand. Then in a near whimper she said, "I don't know what he is. I just know what he did...and now might do."

Forgetting that moments before he had been afraid to confront her for fear of triggering more alarm, he pleaded, "What's going on, Amy?"

She raised his hand and held it to her cheek and moaned, "Oh Matt, it's all so unfair, and it will change the way you see everything about Mom and me. But you're right. You're part of it now too. You have to know."

Matt had no chance to respond before Amy suddenly stood up, let out a muted scream through gritted teeth, and began hammering the wall beside the couch with both fists. As quickly as her vulnerable, helpless state had consumed her, it just as suddenly gave way to a raging tantrum that continued until Matt wrestled her away from the wall and pinned her arms to her sides. "Cut it out! Cut it out! Quit! It's okay! Stop it, Amy! Stop it!" Once she no longer could move her arms, her crying became hysterical but short-lived. Matt picked her up, carried her into their bedroom, and eased her onto the bed where she lay awake, subdued and silent, while he stayed near by, unnerved and unsure of what to do. Her mother arrived some ninety minutes later.

Janice Clark was a handsome woman who looked younger than her forty-nine years. She worked hard at maintaining her figure, and though she continued to be much admired and pursued by men whose intentions ran the gamut from honorable to unabashedly despicable, she had not remarried after her divorce from Amy's father fourteen years earlier, when Amy was ten.

Janice retained her married name because it was Amy's name as well, and, as she liked to tell people, her maiden name of Swindell seemed considerably less than confidence-inducing for a real estate broker—the profession she'd learned after the divorce.

Matt met her at the door and she entered with the calm determination of a plumber come to control a leaking pipe that threatened to break open and flood the kitchen. Janice had a lovely smile that she rationed to punctuate her common expression of serious concern, an expression that she had acquired over ten years of selling houses to middle-income people moving up from small tract houses to large tract houses they could not afford. Putting down her attaché case, she said to Matt, "So, what do you know?"

This was not the informal "what do you know" greeting whose usual response is "not much." Janice actually was asking a question she hoped would be answered: what did Matt know about the circumstances that made a congratulations-on-your-marriage card from Josh Wilcox a traumatic event?

Matt grimaced in a spontaneous expression of innocence. "Nothing. But I hope somebody is going to fill me in soon."

As he was speaking, Amy came into the room, and she and her mother embraced in a heartfelt, spontaneous hug that one associates with the silent expression of shared grief over someone's death. "All poor Matt knows is that his little wifey freaked out at the first sign of Josh Wilcox," she said, moving to take Matt's hand. "It's your story, Mother. It's up to you to tell him, don't you think?"

Matt caught the edge in Amy's voice, but Janice's expression didn't change. "So what's this all about?" she asked. "What do you mean 'Josh Wilcox has surfaced?' He came here to your apartment?"

Without responding Amy handed her the card, which Janice read, turning it over, then reading it again. Amy showed her the envelope and on closer examination the three of them decided that it had been postmarked in Winslow, Arizona, five days before. "How did he know I was married?" Amy asked in a tone of disbelief. "Arizona is two thousand miles from here!"

"Thank goodness for that!" said Janice. "Your wedding announcement was in *Newsday*, but that doesn't explain how he could have your address. And of course his mother still lives on Long Island—I assume."

"You don't know?" asked Amy.

"Well, yes. As far as I know she's still here. But there's never been any indication that she knows about me—or you." Janice slumped into their one overstuffed chair, stretching her legs and dangling her arms like an exhausted fighter resting between rounds.

"You want a drink, Janice? I think all we've got is wine and beer," said Matt, moving toward the kitchen.

"I'd love about a 12-ounce vodka martini, but I have to meet this couple in Huntington at seven. A Coke? Do you have a caffeine-free coke? I've already had a week's allotment of coffee today." Her voice was weary, her eyes stalling for time.

Amy began to play with her wedding ring; it felt strange to her hand. She and Janice were silent until Matt returned with two glasses of cola, handing a glass to each of them even though Amy had not requested one. "Look, let me get a beer and then somebody has to tell me what's going on," he said with evident exasperation. "Enough is enough."

When he returned and settled on the couch beside Amy, Janice took a sip of her drink and sounding unnaturally dramatic said, "Right. Now, there's no way around this." She paused, then choosing her words slowly, continued: "Josh Wilcox is the son of Blake Wilcox, who was a well-known divorce lawyer—my divorce lawyer, as a matter of fact, and"...here she paused, slowly turning her head from side to side and smiling weakly before continuing, "as a very sad matter of fact, Blake was my lover for five years."

She rose from her chair, put her glass on a bookshelf and

looked at Amy. "You know, Amy…you know I've never told what happened to anyone before except you, and for years I've dreaded ever having to tell it again. In fact, I began to believe I'd never have to. But now …and this is really awful…it doesn't seem so bad. It doesn't seem that what I did was so bad. But it is still here to haunt us both."

"No Mother—not both. There are three of us now," said Amy, her voice indicting more than correcting.

Janice chose to stare out the window rather than respond directly to her daughter's gibe, and her gaze stayed there as she continued. "During my divorce from Charlie, Blake Wilcox of course became quite knowledgeable about the nuances of our marriage. Charlie had initiated the divorce—he wanted to marry Marilyn, which, as you know, he did." Then, turning to face Matt, she asked, "And weren't they a lovely couple at your wedding?"

Matt laughed, not knowing how else to respond, and said, "Well, I don't know that I'd call them lovely, but, yeah, they were okay. Maybe a wee bit too comfortable."

"Comfortable. Yes. Well put, Matt. They really made a show of being comfortable, didn't they? Well, Blake and I had long, long discussions, strategy sessions that would have cost me a fortune in legal fees if we hadn't been falling in love and he actually had billed me—which he didn't. But falling in love cost me much more than any fortune."

She suddenly was feeling very uncomfortable standing before them, as if she were assuming a dramatic presence to fill stage space. She returned to her chair and continued, her voice taking on a hardened sincerity.

"I tell you again, Amy, and emphasize to you, Matt, that this was a love affair. Blake was not a womanizer taking advantage of a vulnerable housefrau on the rebound from having been abandoned and humiliated. I may have been those things, but I loved Blake and he loved me, and I honestly believe that our relationship was better for me than for him. Virtually from the beginning of our relationship I had no husband, and up until months after Blake died, Amy was never involved, never a pawn, never a source of guilt—which I suppose speaks volumes about my selfishness, my, shall we say, romantic delusions."

She sipped from her soda, and when she looked up her eyes shone with a hint of tears. "Well, Blake had a wife, a fine woman he told me, who I have to this day never even seen and who he never put down, but who he just didn't love anymore. But he did love Josh and Josh's two younger sisters, Claire and Katy, who, by the way, I've never seen either, and though Blake never said so, I knew he would never get a divorce. We never planned ahead. We just loved each other for five years. We were extremely discrete— incredibly careful about not being seen together in public. I mean, this is sprawling suburban Long Island, but Blake was well known, rich, and who knows who we might run into?"

"One time—and this is the only anecdote I'll tell you— Marilyn and the kids had flown to Arizona on a winter school vacation and..." Amy interrupted ... "Arizona? That's where Josh's card was postmarked!"

Janice looked startled but shrugged and said, "You're right, but I can't make any connection. I don't remember anything about where they were going in Arizona or if there was someone there they visited. Anyway, I met Blake in the City—took the train in. He was so afraid of discovery that he wouldn't even let us ride in together, although he did drive me home. So we met at Le Madeleine, this neat little bistro on West 43rd near Ninth Avenue, and Blake insisted I take a cab from Penn Station even though it wasn't much of a walk—he thought the neighborhood was a little scary, but it wasn't."

She smiled as she recalled this, and Matt realized for the first time how attractive she must have been. It was clear why someone could have taken risks to love her.

"So Blake was there when I arrived. He had the best table, back in the far corner of the room, which gave both of us a full view of the place—not that there was anything to see but other people. We had just toasted each other with our drinks when Blake muttered, 'Oh Jesus H. Christ, there's so-and-so'—I don't remember what the guy's name was, but he was another lawyer Blake had known since law school and who from time to time socialized with him and Marilyn. Blake asked, 'Did he see us clink glasses?' Well, this guy was with his wife and another couple, and it ruined our evening because we were frantic to come up with a story about who I was and what we were doing there. We could think of no good cover story and finally Blake said, 'If they come over here, I'm gong to introduce you by your real name, say we've just litigated a particularly nasty divorce case and are celebrating on your ex-husband's money.'"

"Well, it was a really lame story and behavior wholly out of character for Blake. But as fate would have it, they never once looked our way. I often have wondered what might have happened if they had."

Janice rose from her chair and again walked to the window where, without looking back, she said, "I don't know why I told you that. I've never told anybody. But I guess it's to show how much we wanted to keep our relationship secret—especially Blake. I was so much in love that I didn't care about scandal for me—but I was afraid that anything suggesting I was an unfit mother would bring Charlie and a custody hearing down around my ears."

She sighed and brought one hand to her mouth before continuing. "So it went. We had a variety of rendezvous spots, not very romantic but pretty safe—hot-sheet motels that were clean, if austere, and where nobody asked questions. Forty or fifty bucks up front. I always shared the cost because I refused to be a mistress—no kept woman I. Then that awful afternoon...."

"Blake picked me up at my car on the second level of Macy's parking garage and we went to the motel, ate carryout lobster salad, made love, and Blake dropped dead—while still on top of me." She said no more for several seconds but continued looking out the window.

Matt, not certain what he had heard, turned to Amy, his eyes showing a mixture of embarrassment and disbelief. Amy squeezed his hand and said nothing. Then Janice turned toward them and said, "Do you know what the odds are of somebody dying while having sex? They are very, very high, yet it seems like everyone knows of such a case—John Garfield, Nelson Rockefeller, some guy down the street. Very high odds. But it happened to Blake. It happened to me."

Again Janice turned to the window and continued. "Actually, Blake didn't drop dead. According to *Newsday's* account he was pronounced dead at the hospital. He had a brain aneurysm, probably a congenital defect, and was brain-dead in an instant. At first I thought he was being silly—playing games with me—but...well it became clear he wasn't. I managed to push him off me and I panicked. I called the desk and told them we needed an ambulance, stuffed my underwear in my bag, and threw on my clothes, all the time looking at Blake, knowing he was dead. Some man showed up at the door to the room, a maintenance guy I think, and he just stood there looking at Blake, never touching him or anything and saying something about the ambulance would soon be there. I held Blake's hand, devastated and scared to death. Then a horrible woman, who must have been the desk clerk came in, really upset, asking me questions, was I his wife, which she clearly knew I wasn't, and actually saying at one point that this was all she needed, and a lot of nonsense I don't remember.".

Janice stopped talking but slowly moved her head back and forth as if trying to deny her memories.

"As soon as the ambulance came, in fact while they were still loading him in, I just walked away and went up the street to an Arby's. I called a cab, got a cup of coffee, and sat there crying, looking over at the motel until the cab came and took me home. Nobody said a word to me in Arby's, and I didn't know or care what they thought. I still don't. They tore the motel down a year or so ago and there's a six story office building there now."

Amy turned to Matt and said, "I never knew any of that until Mom was forced to tell me. I was away at Disney World with Dad and Marilyn when Blake died. I didn't even know he existed, and if Mom ever mourned him after I got back, it escaped me."

"I hope it escaped everybody. His death in that motel was so ugly—his white body that I loved so much became in an instant this lifeless thing that...."

Amy interrupted her with a screech, "Mother stop!" And Janice, startled, turned toward Amy and Matt, nodding her head in agreement and raising both hands in surrender.

A long silence followed, then Janice again sat in the chair, leaning back with folded hands, as if self-consciously waiting the end of a long, dreary selection of uninspired music. His curiosity getting the better of his instinct to keep silent, Matt quietly asked, "So did anyone find out about you being there?"

"Do you want me to go on, Amy?" asked Janice, giving no indication of her own desire in the matter.

"Well, you have to I suppose, but can we leave out some of your personal details? I don't want to know things you haven't told me before. You're my mother, for God's sake."

"Sorry," said Janice, her response flat and unapologetic. "I'm trying to do justice to everybody here, and...well, I'll never be able to explain some things. But, yes Matt, Josh Wilcox found out about me being there. I've never been able to figure out how." She sipped from her soda again, her hand unsteady, and continued: "At first I thought no one knew I had been there. But of course the handy man and the desk clerk knew, though they didn't know my name, and Blake's family—at least his wife and Josh—had to know that he had died in the motel with someone. Although the newspaper account said what he died of, there was no mention of where he was stricken. There must have been rumors, but I had no way of hearing them. I had horrific feelings—not exactly guilt, but a sense of terrible irresponsibility, of having let Blake down, of being party to his family's sorrow and humiliation and to the total sense of betrayal that would forever be their memory of him. But I was scared to death, too, that if I got found out, I'd lose Amy. Then came Josh—out of the blue."

"Twice," said Amy. "Out of the blue twice, counting today."

"Oh yes. God yes!" moaned Janice. "And here's where Amy got involved. It must have been a month after Blake's death that just after dark one Saturday evening Josh appeared at our door. He asked for me, and Amy said just a minute and came to get me from the kitchen. When we both came back into the room, Josh had come in and stood glowering at us. He looked so much like his father that I was stunned, and before I could say a word he said, 'I'm Josh Wilcox. I know about you, you....bitch.' I remember his exact words because he paused and seemed to be having trouble saying bitch—I guess he couldn't think of a word that was bad enough."

Before Janice could continue, Amy said, "Then he pulled out this gun, told us to get over by the couch and take off our clothes. His hands were shaking and he began to scream, 'Don't mess with me—I'm not kidding—get over there.'"

"We were both too scared to move—he was clearly out of control," said Janice, "and he continued to scream at us, calling me names and making all kinds of threats, and we both thought we were dead or...."

"Raped," interrupted Amy. "Raped. Why else would he make us take off our clothes?"

"So we did what he told us. We stripped completely and stood there shivering and crying and God knows what—and he looked so much like Blake must have looked as a teenager that somehow for me it made the whole scene seem so nonsensical, so grotesque. It curdled my blood!...Still does." Janice looked away and reached across her chest with her left hand, gripping her right biceps in a one-armed hug.

"But he wasn't even looking at you, Mom. He was standing there pointing his gun at us and staring at my pathetic little thirteen year old breasts. I know, because through my own hysterics I was looking at his face, and his ogling or staring or whatever it was just broke into a contortion and he moaned, 'Oh, this isn't right, it just isn't coming out right,' and he began to cry too."

"He was staring at your breasts?" asked Janice. "You remember that? I don't remember that—I just can see him staring at us both in this awful male stare as if he were embarrassed at being embarrassed. But he couldn't look away until he said that about it not being right and beginning to cry and then...." Janice stopped, put her hands to either side of her face, and looked at Amy.

"And then," said Amy, picking up her mother's account, "the worst part...." But before she could continue, Matt interrupted in a flat voice, "He raped you."

"No," said Janice. "He didn't touch us. I don't know what he wanted to do to us, but he put the barrel of the gun in his mouth and pulled the trigger three or four times, threw the gun down and ran out the door."

"What the hell?" asked an unbelieving Matt.

"The gun was a toy. It looked very real, but it was a toy." Janice's answer carried a tone of self-contempt, as if ten years of distance had allowed her to judge that she should have known it was a toy all along, and that the whole charade had been a childish put-on she should have seen through from the beginning.

"It was a toy, but we didn't know that until he left. How could we? It scared me to death. The whole thing was a nightmare," said Amy, her eyes closed, shaking her head. "And now it's beginning again."

"Unbelievable!" said Matt. "Did you call the cops or anything?"

"Well, we were hysterical for hours. We immediately locked the door, got dressed, and sat around shaking," said Janice.

"I picked up the gun thinking, I guess, we could use it for protection" said Amy, "but it wasn't real. I begged Mom to call the police, but she wouldn't hear of it."

"These are all old wounds, Matt," said Janice. "How could I call the cops? For years I'd been sleeping with this boy's father, who died having sex with me in a hot-sheet motel. If the gun had been real I'd have called the cops, but how could I bring all of this out and humiliate Josh's mother and sisters, Amy, and...me?"

"He called you horrible names, pulled a gun on us, and made us strip naked, Mother! He was crazy—uncontrolled. And now he wants us to know he hasn't forgotten. God knows what he'll do next, and you could have stopped him back then. Humiliation? Jesus, what do you call this?" asked Amy as she got up from the couch and stormed into the bathroom.

Janice yelled after her: "Well, what if he hadn't turned up now? Would you still be shouting at me? You were thirteen years old! Would you have wanted that kind of attention in junior high? And, god dammit, I loved his father! I wasn't just whoring around."

Janice, fighting back tears, her hands shaking, sat down

and looked away from Matt, who never before had been so uncomfortable and unsure of what to say or do. After a few moments of silence, he walked to the bathroom door and called gently, "You okay, Amy?" He heard her sobbing, but she managed to croak out "Yes," and he returned to the living room and Janice, who looked defiant and suddenly every day of her forty-nine years.

After more tense silence, Matt, searching for something to say, and with no thought as to how it might be received, asked, "Why do you suppose he made you get naked?"

Janice looked at him without altering her defiant manner for several seconds before a soft smile changed her appearance markedly. "Well, Matt, why do you think he did it? Curiosity? Revenge? It was rape! He never touched us, but it was rape just the same. He wanted to humiliate us, make us grovel, scare us to death. He probably wanted to see what his father saw in me. Who knows? But it was Amy that changed everything. I see that now. I never realized that, but she said he stared at her breasts, and maybe he saw her as this innocent little near-woman who was just as much a victim as he was...and he had to stop. What do you think?"

"Well, it's pretty grotesque—the whole thing. I mean, the fake gun and acting like he was killing himself. He sounds like a *real* nut case to me. I think we need to do something to protect ourselves—like get out an order of protection to keep him away."

Janice's smile was void of hope. "How do we do that? We go to the police or district attorney or whoever and tell them the story we've just told you, then we show them a marriage congratulations card that has nothing approaching a threat in it and ask them to track down Josh Wilcox, wherever he is, and tell him to stay away or go to jail? Please! After getting their jollies from Blake's 'death in the saddle,' they'd undress both me and Amy with their eyes and laugh in our faces."

Janice sighed. "I don't think Josh Wilcox is dangerous to

us. What does he say on the card? 'Hope you have healed. I never will'? I can't see someone giving us an order of protection based on that."

Unobserved by Matt and her mother, Amy had returned and was standing in the doorway from the hallway. "Or from what his father and you did to me?" asked Amy. "You didn't get the card, Mother. Matt and I did. He knows where we live and I can't go on until I'm sure we're safe." She crossed the room and sat beside Matt.

Her voice tired but void of disapproval, Janice asked, "And how will you know when that is? How does that come about?"

"That's up to you to figure out, Mother. Ever since this was forced on me I've gone along with your assurance that ignoring what happened was the smart course, the safe course—all would be well. And most of the time I believed it was, even though I don't think a day has gone by that I don't relive some part of that God-awful night. Everything has changed. Josh Wilcox is out there still thinking about me, thinking about my tits, thinking about naked you and his father, thinking about making us pay. It has to stop. You have to make it stop." There was a firmness, a finality in her voice that Janice had never heard before.

The three sat in silence, no one moving except Matt, who worried a piece of lint he had picked off the sleeve of Amy's sweater. Then Janice pushed up from her chair, gathered her coat and attaché case and said, "I have to meet those people in Huntington. Give me the card and the envelope."

Amy and Matt were startled by Janice's sudden decision, but Amy took the card that had been lying beside her on the couch, rose and handed it to her mother. Matt rose as well, and he and Amy exchanged perfunctory pecks on the cheek with Janice, who said, "The sins of the fathers is the way that phrase usually goes... the sins of the mothers sounds strange, but...well, you know how sorry I am Amy…and always have been. I'll call you in the morning. Try not to worry."

Amy and Matt were silent as they followed Janice to the door. Then Amy called after her, "Be careful on the way home."

Without turning around, Janice waved her hand in acknowledgement. Amy walked to the window and looked out. "What do you think she'll do?" she asked, a mixture of contrition and fear in her voice.

Matt slumped heavily back onto the couch. "What can she do, honey? What in the world do you think she can do?"

*　*　*　*　*

Sleep came for Janice at 5 a.m. the next morning, and then it was in ten-minute intervals that gave her no more rest than if she had dozed off and on in an uncomfortable chair. Her mind repeatedly backtracked ten, twelve, fifteen years, groping through fragmented sensual memories and unconnected sordid interludes, yet always returning to the dilemma triggered anew by Josh Wilcox's card. Her clock radio, airing a patented Don Imus diatribe calling some fringe politician a "weasel," brought her dimly awake at 7 a.m. and she moaned, weak from lack of sleep and worn out from wrestling with her mind's demons.

More out of habit than resolve, she got into the shower and slowly became a rational, though still unhappy, person resuscitated by pelting hot water to the point where fatigue's despair gave way to a nearly foolhardy resignation to act: she would cast off the caution of the past ten years and chance being discovered, labeled, shunned as the woman who fucked Blake Wilcox to death; the fright, the anger and resentment seen last evening on Amy's face demanded nothing less. She had to find out what one could expect from Josh Wilcox.

Sipping breakfast coffee that tasted more poisonous than restorative, Janice tried to formulate a plan, but none would take shape. She knew no one who was friendly with the Wilcox family, and she knew no one in Blake's law firm, which still carried his name though he'd been dead for a decade. The only person she knew at all who had been associated with Blake was his secretary, Carla Christian, and Janice, who had talked with Carla several times on the telephone, actually had seen her only once, and that was when Janice first consulted Blake about handling her divorce. The possibility of any help there seemed vague at best.

While checking her voice mail she was reminded of the telephone's usefulness, and she called the information number for Winslow, Arizona's area code. No Josh Wilcox was listed. She tried Arizona's Phoenix area code with the same result. Had she gotten a phone listing for him she wasn't sure what she would have done, but knowing where he was would have been somehow reassuring—especially if he were far away. And it would give her a starting point for a private detective, whose snooping, though fundamentally repugnant to her, was beginning to take shape as her best plan of action.

Purposefully waiting until she was certain Amy and Matt had gone to work, she called and left a message, upbeat in tone: "It's Mom. Hope the dreck from last evening didn't keep you sleepless. I'm working on a solution, so don't worry. I'll work this thing out. Give me a ring tonight...or when it's convenient. Love ya."

After hanging up, Janice sat staring at the phone, exhausted from lack of sleep and depressed from adding more lies to the hundreds she had voiced over time in an effort to shield Amy from her secrets. Nausea suddenly jolted her, and she barely made it to the bathroom before retching up everything but her despair.

Slumped with her back against the tub, sobbing, her mouth and spirit sour and bitter, she wept for many minutes until the tears stopped, and she actually dozed long enough for a mere seconds-long dream to form of her in labor with Amy. She awoke with a jerk that thrust her torso forward and brought her wide awake and furious. "God damn it!" she shouted. "Just God damn it!" And in that instant she resolved to call Carla Christian.

Janice's call to "Bishop, Bishop, Wilcox, Clausen, and Dorsey" (the latter Blake's replacement) revealed that Carla Christian had left the firm some time ago. "Retired, I believe," said a young woman receptionist's voice, but Janice could get no more information from her. "We can't give out information about former employees," came her curt reply that was hardly tempered by "Perhaps she may have a listing in the telephone directory."

"How long have you worked there?" asked Janice.

"Why do you ask?"

"Well, I'm just curious as to what you may or may not know concerning your firm's history."

"Three years, but I assure you that any information I give out is accurate," replied the snide voice.

"Oh, I'm sure it is," came back Janice. "It's been nice talking with you." Janice clicked off the connection, muttering; but following the voice's suggestion Janice found a "C. Christian" among a half column of Christians—the lone initial C a clear indication that the listing was of a single woman fearful of getting unwanted calls should she list her full female name.

Janice dialed and when C. Christian answered, Janice asked, "Is this Carla Christian of Bishop, Bishop and Wilcox?"

There was a pause and then, "This is Carla Christian, but I've not been with the law firm for six or seven years."

The voice was strong and cautious and familiar to Janice, who began to speak, not sure what she was going to say. "Miss Christian, this is Janice Clark. Several years ago I was a client of Blake Wilcox and...well, it's a long story that I won't bore you with, but after Blake's tragic death I lost track of Blake's son Joshua, who I recall had an interest in... I guess you'd call it a hobby...in Star Wars collectibles, and I have several Star Wars figures that I think may be fairly valuable, and I thought he might be interested in purchasing them. By chance, would you know how I could contact him?"

The pause was so long that Janice was about to ask if Carla was still on the line when the latter said, "Why did you call me, Mrs. Clark? His mother still lives on the South Shore and is in the phone book."

Janice had the urge to hang up, but instead tried to give a reasonable response. "Well, yes, I thought about calling her, but we've never met and.... Well, I thought that some stranger calling out of the blue about a trivial thing like this might somehow stir up sad memories in conjunction with Blake's passing...and...I don't know, it just seemed awkward, and you had always been so gracious and helpful to me as a client when Mr. Wilcox was handling my divorce that I thought you might have some notion of whether Josh still collected things."

Before Carla could respond, Janice had an inspiration as to how she might make all of this seem reasonable and added, "And, well, to be frank, I could use the money—some of these dolls fetch amazing amounts."

"I see," said Carla, pausing again before continuing. "I think I can perhaps help you out, but not over the phone. Would you like to meet for coffee? Where are you located?"

Janice was caught short; the idea of meeting Carla Christian face-to-face had not been part of her improvised scheme, but she saw no way out of it if she were to learn anything at all about Josh Wilcox. "I live in Dix Hills and have a fairly flexible schedule—I sell real estate. Sure. Coffee would be fine. Where do you suggest?"

"Would Bay Shore be too out of the way for you? There's

a nice bakery-catering place near the ferry. Josephine's. We could meet there at your convenience."

"No problem. Bay Shore is fine, and I know Josephine's. Wonderful prune Danish. How about...would, say, late this afternoon...tea time...four o'clock?" said Janice, her enthusiastic tone belying the dread she felt.

"Four would be fine," answered Carla, but before she could hang up Janice hurriedly added, "I'm wearing a forest green pants and blazer outfit and..."

Carla Christian interrupted, "Oh, I'm sure I'll recognize you. I'll be there at four."

Janice spent the time until the meeting going through the motions of showing two houses to two couples, both of whom spent most of their time arguing with each other about just what it was they were looking for in a house; there was no chance for a sale with either couple, and Janice's thoughts wandered to Carla Christian and how Carla would respond to her far-fetched questioning when they met. Then there also was the tone of Carla's saying, "Oh, I'm sure I'll recognize you," which had a mocking quality, or at least a confidence, that Janice found troubling. Battling these misgivings and her queasy stomach, Janice arrived at Josephine's at 3:45 and sat at one of the four small tables facing the door until Carla walked in exactly at 4 p.m.

Only one other table was occupied—two teenaged girls making a show of drinking coffee and acting bored—but Carla never even glanced their way and approached Janice as if they had been meeting there regularly for years. Janice made a quick calculation that Carla must be at least seventy. She was completely white-haired, immaculately coifed, slim, dressed in sandals, chinos, and a simple but expensive long-sleeved white shirt; her sole jewelry was small, loop, gold earrings, and the only lines in her face were so naturally situated that they gave her a sense of healthfulness that a thirty year-old would envy. In appearance she would have been perfectly in place in Manhattan, Santa Monica, or Bar Harbor. She smiled, held out her hand, and said, "So, Mrs. Clark. How are you?"

Her greeting was more genteel good manners than warm sincerity, perhaps the professional mask of years as a divorce lawyer's receptionist-secretary and buffer against clients' apprehensiveness. After some awkwardness in settling on what to order, hazelnut decaf for Carla, cappuccino and a day-old prune Danish for Janice (queasy stomach and all), Carla asked, "Now, just what is it that you think I can help you with? From our phone conversation it has something to do with Joshua Wilcox."

One long look into Carla Christian's eyes convinced Janice that this woman had never betrayed a confidence in her life and would be willing to lie to keep her record intact. If Josh Wilcox were the Wilcox family's black sheep-loose canon, Carla Christian would never confirm such a thing unless he was a real danger to, as they say in the press, "himself and society." But before Janice could say a word, Carla confounded her by saying, "I want you to know that I am aware that you were the woman with Mr. Wilcox when he died. Mrs. Wilcox knows it. And, of course, Joshua knows it, which I take it is the reason we're sitting here talking. What is it you think I can tell you?"

Janice was unable to breathe for several seconds and was saved from attempting some gasping response by the arrival of their coffees. Cold electrical shocks ran along her spine to her stiffened neck; she felt as if she instantly had been revealed to be naked, ogled, reviled, and pitied in one stroke by a world she'd hidden from for more than a decade. Showing no more emotion than if she had just told someone the time of day, Carla stirred an envelope of Equal into her decaf, seeming neither to avoid Janice's eyes nor to look into them.

Gaining the barest control of her voice, Janice managed a "My God...you take my breath away" that came out as a half-gasp, half-giggle.

Stirring her coffee and not looking up, Carla said matter-of-factly, "I dare say, but I think it is best that we be honest with one another."

Trying to collect her thoughts, and with shaking hands, Janice raised her cappuccino to her mouth and took a scorching sip that left a ring of froth on her lips that she dabbed away with her napkin—an action that made her feel clumsy and ill-mannered in front of this woman whose every move was perfect and natural, and who had just bared Janice's secret life as casually as she stirred her decaf.

Finally, Janice could speak. "Well, what else do you know about me?"

"Just what is in the files of your divorce and anecdotal things Mr. Wilcox related. I was not one to snoop into the personal lives of clients. As for Mrs. Wilcox and Joshua, I'm not sure, but I imagine they know quite a bit more than that since they knew you were the woman in the motel."

"The woman in the motel? The woman in the motel?" repeated Janice, anger beginning to replace the shock of discovery. "I was a good deal more than that. I'm not a whore, Miss Christian. Blake and I loved each other and we met in motels because there was no place else Blake felt safe and it's ironic that...." She stopped abruptly, reining in her anger, and Carla looked directly into her face to see if Janice were going to cause a scene.

Janice took a deep breath and continued—her hands trembling but her voice calmer though still defensive. "I knew Blake was dead when I left the motel. Do you have any idea what that awful experience was like? I left when I knew he was dead. I had called for help. It came and I left, panicked but hoping that somehow our relationship would never be known and Blake's reputation would not be destroyed, which, as far as I've seen, it hasn't been. Yes, walking away was cowardly, but it also was because of love...and sudden, wrenching grief. Can you understand that? Any of that?"

"More than you can imagine," was Carla's instant reply, followed by silence as she played with her coffee mug, her gaze off somewhere in the distance beyond Janice's tense form. Sipping her coffee again she asked, "And Joshua? This made-up story about Star Wars trinkets?"

Wanting to do something with her hands, Janice broke a piece from her Danish and barely nibbled it before returning the piece to its plate and saying, "I don't know why I ordered this." Trying to appear composed, she leaned forward on both elbows, striking a posture for intimate conversation with Carla across the table. "How well do you know Josh?"

"Well," was Carla's serious response.

"How did he find out about me?"

Carla actually appeared uneasy as she answered, "We needn't get into that—nothing will be served. Joshua idolized his father, and he demanded to know details of his death—everything. Suffice to say he was given information in an attempt to lessen his sorrow and very, very serious depression...too much information, as it turned out."

"What is that supposed to mean...too much information?" asked Janice, playing again with her Danish.

"Well, you'll have to fill in the blanks there. As I understand it, Joshua came to your house and there was some sort of confrontation. That same day, or perhaps the next day, he swallowed all the pills he could find. Aspirin, cold remedies, even his mother's codeine pills for menstrual cramps—a terrible assortment of stuff, but fortunately he vomited most of it up and the rest was pumped out…and he became a very sad young man." Her voice became energized then, and she asked, "But why do you ask about him now? That was years ago."

"A sad young man? Is he also a dangerous young man?"

Carla shook her head slightly. "I shouldn't think so. What leads you to ask that?"

Janice, feeling somewhat in command, replied, "I suspect the same thing that led you to suggest we meet today—Josh Wilcox's state of mind and your concern about it. Do you know what went on when Josh came to my house—the 'confrontation' as you put it?"

Carla breathed deeply and again gently shook her head. "Only that there was some unpleasantness that greatly upset him—and frankly I've assumed you were the source of that unpleasantness."

"Source?" asked Janice, angry in disbelief.

Carla raised her hand in a gesture of peace. "Perhaps I over-dramatize things in my mind, but do you know the play *The Death of a Salesman* when Biff discovers his father in the hotel room with the prostitute and how that changes Biff's relationship with his father forever? I think that's what happened to Joshua. He felt so betrayed—everything changed. And you were the woman in the hotel room—not that you were a prostitute—but nothing could be believed in anymore. I'm afraid Joshua's never gotten over that betrayal."

"In a very real sense none of us has—especially the innocent ones, and I don't include myself with the innocent ones," was Janice's barely audible reply.

Both women stared blankly at their coffees for several dead seconds, until Janice said, "Josh came to my house with a gun. He shouted every obscene name he could think of at me and ordered me and my daughter, who then was only thirteen, to undress—which we did, all the time expecting to be shot or raped. He continued to call me names until we were naked and then he said something like 'This isn't right,' began to cry, put the gun in his mouth and pulled the trigger several times, threw the gun down and ran out the door. The gun turned out to be a toy, a very realistic-looking toy gun. My daughter was hysterical for days after, and I was paralyzed out of fear for my daughter and fear of being dragged into some public, disgraceful legal action in which I'd lose custody of Amy. So I did nothing, except sell my house and move into an apartment. And nothing more happened. Amy and I never told a soul about what had happened until yesterday—and now I've told two people in less than twenty-four hours. Amy's husband and you."

While Janice was talking, the soft stoic demeanor of Carla's face slowly changed to one of obvious pain. "My goodness," she sighed. "I had no idea." The pained expression remained as she asked, "But why are you telling me this now?"

"We have had no contact of any kind with Josh since that horrendous day, until yesterday when Amy got a very conventional, tasteful greeting card from him congratulating her on her recent marriage, and it included a handwritten message that said, 'I hope you have healed. I never will.' It was mailed from Winslow, Arizona, and...well, Amy has just fallen apart. Of course, I had to tell her husband the whole sorry business, and I think he feels nearly as threatened as she. And both of them see Josh now as some kind of a stalker—and why wouldn't they?" Janice breathed out a long breath of relief and fatigue and asked, "Is he?"

Carla put her hands together in a gesture of prayer and leaned her chin against her fingertips. She shook her head, not so much in answer to the question, but as a silent comment of disbelief in all that had been said. "He certainly is not a stalker, and I don't think he would harm a fly. But I must say that I am overwhelmed that he did what you say he did and that he sent a card to your daughter after all this time."

She continued to slowly shake her head and look away from Janice, who, sounding accusatory, asked, "Well, just how is it that you know so much about Josh Wilcox and can be so certain about his behavior?"

Carla's head quit its negative movements and began the same slow-paced nodding, but in a gesture of affirmation. "I'm his godmother. I've known and loved him since his birth. He's the only member of his family that I've really stayed in contact with since I left the firm—actually, I've had very little contact with Mrs. Wilcox and the girls since Blake's death."

It was the first time she had called Blake Wilcox by his first name—a loosened formality Janice immediately noticed.

"So then you must know where he is, which is the main reason I called you. I have to know what to expect from him and put a stop to anything that might harm us—especially Amy, who is frightened and angry. And you have to realize that her husband Matt sooner rather than later is going to try to resolve this mess with little regard for anyone's reputation. After all, Amy is totally innocent of wrongdoing. She feels cursed."

"I understand," said Carla, still nodding in agreement. "Yes, I know where he is. He's in Arizona. When he learned of the circumstances of his father's death he dropped out of college, and after the suicide attempt there were months of psychological counseling—care really—when he did nothing but brood and remain what seemed to me to be clinically suicidal, if there is such a term. I despaired of his living out the year. But gradually his spirits picked up--from the counseling and some kind of mood-enhancing medication which he soon quit taking. The family had plenty of money—they still do—but Joshua was bothered by not earning his keep, so he moved into a tiny but nice garage apartment and took a job driving limousines to and from the airport—God knows why." She sipped from her coffee, now grown cold, made a face, and continued.

"He did that for several years and loved it. He became a kind of legend and had dozens of regular customers who would always request him when they called for limo service...he particularly enjoyed working at night and early in the morning before traffic got heavy. He kept journals of conversations he had with passengers, and he would read passages to me—strange tales that his passengers told him or funny things about his passengers' appearances or eccentricities. His journal entries never chronicled unpleasant things or criticized his passengers' often deplorable behavior, and he began to talk about trying to condense his journals and publish them in a book. All in all he seemed content, but I must say that the way he lived during that time was eccentric in that he had no friends. He had no relationships with women that I'm aware of, and he was as reclusive as one can be who earns his living in a very public way." She looked down at her coffee mug, frowned and pushed it away.

"Would you like your coffee warmed up? Let me...." Janice reached for her mug, but Carla waved her hand away. "No thanks. I don't need any more—it's a bad habit."

"Well," began Janice, eager to know more about Josh. "So what does Josh do in Arizona?"

"About two years ago he joined a group of Franciscans near Winslow. I don't know if he's taken holy orders or not—I didn't ask—but my understanding is that he is a kind of lay brother, yet very much a part of their group. He was back shortly after Christmas last year and we saw each other twice. He doesn't wear any kind of religious garb—no robe or anything like that, although he may when he is in Arizona, but he was laughing about being somewhere between a monk and a refugee, and for some reason

I didn't pursue it. He bakes bread for the brothers and sells most of it in town, so he isn't leading a cloistered life exactly, but a life that allows him time for contemplation, reading, and the limited contact he wants with the rest of society. We correspond every now and again, and I subscribe yearly to the *New Yorker* for him as a Christmas gift...and I know that he gets the Sunday *Newsday* by mail, which probably accounts for his knowledge of your daughter's marriage. Was the announcement in a Sunday *Newsday*?"

"Yes, it was. About three weeks ago. But how did he get her address? And why would he send such a message? Have you had any hint that he was...well, depressed? I mean, the bit about never healing?"

Carla shook her head again in what now was becoming a familiar gesture to Janice. "I don't know how he got the address. He had her married name from somewhere and, given that, it isn't too difficult to get an address, even if you live in a monastery or friary or whatever." She cocked her head in a questioning pose and continued, "What's curious to me is what was he doing reading marriage announcements? I would think that would be something he'd pass over."

"Her picture was there, too. But she doesn't look much like she did the last time he presumably saw her—when she was thirteen," said Janice.

"Presumably?" asked Carla, raising her eyebrows in an exaggerated manner. "I, of course, have no knowledge whether Joshua saw your daughter after age thirteen or not, but he's not a stalker, let me assure you of that."

Janice waved both hands, signaling cancellation of any negative implication made by her use of "presumably." But she followed with, "What I would like to know is how Joshua knew who I was, which, of course, started this whole insane business."

In tones void of emotion Carla answered, "I told him."

"You told him?" questioned Janice. "You told him?," her voice rising in indignation. "But how did you know?"

Again, sounding calm and dispassionate, Carla answered, "I knew about you from the beginning—or near the beginning. Blake told me about you."

This was the second time she had called him Blake, and there was no doubt this time that by dropping the formal "Mr. Wilcox" an intimacy was intended. Janice shifted in her chair, moving forward, her upper body and head again inclined half way across the small table. "He told you about me? I find that very hard to believe! Very hard!" She slumped back, her defeated posture unsupported by her defiant words, and asked, "Why in God's name would he do that? He was always scrupulous, maddeningly so, about hiding our relationship!"

Carla looked around, but there no longer was anyone in the place except the clerk-waitress, who was busy boxing up pastries behind the counter and paying no attention to them. "Look, I don't want to cause you...." She stopped, then standing said, "I think I'll get more coffee after all," and carried her mug to the self-serve island holding various thermos dispensers. Janice sat stunned and began to play with her Danish, as if her fingers moved independent of her mind.

Carla returned, and they both sat silent, neither looking at the other, while Carla methodically stirred Equal into her mug. Then she said, "Coming here today, it was not my intention to cause anyone distress, but it is obvious that I'm inextricably caught up in all that has happened, and I can just leave and hope that somehow things will work themselves out to a...I was going to say happy conclusion, but happy conclusion seems unlikely. So, I can leave or I will stay and try to answer your questions...but you are not likely to be pleased with what I say. It's up to you."

"But why would Blake confide in you about me?" pleaded

Janice. "I mean, what's the connection?"

"We were friends," said Carla. "It's as simple and as complex as that. We were friends from the time he came into the firm. Friends. He asked me to be Joshua's godmother—Martha, Mrs. Wilcox, concurred, although I don't think she really cared one way or the other. He told me about you. I didn't inquire—I didn't want to know. But he was proud of his relationship with you. Proud is the way he talked to me about you. Love? I can't make that judgment, but he certainly admired you. Anyway, I protected your affair, although I didn't approve and told him so. I took my godmother role very seriously, and I still do. So when Josh learned about the way his father died, he came to me, crushed, angry, vowing to find out who the woman was who had 'caused his father's death,' as he put it. Curiously, Martha was indifferent about who the woman was. She was grief-stricken, but her attitude struck me as that of a person who expected sudden death—like she knew it would happen. And by the way, I never told her who you were. Josh told her after I told him—which brings me back to why I did—a decision I've questioned ever since."

She began to sip her coffee, but sensing it was still too hot, returned the mug to the table. "I was devastated by Blake's death. We were never lovers or anything like that, but I loved him... perhaps as much as you did. He always treated me as an equal—not as an executive secretary, but as a close friend, which we were... very close friends. And I was very jealous of you. Very jealous. Blake never saw me as a sexual being at all, but he had the poor taste or the insensitivity to tell me about you. Oh, he never went into any kind of clinical detail about sex with you, but I covered for him whenever he would meet you during the day. Of course I knew he had gone to meet you the day he died...but, ironically, it was after he had left the office that day that I determined to tell him that he made me feel like a pimp, and that if we were to remain friends I didn't want to hear about his affair...that's what I called it, an affair...with you or anyone else."

"Anyone else?" asked Janice, her tone a mixture of alarm and hope that there was no one else.

Her coffee now cool enough, Carla sipped from it before answering, "Oh, please. You don't really think you were the first woman he'd...done this with?"

Carla's tone of superiority irritated Janice, and she answered quickly with no attempt to disguise her annoyance, "Well, naive me! As a matter of fact I did think I was the only woman. Did you pimp for the others too?"

Showing no hint of annoyance herself, Carla answered, "No, the occasion never came up, but you clearly were the...the lover he preferred, and I disliked you for it. Enough that when weeping, betrayed, young Joshua came to me for explanations... for comfort...I told him that you had been a long-time friend...I think I said friend...of his father's, and when he asked your name, I foolishly and vengefully told him. I had no idea what he would do, but at the moment I didn't really care, and I didn't think you should get off scot-free. Very stupid of me I see now."

"Scot-free?" sneered Janice. "Terrific! We all got off scot-free, didn't we?" She sat in silence, her angry gaze avoiding Carla; then she asked, "How did it all—me, death by sex, the motel—stay out of the papers? The whole press coverage of his death was totally sanitized."

"Of course the whole legal profession knew almost at once how Blake died," answered Carla. "But it is a very old firm, and status and money can do almost anything in an old boys' society. The firm had an understanding of some sort with the press and never got bad coverage about anything. Long Island has no muckrakers and the Manhattan press couldn't care less—it slipped right by them."

"But it didn't slip by you and Josh, did it?" asked Janice, with a bitter smile.

"I'm afraid not," answered Carla, who then added, "But we didn't shout it around, either."

"Perhaps it would have been better if you had," sighed Janice. "Martha would have been pitied as the wronged woman, Blake would have been canonized by his fellows as the ultimate stud who died in the act, I would have been pilloried as the scarlet lady, and Josh might have left us alone."

"Perhaps," replied Carla. "But any scenario, I'm afraid, would have left Joshua with...how did you say he put it, unhealed scars?"

Janice sighed, "Yes, of course you're right. Which brings us... me...back to what to do about Josh now that he's come back into our lives. What do you think?"

Carla absently stirred her coffee, her face showing concentration behind eyes that stared but saw nothing in front of them. Finally she spoke: "I'm very conflicted. Before talking with you today, I would have said that Joshua is absolutely harmless, and for the most part I still feel that way. But, it comes down to, what do I know? What does anyone know? Joshua forcing you and your daughter at gunpoint to undress and then simulating suicide while no doubt wishing the gun was real...well, that certainly makes me question my ability to judge him. He did get a good deal of psychological help after that happened, and there's been nothing in his behavior that I'm aware of since then that would suggest he would injure himself or anyone else. Can I guarantee that he's harmless? Can I guarantee that he won't contact you again? If there's such a thing as a ninety percent guarantee, then yes, I don't think he'll harm you. But the ten percent's still out there, isn't it?"

Neither spoke for several minutes—each searching for some meaningful way to conclude. Then Carla said, "I don't think you could get a restraining order based on the greeting card and what happened ten years ago—besides they are generally worthless. And if you contacted him and asked him to please not contact any of you ever again, it might serve that purpose, or might open old wounds—ones that he says aren't healed anyway—and cause an unwanted reaction." She shook her head and added, "Sweet Jesus, what a dilemma! But if I were you I would ignore the card and the message and hope for the best."

Hearing Carla profanely invoke Jesus seemed so out of keeping with her very proper demeanor that Janice was at first shocked, but thinking over what Carla had said, Janice agreed with her view. "Sweet Jesus, indeed," said Janice, slumping back in her chair.

After some few moments, Carla began searching her handbag for money, and Janice quickly said, "No, no. Coffee's on me." And then added, "I don't think you can imagine how much your coming to talk today means to me. It was something I had no reason to expect you to do...I'm very grateful."

Seeming just a bit flustered, Carla said, "Yes...well I see now that what I had thought was ancient history unfortunately still has a life of its own, and I just wish I had the magic holly stake to drive through its heart...but...." She smiled, shook her head and got up to leave. "Good luck...to us all," she added, and showing her first hint of self-consciousness, moved quickly to the door.

Janice sat alone, trying to absorb all that had been said. Carla Christian had been at once formidable, appealing, infuriating, and wise, and she had left Janice with a sense that she had come not only to protect her grown godchild but also to gloat over her intimate knowledge of Blake—his strengths and weaknesses—and their special relationship that bore no taint of scandal, unlike Janice and Blake's love affair that she now saw would grow more tawdry with the passage of time and memory. Yet Carla seemed, if not eager, at least genuinely willing to help Janice in so much as she could provide true history and offer careful, well-reasoned advice.

Janice had a sudden urge to get out of Josephine's, so she went to the counter and paid the bill, but on the way out she stopped and wrapped her mutilated prune Danish in a napkin and took it with her.

She walked a block to the ferry landing and sat on a bench looking out toward Fire Island. The sun was at her back and was muted by smog drifting down from the expressways, so that she felt as if she still were inside a stuffy building. She wanted an onshore breeze to clear the air, but the water lay in a mirror-like calm, unusual for that time of day. What to tell Amy?

She'd tell her part of the truth—tell her what Carla Christian had said, leaving out Carla's both poignant and pathetic declaration of love for Blake Wilcox and her shaded skepticism about Josh's state of mind. She would say that Josh was in a holy order, was at peace with the world, and that his card probably was an easing of his conscience in keeping with his new-found religious faith—all of which actually might be true. She'd say that Josh Wilcox was a man recovering from a great sense of betrayal in the loss of his father, but that he had undergone psychological treatment and has led an exemplary life for ten years...and that he was a man who, as his godmother put it, "wouldn't harm a fly." So, verily, verily, Amy, go out into the world and multiply—the peace dove has reached land.

Janice eased against the slats in the back of the bench and spread her arms full length on either side away from her body, one hand still clenching the napkin-wrapped Danish. She closed her eyes and breathed deeply, but the polluted damp air caught in her throat, and any hope for some cleansing sign from nature disappeared from her imagination.

Carefully she unwrapped the Danish and began to nibble the larger pieces, letting crumbs fall onto her lap. Even though a day old, the Danish was as good as she remembered them.

COMMENCEMENT

Amy Macklin more often than not was pleased when people thought she was ten years younger than her forty-six years; but this time, as she scanned the other women scattered throughout the audience with their graying, tinted, bleached assortment of hair colors, crow's feet framing squinting eyes, and facial flesh perilously near collapse, she felt a longing to look her age, to be taken for one of them.

There was more than her misleading appearance that set Amy apart from the other mothers and fathers gathered under ancient oak branches to revel in the college graduation of their children: there was the loneliness of the self-exiled, the determined aloofness of the wary, and the arrogance of success fairly won and unaided. A sadness she could not shake hid behind fashionable sunglasses and the steady tilt of her chin.

One needed a ticket for the commencement exercises, and every folded chair was occupied by a family member, near relative, or fat-cat alumnus, with the latter having, by way of endowments, commandeered aisle seats for quick exits to greet celebrities, potential business prospects, or a calculated chance face-to-face with an old lover. Jack Baker was one such alumnus occupying the space to Amy's left; but rather than sitting he stood half in the aisle scouring the gathering crowd in search of a trophy to be pursued or any number of competitors to be avoided.

Spying no one of interest, Baker caught sight of Amy's shapely bare knee and the crossed leg showing discreet thigh edging out from the hem of her pale-yellow linen dress. He smiled while turning to directly examine her face, and seeing that she was looking away from him, he checked out her breasts and her fit tanned arms and manicured fingers showing no rings or marks of hard use folded in her lap. Amy, though looking away from Baker, intuitively was aware of his ogling and prepared for his unwanted attention.

"Lovely day for these wonderful festivities, isn't it?" said Baker, beaming as if his comment legitimized him as an insider and expert on all matters celebratory.

Thankful for her sunglasses, Amy turned her head so that she was looking obliquely past him and gave no hint that she was eager to say more than a quiet, steady, "Lovely, yes."

With barely a pause, Baker pivoted his body until his knees touched her leg and, still smiling, stuck out his right hand and asked, "You have someone graduating?" and before Amy could respond added, "By the way, I'm Jack Baker, class of '68."

Amy took his hand in a quick, firm grip that allowed him no opportunity to prolong his hold. "Yes, my daughter Sarah… Sarah Charles."

"Daughter? Oh, please! You must mean *sister*…unless you gave birth at age ten," said Baker, drawing back in mock surprise.

Amy was used to the Bakers of the world trying to ingratiate themselves via absurd exaggerations about her looks. "Well, no. Actually, I was 11, and she was my second child," said Amy, giving no hint of irony and looking off into the crowd.

Baker, unsure of how to respond, paused and then laughed too loudly. "Good response, good response. Anyway, you know what I mean. You look much too young to be the mother of a…

what, a twenty-one year old?"

Under different circumstances, Amy might have bantered with Baker a bit before signaling the end of his unwanted attention, but she felt edgy and out of her element and froze Baker by merely not responding. She continued to look away, ignoring his presence, and he, while wanting to call her a bitch, said no more and again took his position in the aisle, looking over the new arrivals filling up the seats.

Amy also was scanning the crowd, not only as a maneuver to distance herself from Baker, but with a purpose that she would have admitted to no one, and which she found painful in a localized aching that made her conscious of her intake of breath: she was looking for Eric Charles—something she had not allowed herself to do since the hours after Sarah's birth.

To no avail, Amy had waited for, or searched for, Eric's appearance through virtually the entire term of her pregnancy. But once Sarah entered her life in the dramatic, vibrant arrival miraculous to all births, Amy vowed to erase all vestiges of romance surrounding Sarah's father. And when early in Sarah's childhood indiscreet people would ask about "Mr. Charles," Amy recited a remembered line from *The Glass Menagerie* that explained away the missing father as one who was "a telephone man who fell in love with long distance"—an answer that left Amy's questioners perplexed, embarrassed, and unwilling to pursue more information.

Eric Charles was far from being a "telephone man." On the night Amy last saw him, he was a theology student at Union Seminary, an avowed agnostic leaning toward a career in "practical ethics"—a field of his own invention and one in which his family's wealth could indulge him. Amy, then a graduate student in theater at Columbia, had ambitions to somehow make a career in the theater but with no thought to being an actress. Their two years living together had been careless but not without purpose as each saw their lives joined by mutual interests in politics (no small matter), the arts, good food, and respect for each other's individuality and independence—a combination easier to profess than maintain.

Amy waited tables and made good money; Eric had an independent family income that permitted him to sit in on business courses and devote time to an endless number of good works his divinity school contacts provided; and his and Amy's pooled resources were shared mutually in a seamless unspoken contract of "being a couple." It all unraveled so swiftly that their friends and relatives had no clues. "Being a couple" simply dissolved in the dark of one night.

Sex with all young couples, married or not, always has been about physical as well as romantic (yea, and spiritual) gratification, and always has had its potential for heartbreak, recrimination, and undying hatred. Amy's and Eric's sex life worked. They loved each other's bodies (their muscles and flesh, their nuanced responses, their unspoken secrets); and initiating their sexual activity had a harmonious schedule attuned to the other's moods with uncanny awareness—or at least it went that way until Amy went off the pill.

It was the time when the long-term effects of the use of estrogen and its possible connection to breast, ovarian, and uterine cancers was being questioned, and women's medical guardians were cautioning against the prolonged use of estrogen-laced contraception pills. Although Amy was a fierce advocate for reproductive rights and all things affecting gender independence, she read and took seriously the warnings that by and large were ignored by young unmarried women her age. Getting pregnant or getting cancer were choices she didn't want to believe in, let alone play off against one another; yet the pills went down the toilet and, with no debate, contraception became Eric's responsibility. He was not happy.

They played condom games, each bringing home the most outlandish ones they could find: those in garish Day-Glo colors, those with nippled or antennae ends and musky scented lubricants, and they would laugh at and mock the absurdity of the marketing ploys supposedly designed to arouse and shock, as if all who used them still were titillated by what used to be judged as objects sinful enough to be sold under counters "for the prevention of disease only." The spontaneity lost by the necessity of fitting the condom bothered them both, but mostly Eric as his erections withered under the pressure of "getting the damned thing on" no matter how much he prepared and anticipated; and "the loss of sensation" (as much myth as reality) began to sour and lessen their "loving" ("lovemaking" was a term forbidden in Amy's lexicon).

Amy relished not having to deal with ejaculate, and the condom lubricant dried up and could be washed away later; but Eric's frustrations increased as did his complaints, which fell just short of pleading for her to go back on the pill or to let him "just go at it bare" when she wasn't ovulating.

"You know what the Catholics call that, don't you? Pregnancy!" protested Amy when Eric first suggested they abandon condoms. But Eric was persuasive, arguing that her menstrual periods were regular and that they were "intelligent people who can count and read thermometers, for God's sake!" Dealing with sex was becoming a burden, so Amy gave in, marked off days on an oversized calendar featuring baby animal pictures (a gift from Eric), and bought a digital fever thermometer. The bloom was off the rose.

The demands of their classwork and Amy's work schedule lessened their time together, and the simple joys of being young and in love were assumed rather than being the dominant flavor of their daily routines. Amy kept scrupulous records of her body's readiness to conceive, but hiding offstage from their sexual performances was a thin dread of the unexpected.

Writing in her bedside spiral notepad one evening she said to Eric, "I feel like if I miss a day with this thing I'm sure I'll get knocked up."

"Then don't miss," said Eric, whose manner was much too cavalier for Amy's put-upon mood.

"Jesus—you're all alike! All you have to do is shove it in, get off, roll over and go to sleep—no consequences, just fucking good fun."

"Really? We're all alike are we? May I ask how many were in your test group?" responded Eric. It was the beginning of a shouting fight with both sides pointing out in vicious detail the other's flaws, physical and intellectual, real and imagined. It was a sudden hate-filled five minutes, frightening, spontaneous, and devastating in the awareness of the damage inflicted by words that never can be taken back.

Amy stared at Eric until he looked away, then she pulled the top cover off the bed, wrapped it around her, and left the room to spend the night on the living room couch. Eric stayed on the bed, left the light on until early morning, and once got up and looked into the living room where he saw Amy staring into the night. He said nothing, and Amy, knowing he was there, remained silent. They spent the night awake in separate rooms, silent and bruised by guilt and confusion. What had taken place left each with a tangible sense that something priceless had been shattered and ground into grit underfoot.

As the sun rose, Amy, leaving the blanket on the couch, went into the bathroom and showered for many minutes. Then, naked and ignoring Eric, she gathered clothes and carried them out of their bedroom. Eric, who had feigned sleep, got out of bed when he thought she would not return and put on his bathrobe— he could not remember the last time he had worn it. Disconcerted by the alien appearance his robe cast in the bureau mirror, he sat on the edge of the bed listening for sounds coming from the living room, but none came and he fell back onto the bed unsure of what to do. In a short time he heard the outside door open and close. Amy had left, and neither had spoken a word.

Amy again was standing staring out the window when Eric returned that evening. She turned to acknowledge his presence but said nothing. He crossed the room and stood beside her looking into the street, their bodies not touching. Eric was the first to speak. "Look, we had a fight, right? We said some awful things that we didn't mean, so how do we get through this?"

Amy looked into his face, and with a half smile said, "Yes, we had a fight all right, but I'm not sure we didn't mean the things we said. At least I'm afraid I meant most of what I said. Things are not the same, Eric, and I won't pretend they are."

"Aw, come on, Amy. I'm sorry for what I said. It was intentionally hurtful stuff, and I'm sorry. So…look…I tell you what. Let's go for a drink…go over to Astoria to Santorini, load up on some ouzo and mezza. We haven't done anything like that in ages. I'll spring for it. Even pay for a cab."

"It's Tuesday. I have to work," said Amy. "I was just about to leave."

"Call in sick. You always show up. Make them appreciate you a little."

"Call in sick?" replied Amy. "Call in sick? Is that part of your so-called practical ethical philosophy?"

"Touché," answered Eric, and reaching out to touch her arm he smiled broadly and added, "Or are you trying to start another fight?"

Amy moved away from his touch, picked up her windbreaker from a chair and headed toward the door. "I'm not sure we've ended the last one yet, Eric," she said, and left him standing across the room. His smile was gone.

Their life together continued in a grotesque détente with Amy stoically behaving as if Eric were an incompatible, arbitrarily assigned dormitory roommate, and Eric vacillating between sullen hurt feelings and manic cheerfulness. Amy continued to sleep on the couch, even after Eric, in a conciliatory gesture, suggested that if she no longer wanted to sleep with him they could take weekly turns occupying the bed. Amy's reply to that was, "I plan to be out of here in a week."

The night she left, Eric came in late, high from wine and fierce debate with his philosophy cronies over whether it was ever possible to do a genuinely charitable act void of ego gratification. Amy was sitting, fully clothed, with a puzzled look of indecision. She was simply sitting, looking off into space, and her appearance was so uncharacteristic that Eric asked, "Are you all right?"

"I'm not sure. Are you?" she asked, her expression unchanged.

Eric, a little drunk, said, "That's the first time you've shown any interest in my welfare since the...whatever we had...breakup? Breakdown?"

Amy nodded and said, "Take your pick." Then she took up her backpack and moved to the door.

An incredulous Eric asked, "You going out? You sure you want to go out? It's two in the morning, Amy," and then, giggling, "It's an evil world out there in an evil city that never sleeps."

"That's why I'm going out. Go to bed, Eric." And she left.

Amy walked a few blocks to an all-night drugstore. She identified the aisle she wanted but walked the length of other aisles looking at the rows and rows of colorfully packaged products that promised relief, beauty, pleasure, and hope for a bountiful future or escape from the present. Then she arrived at what she had come for, the store-brand "One Step Pregnancy Test" in its shaded purple carton that announced in a square design of brilliant yellow: "Twin

Pack." She lifted the carton from the shelf and saw that it was on sale for $9.99. "Why two?" she wondered, and muttered, "Oh, I get it—for those hoping they *are* pregnant...if at first you don't succeed."

She read the instructions on the package and carried it to the cashier, a young black woman, alarmingly thin, who welcomed Amy's patronage as a break from the tedium of her boring dead-end job. Amy handed her the test kit and said, "I think this thing is way overpriced. Ten bucks?"

"I guess it depends on how bad you want to find out. Fifteen-year-olds shoplift them all the time," said the cashier, her melodious voice belying her message.

"Well, I'm more than fifteen and convinced I'm pregnant, so why am I buying this?" asked Amy, sounding self-deprecating.

The cashier held the carton away from the bar code scanner and replied, "To convince somebody else? You still want to buy it?"

Amy nodded, paid, and left. A coffee shop near their apartment was alive with two distinct groups of night people: students in clusters, who were mostly animated in their conversation, and loners who played with their coffee and were given to blank stares. Amy, with no outward resolve, slowly entered, purchased coffee, and sat as far away from anyone as the crowded space allowed. Though nothing had been added to her coffee, she stirred it for several minutes before taking the pregnancy test from her back pack and reading the carton's print. Then she opened the box's end flaps and drawing out its contents studied the two plastic objects through their transparent coverings and read the enclosed instruction paper. As she was returning everything to the carton, two expensively but casually dressed young women passed her table and one, without stopping or looking back, said, "Knocked up, huh?"

The comment, startling in its gratuitously snide tone,

shocked Amy into gathering up the test container and hurrying to the apartment.

Eric had claimed the bed. Open mouthed, he was sprawled face down snoring in arrhythmic snorts. Amy went into the bathroom, read and reread the test's directions before, and again after, the test proved positive.

Sitting on the edge of the tub, she repeatedly ran her fingers through her hair, seeking out something hidden there. *Pregnant!* Good or bad with no chance to second guess.

She went into the bedroom, turned on the overhead light and jerked the pillow out from under Eric's head with such force that his face pushed into the mattress.

"Wake up and listen, damn you," she said, her voice steady and raised barely above its normal volume. "I'm pregnant. Have you got that? I'm pregnant."

Eric looked up then closed his eyes and lay still for several seconds before pushing himself into a sitting position. His face was that of an irritated teenager being prodded to get dressed in time for school. "Pregnant, huh?" he asked, and fell back as if to resume his sleep.

Amy stared at him with silent malice, and he again sat up and asked, "You sure?"

"I'm sure."

Eric, rotating his head and grimacing at the stiffness in his neck, said, "So, is that a problem…I mean, how big a problem is that? What should you do?"

"Is it a problem? Is it a problem? Is it a *big* problem?" Her voice rising with each repetition suddenly dropped to a soft, slowly enunciated "Eric…are…you…awake?" before becoming a shrieked "I…AM…FUCKING…PREGNANT!"

Waving his hand to signal he heard her and as a silent appeal for her to stop talking, he said, "Okay, okay, I get the message. It's some god-awful time in early morning, so what do you want from me? A pledge or something?"

Amy stared at him, trying to grasp the moment and make sense of it. She began to feel detached, the way an oncoming fainting spell shuts down one's hearing. She had to move and walked into the living room. Eric, very much wanting to remain on the bed and fall back under its covers, slowly pushed to his feet and followed her. She stood in what had become a familiar pose staring out the window, and he moved to look out the window as well. Night lights of the Village's neon world blended into what could be seen of the sky between and above the buildings and gave no hint of time. Nor did the occasional sounds of traffic, nor streets void of pedestrians hint that morning was imminent.

After awkward moments, Eric stepped behind Amy, placed his hands on her shoulders and nuzzled his chin on top of her head. There was no response—no tension or softening of muscle or flesh—and Eric said, "Okay, you're pregnant and I am to assume that I'm the father, so have you thought any of this out...like an abortion or what? I mean...this wasn't supposed to happen."

Amy pushed away, gathered her jacket and backpack and left the apartment without a word. Eric slowly followed and called down the hall to her as she stood waiting for the elevator. "So, what are you doing, Amy? Don't do anything crazy."

Looking back at him she said, "I've already done that, Eric," and stepped into the elevator.

Amy moved in with two other waitresses and aspiring-actress friends. Her relationship with Eric since the night she left was surreal, with sparse communication carried on through email or third parties who seemed as disengaged as Amy and Eric. Eric's attitude was that of a winter caretaker of someone's summer cottage, the demands of which consisted of occasionally checking to see if the building still stood. Amy made no inquiries into Eric's life and responded to his emails only if they bore on her financial situation related to her pregnancy, and then in the most perfunctory, legalistic language possible.

After quitting her waitressing job and taking a leave from Columbia, she moved in with her parents on coastal Maine and sat out her pregnancy with a detached anticipation that showed neither anxiety nor self-pity; she would have the baby without face-to-face contact with Eric and then manage her life free of a long-term commitment to anyone but her child.

Deep into her pregnancy she showed what to outsiders was an unreasonable contentment. She read the prenatal good-mother books, abstained from alcohol, ate healthful food, and watched her weight. And while others might have brooded, Amy concentrated on acquiring the knowledge necessary to become a licensed real estate broker. Though she often was the subject of "talk," being pregnant with no husband in sight was not grist for scandal in her small Maine town where the divorce rate easily topped the national average and unwed pregnant teenagers coming from some of the best families seldom turned a head. No Scarlet Letters here.

On her birth certificate Sarah bore Eric's surname of Charles instead of Amy's last name of Macklin, and this would be a point of confusion forever to those who did not know the history of Sarah's conception and birth.

Eric appeared at the hospital the day after Sarah's birth, having received an email from Amy's friend Joan, whom Amy had designated for that chore. Sarah had just been returned to the nursery after Amy's breast feeding, and Joan was looking through the nursery window at all of the babies when Eric appeared by her side. Joan had no idea who Eric was, and he, without identifying himself, asked, "Do you know which one is Amy Macklin's baby?"

"As a matter of fact I do," answered Joan, and then with a flat, suspicious tone asked, "And you are?"

Eric looked at Joan, carefully examining her face and then moving downward as if checking for something concealed. Turning away and again looking into the nursery he said, "I'm the designated father, Eric Charles. Now is it okay to identify the baby for me, or should I hunt up a nurse or somebody and offer to give a sample of my DNA in exchange for showing me my baby?"

Joan, herself a nurse and a friend of Amy's since childhood, was inexperienced with condescending, sarcastic, smartass New Yorkers, but she had the strength of intelligence and the confidence that comes with being on one's own turf and replied with a smile, "Well, really I'm just a friend of the *actual* mother, and I think you would be more comfortable dealing with the aide who is coming into the nursery now, and who I suspect isn't all that interested in your DNA." She nodded toward the nursery where a uniformed young woman had come in from the rear door and continued, "I'll see if she will help you."

Opening the door Joan said, "This is the Baby Charles' father. Could you roll her bassinet over to the window for him?" Then, turning to Eric she added, "Nice meeting you Eric. I'm Joan Robinson, Amy's friend who emailed you," and walked down the hall to Amy's room where in agitated rapid speech she told her of Eric's appearance at the nursery. "And can you believe he actually called himself 'the *designated* father'?"

"Is he coming in here?" asked Amy, propping herself up with a pained grimace.

"I don't know. I have the sense he likely barges in wherever he goes. He seems nasty, Amy," said Joan, moving to help Amy with her pillows.

"Nasty or angry?" asked Amy.

"Nasty. Angry. Maybe both…Oh, I don't know," replied Joan, who then added with a self-conscious giggle, "I don't like him much."

Both fell silent, waiting. But Eric did not appear. Instead, he left a note at the nurses' station: "Nice job. Beautiful little girl. I'll take care of her. Eric."

Eric was true to his word. Through his family's law firm, a $250,000 trust fund was established in Sarah Charles' name, and it would triple in value by Sarah's twenty-first birthday when she became free to spend and administer it as she saw fit. The trust had stipulated that Amy could draw on it for "reasonable expenses" for Sarah's benefit, but other than her college tuition (which included a junior year in Spain and Italy) and a "sensible" monthly college stipend, Amy drew not a cent—a decision that Amy's family and friends viewed as prideful and foolish given Amy's precarious financial state before breaking into lucrative real estate sales during Sarah's early childhood. Amy's hoped-for career in theater had given way to the pleasure and financial success she found in imagining, dramatizing, and ultimately manipulating the lives of her wealthy clients.

As for Eric's participation in Sarah's upbringing, there was none. His note to Amy left at his hospital visit was the last direct communication of any kind from him. He simply dropped out. And Amy's discreet letters to Eric's parents informing them about Sarah's development and activities never were acknowledged, nor were inquiries about Sarah forthcoming from any of Eric's family. Amy assumed that Eric had denied fathering Sarah and had portrayed her as a fortune seeker who was best bought off than litigated against given the sordid publicity that would result; yet Amy was reluctant to create and accept such a scenario since it was so antithetical to the humane Eric she had loved and whose competitive business ethos she always had felt was an anomaly. But there it was. What else could she think?

When Sarah reached puberty, she became increasingly curious about her father. Many of her friends' parents were divorced, and some had remarried and had children with new mates, so Sarah was familiar with broken families and other single parents. But though all kinds of domestic problems were evident in the home lives of many of her acquaintances, all but she and one other friend had a visible father, and that friend's father recently had died of a heart attack. For Sarah, a corporeal real live father never had been seen or heard from and existed only in her imagination.

That imagination was helped along by Amy's openness regarding Eric. Even before infant Sarah was curious that there was no father in her life, Amy would tell her that Eric had gone away before she was born. He always was referred to as Eric, never as daddy or father, and before Sarah knew to ask where he lived, Amy played a game of "Let's imagine where Eric lives," which continued through her childhood, although as Sarah aged, "Let's imagine where Eric lives" was played less and less and became a way to pass time while waiting for real people to appear or public events to begin.

When she was nine, Sarah began to place Eric in spots she would like to visit, ranging from Disney World to Hawaii; but soon she began to imagine him in a recurring spot, a village high on a forested mountain where he painted pictures of all kinds of bizarre subjects: huge racing bicycles, furry animals that grinned and had multicolored coats, Christmas trees with watermelons— any number of objects or people that were unlikely to be seen depicted but that always drew quizzical looks and comments from whomever Sarah shared her descriptions.

In time, however, Eric's whereabouts more often became a topic of serious discussion between Amy and Sarah. And as Sarah neared adulthood, Amy for the first time sought information from Eric's family.

Certified letters were not answered, and an unlisted phone gave her no access. Amy then called the law firm administering

Sarah's trust. At first she was told that "they were not at liberty to give out personal information about their clients." Amy explained that she was seeking only medical history for Sarah regarding Eric and his family that possibly could be valuable in making life-changing decisions based on inherited traits and genetic markers. After a short pause the woman said, "Yes, I understand, but the best I can do is convey your request to Mr. Charles' family. I have to tell you, however, that I don't find in the trust's file any contact with Eric Charles regarding the trust since it was established. I'm sorry I can't be more helpful, but your concern is clearly one in the best interest of the trust's beneficiary and I'll pass on your request for information to Seth Charles, who, as you know, is the family trustee."

She had not known this; she knew only that Seth was Eric's older brother, and he was the only member of Eric's family she had met during their two-year relationship. Eric had disliked Seth but not with the contempt he held for the rest of his family— his sister Harriet, his mother, and his dead father, whom, the few times he mentioned him, Eric referred to as "the Overlord." The one time Amy had met Seth she found him well-mannered with an outmoded detached demeanor that appeared learned—how one behaved to get along. The three of them had eaten in an Italian place she and Eric liked, though Seth, without complaining, intensely scrutinized everything about the restaurant with his head jutted forward, eyes squinting in a skeptical expression as if he were protecting himself from being physically harmed or cheated. Speaking only when spoken to, Seth hurried through his meal, placed money on the table to cover the entire tab, said a perfunctory "Nice meeting you" to Amy, and left without even a final nod in Eric's direction. "Asshole," had been Eric's softly spoken response.

Amy held out little hope of hearing from Seth or anyone else in the Charles family. Nonetheless, a note signed by Seth came within days of her conversation with the legal assistant, the language of which appeared to have been carefully vetted to disavow any legal claim to a blood connection between Eric and Sarah:

"No acknowledgement of parenthood by my brother Eric ever has been made regarding Sarah Charles (a surname you chose with no legal basis). His establishment of a trust in her name is not proof of parenthood and was no more than a sentimental gesture of philanthropy on his part. Therefore, since there is no established blood connection between the Charles family and your daughter, the release of the Charles family medical records is unwarranted and would be an invasion of our privacy. Of course, if Eric chooses to give you his medical history that is his choice, but since he has not been heard from in more than 16 years, and there is no evidence that he still lives, his cooperation appears unlikely if not impossible. On a personal note, however, for whatever 'medical' information you may be seeking, it is safe to say, Eric is/was a fool!"

The unforeseen heartless content and tone of Seth's note shocked Amy, and repeated readings culminated in her actually shuddering and led her to consider burning the note as an act of exorcism. Instead, she buried the note in the back of a portfolio of documents containing Sarah's shot records and miscellaneous clippings and old report cards. No further contact between Amy and Eric's family took place in the next four years leading to Sarah's college commencement day.

During breakfast that morning with Sarah at a jammed Bob Evans, Sarah asked, "So. Do you suppose Eric will show up today?" Although caught off guard, Amy recognized that the question was meant to start a conversation about Eric and was a variation on a question Sarah often had asked since she had become aware of who Eric was. As a child Sarah's questions were: "Where does Eric live?" "Will Eric come see us?" "Why did Eric go away?" But in her early teens she once asked, "Do you think Eric is still alive?" Without pausing, Amy had replied, "You know, I have a feeling he is not, but we really don't know, do we?"

It was a typical truthful answer that Amy always gave to Sarah's questions, and speculation on whether Eric lived or not would not be mentioned again by either of them. But this morning, breakfasting among festive family groups in this small Indiana college town, Amy had asked herself that same question—"Will Eric show up today?—and immediately had felt foolish that she'd even considered Eric's sudden appearance. Thus she almost began her answer with "Funny you should ask," but instead she replied, "After all this time I think it would be highly unlikely. Does he know anything about us? Would he even know you're graduating? You aren't feeling creepy about him all of a sudden, are you?"

"I've felt creepy about him forever. It's just so strange," said Sarah, who, looking straight into her mother's eyes, continued, "I think he's dead…been dead for years."

Amy saw defiance in Sarah's eyes—a final judgment not to be challenged, and a judgment masking enormous disappointment.

A sense of failure swept over Amy and she leaned back in her chair as if she were easing a sudden stomach cramp. Throughout Sarah's life Amy had made Eric a topic and a figment, almost an imaginary friend to them both. Amy's Eric was as she saw him last: handsome, angry over having impregnated her, and embarrassed by feeling somehow victimized. She no longer remembered their happy times together. Her images were of their bitter disputes about sex, reinforced by Eric's silent accusations that someone else's sperm had fathered Sarah; and these images had grown larger and more vivid over the years.

For Sarah, who had seen Eric solely in goofy poses in old candid snapshots, Amy could only guess how he actually must have appeared to her. At every question from Sarah about his physical appearance, Amy had described him as accurately as she could remember and never had played on the fact that she and Sarah had been abandoned; but now Amy wondered if all the games in which she and Sarah imagined Eric over time had built hopes that someday he would materialize as an actual living father.

Before Amy could respond to Sarah's conviction that Eric was dead, a man at an adjacent table bellowed, "For Christ's sake," and began berating a young boy who had upset his glass of milk: "If you'd pay attention you wouldn't...." The man grabbed napkins from others at the table and furiously mopped at the milk dripping onto the floor, his now-lowered voice trailing off into, "Get your head out of your ass." The boy's stoic face could not dam back tears of humiliation, and an elderly waitress quickly appeared, mopping up the milk with a sponge cloth and reassuring the boy with "Not to worry, no problem. It's only milk. No problem."

Amy pushed away her plate and took a last sip of coffee. "I'm ready," she said to Sarah, who replied, "Me too," and they left the restaurant without another word or glance back at the father and son.

On the drive back to campus, Sarah talked about all the things left undone that would have to be dealt with before she cleared out her room, and Amy said she would stop at a liquor store for book boxes. Sounding more hopeful than concerned, Sarah said, "It's Sunday, Mom. There's only one liquor store and it's closed. We can make do." Then she added, "Could we stay over tonight?"

Amy nodded and smiled. "You had this all figured out, didn't you?"

"Not really...but maybe a little," said Sarah after a long pause." Then she added with a shrug, "But after today I guess I'm grown up, huh?"

Reaching over to pat Sarah's knee, Amy said, "You've been grown up since you were about five, so one more day at college won't make a difference. Do you want to stay in the dorm or with me? I'm sure I can extend the motel."

Amy dropped Sarah back at her dorm, and becoming increasingly dispirited changed clothes at the motel and drove to the campus commencement site.

The scene around her was one of cautious merriment—the air soft with late spring odors and the sun highlighting colors into shades of brilliant green were perfect for the ceremony to come, combining joy and melancholy in this traditional rite of passage. Amy wished there were someone to talk to—to ground her in trivia—but starting a conversation with intrusive Jack Baker would set his testosterone-addled brain into false assumptions, although trivia was sure to be his strong suit.

She scanned the crowd, a third of which was in her immediate view. She felt Sarah's sudden interest in Eric was a rebuke of her as a mother; the one thing Amy had not been able to provide Sarah was what Sarah wanted most—a father. Amy looked at the males in the crowd, who she judged could be Eric's age and who surely could be fathers of the graduates. Most were with others as couples or in family groups. She saw the man and his family from the restaurant and his chastised son who now played a hand-held video game.

What would Eric now look like? The absurdity of her missing-person's search caused her to close her eyes, shutting out possibility.

Indifferent to what anyone looking at her would think, Amy sat with closed eyes breathing in the scents of cut grass, overly perfumed bodies, and the faint distant odor of a barbecue's smoking charcoal until a string trio struck up a thin version of "Pomp and Circumstance." She opened her eyes and saw Sarah, radiant yet vulnerable, near the front of the line of graduates filing onto the outdoor stage, and she said in inaudible rage, "Eric Charles, you son of a bitch!"

HENNY YOUNGMAN
CANCELED MY WEDDING

I am fifty-four years old and have never married. Which is not to say I've not— what's the legal term—cohabited? In fact, if you add up the number of years I've lived with men and divide by seven (which is how you determine a common-law marriage, isn't it...or is that how you figure a dog's age in human terms?), you could say I've been married four and a half times—not to mention one-night stands and weekend trysts. I've come close to marrying several times; one time we even had a license. But I'm sounding flip, and I don't want to give the impression that I think marriage is silly or a convention that has seen its day. On the contrary, I revere marriage as a wonderful, romantic ideal, which, I suppose, is why I've never quite done it.

I likely would have married, though, if it hadn't been for Henny Youngman. Barton Crandall II was my husband-to-be, and his name alone goes a long way toward giving an accurate description of him. Bart affected being Mr. Harvard MBA: confident handshake; wondrous black hair that changed with each new style as if it determined its own length and cut; the long-limbed, tempered body of a rower; and the face of a model for crewneck sweaters in a Sunday *Times* Men's Fashions supplement— handsome but nearly anonymous in masculine features so perfect that a police artist trying to draw a composite face of him from others' descriptions would quit in frustration. He was, in short, a Barton Crandall II. I'm sure you've seen him.

It was in the late seventies, and looking back now the decision to get married was a bit unconventional since everybody else was getting a divorce. I'm a singer, and I was good enough and young enough to think I had a career. I worked about eight months a year and sang in some clubs around LA, once did three weeks as a warm-up act for Mel Tormé in Vegas, and actually was on Johnny Carson twice that year, although I was so poor that I bought dresses for both gigs knowing I would return them the next day. The second time I got into a classic New York confrontation with a sales woman who didn't want to take the dress back because of the sweat-stained armpits. I was great! I feigned indignation and arrogance so outrageously that I actually ended up shouting, "Do you know who I am?" Fortunately, the sales woman didn't, and she credited my MasterCard rather than risk offending someone who might have been—well, someone. When I got back to LA and told Bart the story, he beamed, hugged me, and took credit for my "balls," as he put it. "See? Living with a financial genius pays off," he said, and took me to Blum's for a hot fudge sundae.

"Financial genius" may have been a bit of a stretch. When I almost married him, Bart was a stockbroker of some kind—I never understood exactly what he did—but he complained all the time about being on the West Coast when all the action that really counted was on Wall Street. "So let's move to Manhattan," I'd say, and he'd say, "They don't have any surf, or we would." It made me happy that he always said "we," and I believed him because I thought I loved him. Maybe I actually did. Anyway, the bit about the surf was part of his fantasy image: he was born in rural New Hampshire, could barely swim, and was scared to death of riptides.

When I sang nearby, Bart would come hear my last set and

drive us home. I'd watch him when I sang, and he would sit there smiling with a kind of mindless confidence, as if he were being judged by how well I sang. He liked the songs I sang and sometimes tried to talk "musicians'-talk," but it irritated me that he wasn't sensitive enough to know that his words were just jargon; yet I'm sure his intentions were kind. I didn't have a clue about buying and selling stocks and made no claim to, so why should he assume that because he could carry a tune he knew subtleties about my music and my singing? And like all performers, I had good nights and bad nights, but Bart thought all my nights were good nights and once good naturedly accused me of faking dissatisfaction in order to gain praise. I started a fight over that, but the big breakup came months later.

We had gotten our marriage license with no set date for a wedding. The license was good for a month, and since both of our families were either indifferent (mine) or disapproving (his) and on the East Coast, we had vague notions of just inviting another couple to stand up with us one day in front of a judge in West LA. It was a Friday morning and the last day the license was valid. We'd talked off and on for four weeks about setting the date (oh, we were so cool!) but nothing had been settled, and here we were lying in bed at ten thirty a.m. with, at most, five hours left to get married.

Bart always woke up looking as if he had just primped for a promotional photo, every hair in place with even his overnight beard blended and groomed and not at all scruffy. There he sat, propped up against the headboard, being beautiful and sincere. "So, what do you think? Should we actually do it today?" he asked.

There was no hint in his appearance or tone that he had a preference. "So the ball's in my court, huh?" I asked, trying to match his blasé attitude with my own smiling, indifferent response.

"Well, maybe we should toss a coin. I'm heads and you're,

of course, tails," he replied, leering like a lecherous silent-movie villain.

"Fine with me. But wouldn't that mean that one of us would have to get out of bed to get a coin, or, hey—we could shoot fingers for odds or evens." I said that with enough sarcasm to cause his mouth to turn down slightly and leave him quiet and fiddling with the cord to the clock radio.

Sarcasm usually accelerates to hurt feelings, or at least to a serious response, but before Bart had a chance to get serious on his own or disarm me with feigned pain, I asked, "So, seriously, why do you want to get married? I mean, we never have *really* talked about marriage. In fact, I can't remember how we even got around to getting the license." My tone was petulant, but with enough controlled anger that it was clear I would not be put off with a smartass answer. I got one just the same.

"Why do I want to get married? Well, why does any man want to get married? So he can punctuate his arguments with the old Henny Youngman bit—'Now, take my wife, please.'"

I was outraged, although I suppose I shouldn't have been; I knew Bart was incapable of being serious about anything that one should be serious about, but it had never been so clear to me before.

I've relived that scene dozens of times in the past twenty–some years, and each time I think I should have said, "You insensitive, self-centered bastard! You can't bring yourself to say you love me, can you?" And maybe I would have if what he'd said hadn't been so tasteless. But instead of attacking the indifference to my feelings such a silly comment expressed, I challenged his sense of humor!

"'Take my wife, please?' You think that's funny? You think Henny Youngman is funny?" I shouted, incredulous and disgusted.

"Hey, come on. Everybody thinks Henny Youngman's

funny. It's un-American not to. I mean, the guy's a classic."

"You're serious aren't you? You actually are being serious for once in your life. The next thing you'll be telling me you think the Three Stooges are funny!"

"Of course they're funny! They're stupid, but funny. All that stuff, poking each other in the eye and slapping their heads—nobody gets hurt. It's make believe—willing suspension of disbelief and all that." He was still propped up on his pillows while I sat naked at the foot of the bed, and his position gave him a natural advantage to stress his argument. "They're funny—but not funny like Henny. Henny Youngman has this great timing, that Catskill resort shtick of his. It's genius, and I'm surprised you, a musician, don't recognize the subtleties, the innate rhythm."

He sat there pontificating and close to sneering. But Bart's seductive-charm genes really couldn't make a physical sneer (just like the genes of some people prevent them from rolling their tongues), and before I could defend myself he said, "For instance, Henny Youngman tells this story about the teenager who goes to work in his uncle's candy store and some guy comes in, buys a pack of cigarettes, and gives the kid a five dollar bill. The kid gives the guy change, and as he's putting the bill in the register he realizes that he'd shortchanged the customer, whose gone by now, *and* he discovers that a twenty dollar bill is stuck to the five the guy gave him. So, his first day of work he's faced with this moral dilemma: should he tell his uncle that he'd shortchanged the guy?"

Bart sat there smiling like he'd just won a poker hand. "That's it? That's the joke?" I asked. "Or, more to the point, *is* that a joke?"

"Oh, come on! Of course it's a joke. Don't you get it? The kid short changes the customer accidentally and he sees that as some kind of moral dilemma, but he doesn't see anything wrong in keeping the twenty bucks—so, of course he can't tell his uncle about the..."

I cut him off and said, "I get it all right, but I don't get why you think that's funny. There's great timing in that? There isn't anything funny in it at all unless you're some kind of anti-Semite—and you, you're half-Jewish, for Christ's sake."

He looked past me, trying to sort out his so-called joke and my reaction to it, and after a few seconds he shrugged and patronized me by saying, "Is that some kind of pun—'Christ's sake'? 'Anti-Semitic'? Believe me, Jews know what's anti-Semitic and that joke's not anti-Semitic. And who said the kid's Jewish? I guess you have to have been there."

He looked me in the eyes when he said, "I guess you have to have been there," and there was a take-it-or-leave-it finality in his expression. I got up and went into the bathroom, and when I came out he was still propped in the same position, but he smiled and asked in a tone that was a little sad, "So what do you think? Do we use the license or not?"

"Not," I answered, dressed rapidly, and left him still propped up in bed playing with the clock-radio cord.

No more was said about getting married that day or any other. We were polite to one another and, since it was Bart's apartment, three weeks later I moved out. Female cabaret singers who survive job-to-job don't take leases on anything, and in my case that included husbands.

So here I am—a hostess-singer in a pricey restaurant on the Connecticut River just outside Windsor Locks. It's a good job. I like it. I am very charming checking off reservations and escorting people to their tables, and every evening about nine o'clock, once the late arrivals have gotten settled in, I accompany myself at a wonderful baby grand piano and sing romantic ballads—hardly ever anything uptempo. I'm good. I take my singing seriously, and with some luck and a good agent I might really have gone somewhere. I work out daily and have a terrific body, if I do say so myself. No wrinkles—I've never smoked or lain around in the sun. Men hit on me every night.

That's the downside of my job. Some of them are very attractive, and all of them are rich—at least by my standards. But for them I'm a perk—a rental BMW or an executive box seat at the Garden for a Knicks' or Rangers' game; and for a few of the older ones I might become a trophy wife for their last desperate years of displaying what, outwardly at least, passes for virility. Such an arrangement, however, doesn't exactly fit my idea of matrimony, let alone virility.

Besides, I have all the sex I want, no sexually transmitted diseases, no physical abuse, and no sticky commitments. I sleep only with married men because they don't want commitments either. And they all, or the ones I choose, feel guilty so they treat me very well. They bring me sentimental, inexpensive gifts, and a couple of them have written me poems—one poor guy even tried to pass off some paraphrased Edna St. Vincent Millay sonnets as his own. He was a sweet guy—very confused and ultimately very impotent. The last night we were together he told me that his wife busted his balls, and then he actually said, "Now take my wife, please." I said nothing, handed him his clothes and walked to the door of my apartment; and when he had dressed and came toward me, looking like a cross between a whipped dog and an Eagle Scout, I opened the door and said one firm word to him: "Out!" He left without a look back and was gone forever.

I don't want to leave the impression that Bart and the phony poet were the only ones who liked to invoke Henny Youngman. Over the years I've had a dozen or so charmers on the way back to their tables from the men's room stop by the piano to make a request—not for a tune but for my body. And it would go something like this: "You've got a great voice, great voice! How do you do that—play the piano and sing and look terrific all at the same time? Not everybody can do that, you know. Now, for instance, take my wife—please!"

I have a stock response for these diners who want to give their wives away. "No thanks," I say, smiling my most kittenish smile. "You're too generous by half—the better half. But I'd like to give you something—a tune especially for you. What's your name?"

Not quite sure of what to expect, but generally pleased with themselves, they'll tell me their first name and return to their tables. Then, after doodling a few bars, I breathe seductively into the mike, "Here's a request dedicated to a special wife by her loving husband Ken," or whatever his name may be, and I sing a very slow-paced, clearly enunciated, sincere-as-hell version of "Our Love Is Here to Stay."

The last time I had occasion to do this was no more than a week ago, and the man who wanted me to "take his wife, please" managed on the way out of the restaurant to smile in my direction while mouthing an unmistakable "Bitch!" It made my night, although as I thought back over the evening I felt a little guilty— the guy's poor wife must have wondered why after her husband publicly dedicated his love to her he was in such a bad mood on the drive home.

But, as I was saying, I'm fifty-four years old and have never married. Right now life is good. People who know how old I am constantly flatter me with comments of disbelief that I could be that old and look so young. A great number of women would love to trade places and bodies with me, and that's fun to know, although I've always thought that envy is the stupidest of the deadly sins. I'm singing better than ever, I have a secure job, good health and few regrets.

But perhaps you're smugly wondering what happens when my looks and voice go? And they surely will. Well, I'm going to get married—a marriage of convenience. You know—marry a gay guy or somebody needing a green card, and that will legitimize my new career as a stand-up comedienne. And I'll say lame, corny things like, "Men just aren't equipped for some simple movements—even male gymnasts, who can do one-hand pushups and do headstands with those parallel rings, just don't have the coordination or muscle mass to put the seat down on the toilet. Now take my husband.... please!"

BETRAYAL

The reality of Peg's death, accompanied by news that he had won six million dollars in a state lottery the same day as her memorial service, had left Stan Hopkins insensate for days, but that numbness was beginning to change to agitation, a new confusing demand on his consciousness. He didn't like it. Was this grief taking over from shock? What *is* grieving, anyway?

It was his first day back at work, and everyone at the library treated Stan with friendly distance, with those who knew him least well trying to hide their self-consciousness and his closest colleagues striving to behave as if it were merely a routine Monday. The schedule had been revised so that Stan worked the reference desk the first thing in the morning—the slowest time since early patrons knew what they were there for and usually didn't ask for help.

He spent free moments looking around the room, examining the place carefully. The rug once had been deep blue with a faint pattern of gold diamonds running through it. The path from the door past his desk to the card catalog and computer terminals was filthy and badly worn with threads of the binding beginning to show through the nap, and the carpet's remaining surface was a dull gray that looked like dust but really was old age. The wall and ceiling paint was similarly shopworn, and thin cracks ran in all directions around the light fixtures. The fixtures themselves beamed silhouettes of dead moths through opaque globes, and the plastic-covered switch plate near the door was bordered by years-old finger smudges. Every place Stan looked he saw, for the first time, worn and aging objects and structures that before today had gone unnoticed in the demands of the room's business.

It was, after all, that business that kept him there. He enjoyed supplying information and the challenge of finding answers to new and arcane inquiries. He cherished the civilized aura that came with the territory and the quiet that signaled respect in an era of persistent clamor. It was a haven of sorts that paid him a decent salary, and as he looked around, seeing things close and clear, he realized he was seeing the library in the past tense. If he chose, he need never come back after today.

The university was on spring break, and the patrons in Stan's reference room were a few die-hard undergraduates obsessed with getting into Ivy League graduate schools, a dour female doctoral student tracing elusive connections by scanning indexes and bibliographic bulk, and an aged townie who, with showy self-importance, hung out in libraries as a substitute for real life.

By late morning Stan had turned down invitations to lunch off campus, excusing himself by saying he had some errands he needed to run during the lunch break. The fact was he had no plans for lunch, but he didn't want to be sociable or be pitied or be the recipient of awkward small talk; so he dawdled until well past time to go to lunch and then walked toward the parking lot where, on impulse, he walked past his car. Glancing back to see if anyone was watching and seeing the lot was two-thirds empty and no one was in sight, he continued walking to where a line of oak trees had been saved. Stan never had looked beyond those bordering trees, but now he walked between them and came to a chain-link fence surrounding a low windowless building that was some kind of utility station. Tangled scrub oaks and stunted hemlocks formed a scraggy strip bordering the road running past the campus's western property line.

Stan was disappointed. He had hoped that beyond the tree line would be an unspoiled vista. Instead, there was merely more leveled land holding yet another ugly functional building around which no life appeared. Turning back the way he'd come, Stan's view of the library filled most of the near horizon with its uninspired design backing the muted shades of blue, gray and green Subarus and Hondas scattered around the parking lot. Everything appeared out of place, and though he had driven into that lot hundreds of times, what he now saw seemed grotesque. He got into his car and drove away.

The through streets bordering the campus featured pizza joints, delis, soft ice-cream parlors, Chinese or Thai restaurants, chain drugstores, and vacant down-at-the-heels storefronts. There was an incongruous garish stagnation about the strips as if they had been brightened up to fail, and Stan seldom drove this way, favoring the slower stop-and-go of the residential streets bordering the opposite side of the campus. Stan drove slowly, tempting the wrath of the impatient drivers behind him as he debated choices for lunch. He retraced his route, going in the opposite direction and beginning to enjoy impeding traffic. A teenager in a Trans-Am blasted his horn and whipped around him shouting something indistinct that Stan took for an obscenity. He decided he would end his foolish game and stop at Dandy Donuts a few blocks away, a place where he and Dave Bryant often stopped for coffee on the way back from shooting hoops.

He wasn't hungry until he was inside the shop and spied his favorite breakfast pastry, chop suey rolls. The roll is a combination of citron, raisins, and colorful bits of other dried fruits infusing an uneven round glob of fried sweet dough. They have veins of cinnamon running through the dough, the fruit sticks up like warts, and the whole roll has a sugar glaze that falls off in shards when one bites into it. Stan knew the roll would lie heavily in his stomach for the rest of the day, but as he took a place at the counter he smiled and felt smug—a forgotten feeling.

The waitress passed Stan twice while serving others and showed no sign that she knew he existed, so he was surprised when going by with someone's order she stopped and said, "I know you. You once told me where I could find a list of schools in America that had programs in physical therapy."

She looked at him with unblinking confidence from a heart-shaped and almost child-like face. The confidence came from her eyes—large agate gray-green that were deep and intelligent, like the eyes of a serious mouser.

"Good god," blurted Stan, who had a near pathological dislike of being identified by anyone for any reason—a foible that was making his yet-to-be-identification as a lottery winner all the more difficult. "Did you find the school you wanted?"

"Not exactly. I'm still here aren't I?" This was said with an edge that disappeared when she asked, "What can I get you?"

His cover was blown. Before ordering, he looked around to see if anyone was eavesdropping before ordering: "Coffee and… uh…I think I'll have one of those, what are they called, chop suey rolls?"

"You actually like those things? Well, so do I. They're really awful but I love them. You drink your coffee black, right?"

"I do, but how did you know that?"

Smiling, she looked at him. There was that confidence again. "I didn't," she said. "You just look like a black-coffee guy."

Stan wanted to look at her closely, but he felt as if he were the one being scrutinized. It was those eyes—those feline eyes that never left his face and conveyed a predatory warmth that he could translate only as a ridiculous desire to lay mice at his feet. She had an athletic build, lovely and feminine—small but strong—a gymnast cum ballerina. A quick glance revealed the collar of her uniform spread to frame a barely perceptible gold chain with a tiny cross. The skin on which the cross lay was flecked with pinhead dots of freckles—an earthy trademark stamping the article to be the genuine thing. "So, what's a black-coffee person like?" he asked.

With no guile she replied, "Like you. A nice man."

A United Parcel driver at the end of the counter waved his check and a bill in her direction saving Stan from an extended embarrassing pause as she moved to take the man's money. As she stood at the cash register, Stan saw that from the waist down she fit the configuration from the waist up. She was a lovely young woman with extraordinary eyes, and he wondered how he could not have remembered those eyes from their conversation when she sought his help in the library.

As she cleared the counter where the man had sat, Stan felt self-conscious about his chop-suey roll. How could he eat the thing in front of her? It was impossible to bite into without causing a shower of sugar glaze and crumbs to dribble down one's chin; and to break it into bite-sized pieces was too prissy. The roll remained untouched when the waitress returned, again stood in front of him, and said, "So, pretty quiet at school this week, I guess?"

"Yeah, vacation time always is, but there are some people who never go away, so we have to be there to earn our keep," said Stan. "What about you? You going to get away some place?"

"I wish. No, I dropped out in December and I work here pretty much full time. Going to school was my vacation."

Stan smiled and played with his coffee mug, "I get the impression from some of my faculty colleagues that you aren't alone in seeing college as a vacation, but I wouldn't have thought you fit that mold."

"Oh, I fit it all too well," she said, looking Stan straight on. "It got so that all I did was party...and it became clear that I'm an alcoholic." What could pass as a confession carried no self-serving weight in her voice; there was neither guilt nor flippancy, just information freely given.

Stan was startled. Her eyes convinced him that she was telling the truth, yet he awkwardly responded, "Oh, come on! You're the healthiest-looking person I've seen in sometime." Some inhibitor that cautioned against anything that could be construed as sexual kept him from adding, "and one of the prettiest, too."

"I'm more or less healthy now. Haven't had a drink—I'm a vodka drunk—since I quit school." Her eyes never left his.

Stan was becoming more and more uncomfortable. Were these revelations part of some twelve-step therapy that called for her to tell everyone she meets that she's a drunk? Those eyes, the cross hovering above breasts that appeared not to need a bra, the story of her life? It was time to get out of there.

He made a show of looking at his watch. "I've lost track of the time and better get going. Could you put this thing in a bag and I'll get to it later...or maybe keep it till breakfast—microwave it, maybe."

She smiled and was the same cheerful person who had said "I know you" when he came in. She wrapped the roll in its waxed paper square and slipped it into a bag while saying, "That will be two forty-seven," and as Stan gulped the still-too-hot coffee he realized he would have walked out without paying had she not told him the price. He handed her three dollars with a gesture waving off change and said, "I hope you can get back to school and do whatever it is...physical therapy?...you want to do."

Her eyes holding his, she replied, "Thanks. I plan to get back in the fall, and I just may make it if I can stay sober and get more twenty percent tips from people like you. It's been nice talking with you."

"Yes, it has been," said Stan as he stood up to leave. "I enjoyed it. I'll look for you."

Back in his car Stan's mood returned to the feisty, perverse state it had been before he entered the doughnut shop, yet he now experienced a lightness, a small contented sensation. It once was a familiar feeling but one that had been missing for months, and he knew the doughnut shop waitress had brought it on. "Fuck the library," he shouted. "Why should I go back there?"

He drove home, phoned the library, and in a firm voice so as not to sound pathetic said he had a migraine and begged off for the rest of the day. Who could question a grieving husband who had come back to work ten days after his wife's funeral? He had lied about the headache but was unsure about his physical and mental shape in light of the surge of emotion brought on by a woman young enough to be his daughter.

The bag with the chop-suey roll centered his attention. He poured a glass of milk, ripped the bag down the middle, and devoured the roll in big chunks, letting glaze and milk dribbled down his chin. He ate every crumb of roll and shard of glaze and defied the roll to kill him. Lust and gluttony. Primal sins? Stan felt no shame, and greed had yet to be factored in. He would take a nap and let the afternoon take care of itself.

*   *   *   *   *

Dave Bryant woke him from troubled sleep. It was nearly 3, and Dave, both agitated and bored, had slipped away from his car dealership and jostled Stan's shoulder as he sprawled, mouth agape, on the porch's chaise lounge. "How's it goin', Stanley?"

It took Stan a few seconds to orient himself, and before he could speak Dave had gone into the kitchen and returned carrying an open beer. "You're out of beer—this is the last one."

"You sneak into my house, wake me out of the first decent sleep I've had in weeks, and steal my last beer. So what are you doing here, anyway?"

Dave took several long swallows of beer, held the can up in a salute to Stan and said, "You're on your porch so I didn't sneak into your house, and if you weren't such a cheap bastard you'd have more than one beer in your fridge—you're a fuckin' millionaire, Stan,...and...I couldn't hack the job anymore. So, let's go shoot some hoops."

"I'm not sure that's a good idea," said Stan. "I left work at noon and called back and said I had a migraine."

"So, who cares! You've won six million dollars and could buy and sell those guys ten times over. I guess you haven't told them yet?"

"I haven't told anybody. You know that. What about you?"

Dave gulped his beer and shook his head. "No. Actually, the reason I left work was I went to collect my so-called winnings, which turned out to be six thousand seventeen dollars and change. Not exactly the windfall I was counting on."

"Why only six thousand?"

"Oh, they explained it all—sort of. There's this complicated formula about a pool of twenty percent of what's left over from something, and that's divided among people whose numbers were only off by one from the big winner. Can you believe there were five of us? And, on top of that, if your winnings are over five thousand they skim twenty percent off for the IRS." He crushed the empty can in his fist. "Shit! I was hoping for at least fifteen grand. One lousy digit made the difference between your winnings and mine."

For several years Stan and Dave had each bought a one-dollar weekly pick-six lottery ticket using the same numbers except for the final digit. Each had chosen their high school basketball jersey number for that digit: 7 for Stan, 9 for Dave. They had never discussed sharing the winnings if one of them won, nor even speculated on how each would spend his winnings. Distracted by Peg's illness Stan had quit buying his weekly ticket, but Dave, thinking Stan should keep their "string" going, without telling him had bought Stan's tickets for him every week for the last two months before Peg died. The winning numbers, 7-18-26-30-38-42, had been drawn the day of Peg's memorial service. Stan's winnings were going to be over six million dollars, and he would not have known he had won if Dave had not bought the ticket and been checking the paper.

"We'll split the damned thing. Add the two together and split it down the middle," said Stan nodding, as if it were all settled.

"Oh, come on! It was your ticket. You won. There was never anything about sharing. You won, fair and square."

"Fair and square? I wouldn't have won diddly if you hadn't bought the ticket and, in fact, I think legally the winnings are yours. The whole thing. You paid for the ticket—handed it to me…and I'm giving it back. It's yours—the whole thing." Agreeing on where the lottery money would go suddenly sickened Stan. It was too much to deal with and he added, "The whole thing, Dave. It's yours. I don't want it. Fuck it!" and he got up and started for the den.

Dave called after him. "Hey, take it easy. I don't want to get into a fight over this. We're buddies, right? We don't fight…I mean…shit!"

Stan returned with the lottery ticket, threw it onto the table beside the chaise and flopped back onto it. They sat silently for a few minutes until Dave said, "I'm not picking it up," to which Stan replied, "Suit yourself."

Long silence was broken when Dave said, "I meant it when I said I came over to see if you want to shoot some hoops."

"Yeah, that would be good. Might clear my head." Stan began to laugh. "Clear my head? That's good because I told them at work I had a migraine—I don't even know what a migraine is supposed to feel like, but I don't want to go back. Where could we go, Linden Tree School? There's no school this week so there may be kids on the courts. And you're right—who cares if it gets back to the library?"

"We can stop for a 6-pack on the way," said Dave.

"We can't drink beer on a school playground, Dave! Jesus! How old are we? We sound like a couple of…I don't know…frat boys," said Stan, laughing and going to change into sweats and sneakers.

There was no one on the basketball court but a couple of preteen skateboarders jumping their boards up and down the short flight of stairs leading to the swing sets. Dave took his basketball out of his car trunk, flipped the ball to Stan, and changed into his sneakers while Stan began taking jump shots. Banter about their individual skills had been part of their friendship since childhood, and it continued today with each deriding the other's skills. Usually they would play "horse," and they were so evenly matched that if a tally had been kept of the hundreds of games they played, no clear winner would be apparent. Today they each won a game, and instead of playing a tiebreaker of "horse," Dave insisted on playing "21" to determine the winner.

Since Stan had won the last game of "horse," Dave took the ball out and ran off four straight jump shots before missing and losing the rebound to Stan. Being so far behind and thinking himself faster off the dribble than Dave, Stan faked a shot, drove around him and went up for a lay-up. Dave was beaten and should have conceded the basket, but he slid under Stan, a move that flipped Stan head-downward. Stan landed on his upper back and shoulders which took enough of the fall that when his head hit the asphalt he was saved from fracturing his skull.

Momentarily unconscious, Stan began to roll from side to side. Dave had committed the dirtiest foul the game knows—sliding under an airborne helpless player—the cardinal sin of basketball be it a schoolyard game or the finals of the NBA Championship. Dave leaned over Stan, not knowing what to do but fully aware of what he had done. Blood began to flow onto the asphalt. "Take it easy, Stan. Take it easy…You okay?...Just lie there. Don't try to get up." The common-sense medical instructions Dave gave came from a realization that what he had done could have killed Stan.

Carrying their boards across the grass, the two skateboarders had walked by just as Stan was flipped and stood wide-eyed at the other end of the court. When it was clear that Dave saw them, they began to run. "Hey, wait," yelled Dave, but Stan was struggling to get up and Dave again turned his attention to Stan and asked more as a plea than a question, "You gonna be okay? Don't try to get up. Just rest there." Stan, like a boxer struggling to get up after being knocked senseless, braced himself on all fours before falling back onto his side. Blood was running down his neck and left arm.

Dave grabbed Stan's sweatshirt from the side of the court and pressed it against the wound. Stan, stunned but conscious, sat spraddle-legged and took the sweatshirt and held it to his head as Dave commanded, "Don't get up. Don't move. Just hang there and we'll get you fixed up. I'm gonna run to the car and get my phone."

Retrieving the phone and sprinting back to Stan, Dave considered getting Stan on his feet and helping him to the car, and then maybe no one would know what happened if he could get him home and patched the cut; but when he saw the blood still flowing and Stan's strange glowering gaze, he called 911 and then sat down, positioning himself behind Stan, one arm wrapped around Stan's shoulder and the other holding the sweatshirt against the bloody base of Stan's head. The Emergency unit was there within ten minutes, a torturous amount of time that allowed Dave to consider what he had done and to speculate on how he could explain it.

The ambulance drove through the parking lot and across the lawn. The driver, a volunteer from the firehouse, was a college student, humorless and self-important, for whom playing ambulance driver was his whole life while he fantasized about getting off academic probation and raising his grade point average enough to somehow get into med school. With him was a middle-aged man, affable and proficient in life-saving techniques as a licensed med-tech volunteer and who, on examining Stan, judged Stan's condition not to be life threatening. After putting a compress on the wound and stanching the flow of blood, they eased Stan onto their stretcher and into the ambulance. Then, sounding an unnecessary short bleep of the siren, they headed for the University Hospital. Dave followed in his car.

An attending ER physician diagnosed Stan as having a moderate concussion, stitched and dressed the wound, and admitted Stan for "overnight observation." He was wheeled to a room to be shared with a man in his sixties who was recuperating from a prostatectomy and who looked away as Stan, behind a pulled curtain, was undressed and helped onto his bed. Dave had stayed behind to call Len Rood, Stan's primary-care physician, and got assurances from the latter's nurse that Rood would look in on Stan that evening. When Dave came into the room he sounded as if he hoped for a positive response when he pushed aside the curtain and again asked, "How you doing?"

"My head hurts…and I'm pissed to be in here," answered Stan, his voice flat and tired, his eyes closed.

This was said with no passion and Dave could not tell whether Stan remembered how his injury came about. Dave came close to confessing when he said, "It's my fault. You remember going up for that shot? We somehow got tangled and you got off balance and fell. I'm *really* sorry, Stan."

What Dave said was shaded in truth, but its ambiguity shielded him from the full glare of fault and guilt; one not witnessing the "tangle" would assume it had been an accident—an awkward move. Carefully fingering his bandaged skull and with eyes still closed, Stan said, "Forget it. We're too old to play kids' games anyway. What time is it?"

Dave's watch was in his car where he had left it when they went to shoot baskets, so he asked Stan's "roommate" if he had the time. The man, sitting in a chair, continued to stare out the window when he replied, "I have no need for a watch. You'll have to ask somebody else."

Dave gestured towards the man's back and shrugged, and for several minutes there was silence until a nurse's aide entered to retrieve the man's supper tray, which sat untouched beside his chair. "Are you finished Mr. Purvis? I can come back if you aren't," her tone suggesting that might be a good idea.

Still staring out the window, he waved his hand and said, "No, take it away. Thank you. I'm not hungry."

The aide was middle-aged, a bit plump and pretty in a former-cheerleader kind of way, and her enthusiasm signaled she was new to her job and eager to please. Stopping beside Stan's bed she looked down and said, "I'll see what they've got planned for you."

"I doubt if it's much. He's got a concussion and they probably don't want him to eat," said Dave. Dave wanted to get out of there, and he asked the aide what time it was, sounding as if he were late.

"Nearly six. It's going to be a lovely evening," she replied, exiting the room.

The men again sat in silence for several minutes until Dave asked Stan, "Do you want me to call someone to let them know you're in here? I mean, you're only going to be here overnight, but somebody might call and wonder why you didn't answer."

Stan took a long time to answer, and Dave was about to repeat his question when Stan, opening his eyes, said, "I guess not. I don't know. I'm a little confused. My answering machine is on, I guess."

"Well, that's right. What about your sister or the girls? They'd think you'd gone out and would check in the morning, wouldn't they? But then if you don't answer they might wonder and...well, not to worry," said Dave "We'll figure something out...."

The room was filled with sadness. Donald Purvis, assuming his sex life was gone and the rest was soon to follow, shied from the other two men and generated pathological hatred for things healthy. Stanley Hopkins, his sensibilities skewed by the death of his wife, inexplicable sudden great wealth, indecision, and throbbing physical pain lay in confusion. And David Bryant, childless, self-pitying, frustrated by a lifetime of under-achieving, and guilt-ridden, wanting only to flee the room, was held back, not knowing how to atone for injuring the one person he had reason to revere. In an angry bellow he said, "Jesus Christ, Stan, I hate to see you in here—especially after Peg and everything. I feel guilty as hell!"

Dave's outburst caused Purvis to abandon his psychic cave and turn toward the other two, but Stan, silent, as if he were translating Dave's outcry, finally said, "Go on home. I'm all right... just got a doozy of a headache."

Dave promised to check with him in the morning and drive him home. "But call me if you need anything tonight. Anything at all." Then, patting Stan's foot sticking out from under the sheet, added, "Get some rest," and left the room.

The evening seemed to have no boundaries, and time was not part of Stan's awareness. Purvis' wife came in and talked in soft tones to her husband. Stan had no interest in what was being said and did not strain to hear, and the rest of the night was a continuum of nurses checking his pulse and asking who is the president of the United States or what month is it. The head wound hurt when he moved, so he lay still, contending with what had become a dull headache and slipping into short terms of uneasy sleep and dreams. The waitress from Dandy Donuts at one point seemed to be sitting across the room smiling at him, and sometime during the night colorful images of spinning slot-machine graphics followed a painful slow examination of his eyes with a bright flashlight's beam.

Morning was announced by an intern who didn't identify himself before asking Stan how he felt. "Awful," said Stan. "Awful. Hung over."

"To be expected. You got a nasty shot to the head. Let's take a quick look and then we'll see about some breakfast for you," said the doctor in practiced amiable tones.

Stan opted for apple juice and coffee, with the latter tasting bitter and stale, and propped up in bed he tried to recount the events that brought him to this hospital room. Not much was clear. He remembered hitting the court and being lifted into the ambulance, but the progression of events after that was vague until finally he was in the hospital bed, and someone had either told him what had happened or he had realized on his own that he had a concussion. It seemed to have something to do with money.

Len Rood came in while the breakfast tray was still on the bedside table and began to kid Stan about getting hurt playing a kid's game he should have given up years ago. Stan had not seen Len outside of the latter's office or the hospital, but through Peg's long illness they had developed a rapport that was comfortable for both doctor and patient, or, to be precise, for doctor and patient's husband. Len had treated Stan only once, and that was years ago for a sinus infection, but they had spent much time together with Peg or outside of her hearing discussing her treatments, her chances for recovery, and finally her assured death. Stan had confidence in Len's medical skills and appreciated his humane sensibilities and sense of humor, and he was able to smile when Len said, "The admitting physician told me that there wasn't much wrong with you except you think you're Michael Jordan, and in fact I wouldn't be in here now if I didn't have to be in the hospital to see someone who's actually sick."

Stan responded to Len's questions as he took Stan's blood pressure, looked in his eyes with a flashlight, felt around Stan's neck, and poked his soles with a pen. He had Stan describe his headache and asked him if he could remember things he wanted to forget? "All too well," replied Stan.

"Good. That means you're fine to go home. Your concussion may make you feel goofy off and on for a few days, but your reflexes are good. You will need some help getting the dressing changed, and I'll leave instructions about that. Take it easy until the headache goes away, and you might give some thought to playing games where you keep your feet on the ground for awhile—if not forever."

After Dr. Rood left, Stan wondered if his admonition to "keep your feet on the ground" had metaphorical as well as literal value? It had been barely a week since he had buried his wife, and some might judge that getting a concussion while playing basketball was a bit out of character for one in mourning. And the waitress and the chop suey roll? And the six million dollars waiting to be claimed?

Purvis was dressed and sat across the room, ignoring Stan and staring into space. Stan wanted out of there and searched out his sweat pants, tee shirt, socks and sneakers in the closet beside his bed. There was no sweat shirt and he worried that he would attract notice if he left wearing a tee shirt and no sweat shirt or sweater on a cool spring morning. Had Dave said he would drive him home?

Feeling no dizziness, Stan walked to the nurses' station and announced he was ready to go home. The startled nurse immediately made him sit in a wheelchair while explaining that procedures had to be followed for him to be discharged. "So follow them," said Stan. "Dr. Rood has seen me and said I could leave."

Pushing aside the folders she had been examining when Stan came up, she found Stan's folder and acknowledge that Len had ordered his discharge. "Is someone picking you up, Mr. Hopkins?"

"I'm not sure," said Stan. "I need to check on that."

"Well, you'll have to gather your things and we need to know someone is looking after you when you leave."

"There's nothing to gather. I'm wearing what I wore in here, although there should be a sweatshirt, too. I think someone is picking me up, but I guess I need to make a call to make sure… and I don't have his number. He'll be at work. Maybe I should just call a cab?"

The nurse called to an aide who had just walked up, "Wheel Mr. Hopkins back to his room and help him gather his belongings, and then we'll see about transportation for him."

Feeling helpless, Stan said nothing until he was returned to his room where the aide looked in his closet and bedside stand in search of his belongings. "There's nothing else. I don't even have my wallet. How did I get checked in here without that?"

The aide was as confused as Stan and again looked into the closet and drawers. "Well, I'm sure your things are safe," she said. "Don't worry. I'll go check for you."

Several minutes followed and Dave suddenly appeared in the door. "How you doin', buddy? You set to go home?"

Stan explained his dilemma and Dave handed him his wallet and told him how he'd shown Stan's ID and insurance cards to get him admitted. "If you're up to it, let's get you out of here. You had anything to eat?"

Stan waved a hand and said, "Not hungry. Let's go."

A nurse insisted on his riding in a wheelchair and an aid waited with him until Dave pulled up in his SUV. Stan welcomed the cool air as he was helped into the car, but he began to shiver as they drove away. "Typically I have my head up my ass and should have thought to bring you a sweater or something. I threw your sweat shirt into our dirty clothes and…" Dave didn't finish his sentence and Stan responded, "I'm okay. Just glad to get out of there." The hundreds of memories surrounding Peg and the hospital where he had just spent the night as a patient had not been among the specters that flickered through his half-awake consciousness during the night, but now he marveled at how he could have been in that hospital and not been tormented by the horrible memories that place called up. "Asshole," he said aloud.

"What?" asked a startled Dave.

"Not you…me. I'm just feeling extra stupid…fuzzy headed," said Stan.

They were silent until they arrived at Stan's. Dave was awkwardly solicitous as he made certain Stan was well enough to be left alone, repeatedly asking for Stan's assurance that he would be all right and offering to get him anything he needed. "Actually, I've got two clients to see this afternoon, but I'll come by afterwards and see about supper and whatever"; and as he was leaving, and with only the vaguest allusion to his role in Stan's injury, he said, "I'm really glad you're okay."

Stan walked Dave to the door, then sat on the couch. Nothing seemed important, but coffee sounded good. Going into the kitchen, Stan saw the light blinking on his answering machine. It would be the library checking on him. There was no way he was going to return their call—at least not until he knew what he would lie to them about this time. Then he saw the lottery ticket on the table where he had thrown it in anger the day before. He picked it up and carried it into the kitchen, placing it on the counter while he got coffee brewing.

Once the coffee was perked, Stan filled a mug, picked up the ticket again and carried both to the patio door. He slowly scanned the yard with its early greenery and budding shrubs and began to sob. With both hands he tried to steady the shaking mug and caused coffee to spill onto his fingers, scalding them and dripping onto the lottery ticket and the rug. He welcomed the pain.

ENLIGHTENMENT

Chuck Tillis' morning had gotten off to a bad start the evening before when Jean Bruder called and, just short of demanding, had implored him to join her and her husband Joey for Chinese food with John and Louise Kellerman.

"I know it's a last minute thing, Chuck, but…well, Johnny is in some kind of remission and actually can eat again, and I think it would mean a lot to them. Louise never really gets out, and anything to lift Johnny's spirits—right? Besides, with Gail gone you're probably just going to have peanut butter and jelly and a beer or something."

Her gasping nervous laugh had given Chuck a moment to scan his desk calendar in hopes of finding an excuse to decline, but he knew there was nothing written on it.

"Yeah, I've been meaning to call Johnny ever since his last round of chemo, but…I guess I'm just a lousy friend. Chinese food, huh? Sure, I can make that."

The Bruders and Kellermans already were at their table when Chuck arrived, and he was embarrassed, thinking he must have misunderstood the reservation time. "No, no. We got here a little early," Joey had said, "and we just decided to take our table instead of sitting out in the lounge. We knew you'd be on time, Chuckie." And then he too had laughed a nervous cackle that after 18 years of marriage was identical to his wife's. Johnny Kellerman's folded walker was wedged against the wall behind his chair, making it clear why the Bruders had opted to go straight to their table rather than go through the awkward, painful business of maneuvering Johnny into and then out of a seat in the lounge.

The restaurant, the Hunan Hoo, was a converted steak house with oak-colored paneling, deep green rugs and a minimum of gilded trim that gave the place a genuine understated opulence unusual for rehabbed Chinese restaurants. The employees were beautiful Asians. Their service was attentive and calm, and the food was excellent, though not worthy of the exaggerated praise Jean and Joey repeatedly declaimed; the Bruders were enthusiasts, the kind who leap to their feet flailing their hands wildly at the conclusion of any concert, no matter how mediocre it may have been.

The meal had been pleasant enough, if one could ignore Johnny's frequent fidgeting movements that raised him up a fraction of an inch and then settled him back into the chair in an effort to ease the pain that cramped up from his lower back.

The conversation had been light and relatively natural as all strove to ignore the obvious—that without a miracle John Kellerman would be dead within a year—and the awkwardness of this being a potential last restaurant meal together never blighted the evening until the fortune cookies. Chuck, recognizing the certain folly in sharing forecasts of the future with a man who had no future, tried to ignore the fortune cookies altogether and called for the check as soon as the candied kumquats had been eaten. The fortune cookies lay haphazardly, seemingly forgotten, still in their cellophane pouches, but Jean had spied them, and in one last outburst of conviviality forced the cookies onto everyone. "Oh, we almost forgot the fortune cookies. Now we can't leave without checking our fortunes—I mean, God, the lottery may be just around the corner."

Chuck had wanted to reply, "Or the Grim Reaper, you stupid twit," but instead he tried to deflect what could be unforgettable anguish; picking up his cookie he threw it onto the table saying, "No one actually eats these fucking things do they?"

Everything stopped, and all looked at him with surprise. These were old acquaintances, if not close friends, and none of them used crude language unless after too many drinks the language was part of a dirty joke. But Jean was not to be thwarted. "Of course we do," she had proclaimed. "Or at least we have to read our fortunes. I mean, after all this is a Chinese restaurant! Right?"

No one replied, and all dutifully went about tearing open their cookie packets. Chuck took some solace in remembering that fortune cookies these days never carried fortunes but instead contained insipid forgettable aphorisms—as if Chinese restaurateurs were fearful of being sued should a prediction of harmful things actually came true. Maybe Johnny would get one that even a dying man could agree with. But when Johnny opened his cookie, there was nothing there at all—no fortune, not even "A fool and his money are soon parted"; no slip of paper... nothing. Johnny crumbled the cookie, breaking it into tiny crumbs and said, "Well, I got nothing at all. There's nothing there. I guess somebody's trying to tell me something."

As Johnny spoke, hopelessness had bowed his head, and this morning, as Chuck hurried to meet his wife at their suburban airport, the memory of Johnny Kellerman's desolation made him view hope for his friend as an absurd delusion. Chuck couldn't get it out of his mind.

The trip to the airport normally would take forty minutes, but Chuck was off to a late start for which much of the blame could be placed on that empty fortune cookie. He had gone to bed angry and depressed. Johnny's hopelessness somehow had become mingled with Chuck's unease about his wife Gail; and in a sentimental gesture he had moved to her now empty side of the bed and had tried to read, hoping written words would erase the misgivings he felt. But barely a paragraph into his book, the bulb in Gail's bedside lamp burned out and he had been left in the dark, unnerved. Sleep became fitful and slow in coming.

Gail had been away four weeks—gone to stay with her mother, who had broken a hip months before and who was convinced she could never walk again although medical wisdom had deemed her inability to walk as mostly her loss of will. Gail and her sister took turns caring for, cajoling, and, if truth be known, loathing their mother for her self-pity and lack of courage.

Chuck felt the distance between Gail and him had expanded far beyond a four-week absence and nine hundred actual miles. For some time before she left, he had been unable to please her in anything he did, and he had found slim consolation in the knowledge that no one else seemed to please her either. She was angry, cheerless, and his attempts to get her to talk about her discontent or to see a doctor unfailingly led to her becoming furious, and then mute or sullen for hours or even days.

Sex? None. She cringed at all physical contacts, be they affectionate or accidental touches; but given all of her outward display of misery directed at Chuck, she managed somehow to function in her job, brainstorming and writing copy for the public relations office of their regional electric company.

Early in their marriage Gail has decided they should not have children and, ironically and cruelly, her desire was fulfilled when fibrous uterine tumors and fear spawned by incipient cancer cells necessitated a complete hysterectomy at an early age. Now Chuck had begun to think his wife's discontent might grow from that history. He read medical journals and whole books on hysterectomy and menopause, and would stand for hours at the magazine racks in bookstores reading romanticized case histories in popular women's magazines of how postmenopausal women can put spark back into their marriages; he even read up on male sexual failures; but nothing seemed to apply.

Yet instead of giving into his frustrations and becoming angry, Chuck's love for Gail took on a paternal desperation, much as that of a parent who suspects a daughter of using drugs or of being anorexic. So it was that when the clock radio came on, his over-wrought consciousness was slow to push off the dead weight of delayed deep sleep, and he had drifted another 30 minutes, paralyzed by false contentment before he was able to get out of bed.

While showering, old accounts of past plane crashes with their litany of ironies paraded through his mind: people who were saved when they missed the flight because of flat tires on the way to the airport, or were bumped and rewarded with a free flight later on; or the businessman killed when he changed his flight plans at the last minute to save 35 minutes of air time; or the man saved because he was in the lavatory when the turbo prop blades slashed through the fuselage where he had been sitting seconds before.

These thoughts and Johnny Kellerman's face suddenly were replaced by Chuck's memory that Gail's bed lamp had burned out, and foreboding rushed over him, causing shivers even as hot water steamed down his body. As Chuck rushed to dress, he knew that above all else he would have to replace that bulb. Her plane was probably already in the air, but he could put in a new bulb before she landed; after all, he reasoned, most crashes occur at takeoff or landing, so maybe he had some slack.

Chuck dressed and dashed for the utility room cupboard, but he could find no light bulbs. He thought about driving to the 7-11, but there wasn't time for that if he were to come close to meeting Gail's plane on time. He would steal a bulb from another lamp.

In his haste to unscrew the bedside bulb, he broke it off at the base and dug a cut below his little finger, which, though not deep, began to bleed enough that he had to stop and wrap his hand with a wash cloth.

"Shit, shit, shit," he bellowed as he ran for his toolbox and pliers to screw out the bulb's base. He remembered to unplug the lamp before grabbing the base of the bulb with the pliers, but he was half tempted to leave the lamp plugged in and hope contact with the bulb would put him out of his misery. His undershirt began to stick to his back. Cursing in a slow cadence to calm himself, he managed to unscrew the bulb's base, but he still needed a replacement bulb.

The wattage of that bulb took on sudden importance—the replacement bulb should be as near a duplicate of the burned-out one as possible if he were to ward off disaster, but he didn't know what the old bulb had been and all that remained were tiny shards of glass and the mangled base. Checking the bulb in his own bed lamp, Chuck saw it was 75 watts and he took the chance that the two bulbs had been the same; as for the symbolism, surely his own bulb would carry more protective weight than a brand-new impersonal bulb?

He screwed his bulb into Gail's lamp, turned it on to be sure it worked, and ran for his car.

The tension created by his tardiness and the broken light bulb increased as he navigated through unusually heavy traffic on the parkway. Repeated glances at his watch made it clear that if Gail's plane were on time it would be landing in 10 minutes, and he was still at least 30 minutes away. But then he calmed, realizing that it was a clear day and, though he'd be late, her plane should have ideal landing conditions. So what if he'd be a half hour late—

her plane would land safely and that was the important thing. He even began to see humor in his silly premonition of doom brought on by the burned-out bed lamp. Still, Johnny and his empty fortune cookie remained at the edge of his consciousness, never leaving him wholly free of a sense of being fated for sorrow.

Traffic thinned, but Chuck's estimate of his own arrival time was off by ten minutes, and by the time he had parked in the short-term lot and sprinted into the terminal, Gail's plane had been on the ground for 45 minutes. He saw her immediately. She was holding her closed cell phone and leaning on the back of the last seat in the row of seats nearest the door. As he hurried to her, she looked up and said, "Oh, how nice of you to come. I gave up and just now left you a message. I hope I haven't interfered with your morning *New York Times*."

Chuck leaned down to kiss her, but she turned away and handed him the handle to her piece of rolling luggage.

"Hey, God, I'm sorry, but...." (What could he tell her? That Johnny Kellerman had gotten a fortune cookie with no fortune in it, and he couldn't sleep because of it; that her bed lamp had burned out; and that when he did finally get to sleep he slept so soundly that the clock radio didn't quite register with him, and then he broke the bulb in her lamp trying to change it?) "Well, it's a long story. You had to be there."

Gail looked at him without a hint of curiosity, but than shrugged and said, "Oh, I'm sure you have a lovely excuse. Everything that happens to you seems to be someone else's fault."

Both of her comments aimed to hurt, and they were common to her—the kind of comments she'd been making since shortly after he had been told that the department had denied him tenure. She had felt near panic, speculating on what could be financial disaster if he couldn't get a new job within the upcoming year of grace the university's union contract allowed; and when attempting to ease her anxiety he had said he would just have to spend every free second trying to finish his book while he still had time, her anxieties only increased.

The reason given him for his failure to achieve tenure was the standard one that he "hadn't progressed enough in his scholarly output," and Gail, he knew, was skeptical he ever would become a publishing scholar. After all, he had known that publishing a book was essential, yet he had spent the last two years doing what he called "research" but which looked to her like doing almost anything but getting down to the business of writing a book on *Sir Walter Scott, The Neglected Iconoclast*—"as if," she once had confided to her sister, "anybody anywhere really gives a shit about Sir Walter Scott."

On mornings when Chuck did not have an early class, he spent hours reading the *Times* from cover to cover, and once she had suggested that a more interesting book might be "a study of the compulsive *New York Times* reader as worthless-knowledge junkie." Chuck ignored her sarcasm but repeatedly told her that it was important for him to keep up with things and that it would all work out.

Pulling her bag along, Chuck tried to make conversation. "So, how did it go back there?"

"The same. Mom is hopeless."

"Have you had breakfast? Would you like to stop somewhere?"

"I had coffee on the plane."

On the ride home, at first he had said nothing since Gail immediately had leaned back against her headrest and closed her eyes. But once when she opened them and looked around to see where they were, he asked, "How about a bagel? You couldn't have gotten a decent bagel in Madison." She didn't answer, closed her eyes again, and remained that way until they pulled into their driveway.

When Gail had been gone they had talked on the phone once a week. The conversations had been short—mostly about mail that had come, some local gossip, and, of course, Chuck's inquiries about his mother-in-law. Usually Gail sounded tired or bored, but there had been none of the hostility that she carried with her this morning and which had been with her off and on for months.

Inside the house Gail scanned the tidy kitchen and said, "Well at least you've kept the place up."

"What do you mean, 'at least'?" asked Chuck. "Why 'at least'?"

Gail looked surprised but then with a wave of her hand, as if waving away an unwanted helping of food, said, "Who knows—a phrase, just an expression. Whatever." Then she sighed and added, "I'm going to lie down. I don't think I slept at all last night."

Carrying her bag, he followed after. "You either? I had a hard time getting to sleep and, as you know, a hard time waking up."

"Tell me about it," she replied, her sarcasm conveying the exact opposite. Fully clothed she stretched out on the unmade bed, shielding her closed eyes with a hand.

"Okay, I will," said Chuck, ignoring her tone. "Jean Bruder called and forced me to have dinner with them and the Kellermans at this new Chinese restaurant, the Hunan Hoo—can you believe that name? Johnny's in terrible shape, you know, so I couldn't turn her down, and I go there expecting a really depressing evening but knowing I should go just the same. Well anyway, Johnny was getting around pretty well with his walker, and the tension wasn't bad—in fact we had a pretty good time until the end of the meal when...." Without changing position or opening her eyes, Gail, in a firm, even voice interrupted, "Chuck, I'm wiped out. Could you just close the drapes and tell me this later?"

Chuck said nothing for a few seconds and then responded, "Yeah, sure. Sweet dreams." But he didn't move. He continued to stare, first at her and then at her bed lamp. He remained staring until Gail, sensing he was still there, removed her hand, opened her eyes, and asked, "What?"

"Nothing," said Chuck. He turned away, but when he reached the door he stopped and looked back. Gail returned her hand to cover her eyes. She looked childlike—vulnerable, yet protected, like Disney's Snow White in her glass-covered coffin.

His eyes moved to his bed lamp and its empty socket. A bulb taken from another lamp would not do for it. He must buy a new one. One that was very bright. Dangerously bright. One whose wattage exceeded that which for safety's sake was recommended by the lamp's manufacturer. Then he would remove the shade and everything would be bright. Everything would be clear. Everything.

THEORY OF RELATIVITY
*A Postmodern Eulogy for Paul Newman
with an Honest-To-God True Introduction*

Paul Newman stole my identity. It wasn't his fault, and he never knew it happened, but it did happen, and here's how. The first syllable of my last name is *New*, and there is a psycholinguistic quirk that often causes people, no matter what I say, to mentally make the second syllable *man*. Thus many people hearing my name—even when I spell it as I state it, "Paul Newlin, N-E-W-L-I-N"—restate it or write it as PAUL NEWMAN.

After Paul Newman became a film star by way of his role in *Cat on a Hot Tin Roof* in 1958, it seemed that half the people I met would mishear Newlin as Newman and respond in scoffing incredulity, "Paul Newman?" My response became an automatic, "Of course. You noticed my blue eyes." I'm five years younger than Newman, started balding at 26, and what hair I once had was blond gone to olive drab. I'm a couple inches taller than Newman, weigh 160 pounds, and have worn glasses since I was 5. We, however, do have in common that one great physical property mentioned above: blue eyes—mine less penetrating and a bit obscured by my glasses, but blue nonetheless. But are they Paul Newman's blue eyes? Hardly. No one could be fooled.

I never met Paul Newman, although I did see him in the

flesh about the time he became famous. I was driving in Beverly Hills and passed Newman and Joanne Woodward walking two large poodles along the upscale shops on Rodeo Drive. Poodles? Could that be right? Poodles and Paul Newman don't seem to match, but there they were. I drove right by. Of course then he hadn't yet stolen my identity, so even if I had had the guts to act out my yet-to-be-evolved recurring fantasy of going up to him and asking, "Aren't you Paul Newlin?," the joke then, as now, would have been lost on everyone but me.

Often when I was not face-to-face with someone, on the telephone, for instance, Paul Newlin also would become Paul Newman. In 1968 I was Vice Chair of the "McCarthy for President" campaign for the state of Delaware, and since Paul Newman nationally was a very visible Eugene McCarthy supporter, my title made me a shade sexier and more estimable than, say, being Vice Chair of a "Harold Stassen for President" campaign in Michigan's Upper Peninsula. One day I was making phone calls trying to raise money for McCarthy, and I began my spiel with, "Hello, this is Paul Newlin, and I'm calling on behalf of Delaware Democrats for McCarthy." The man on the other end squealed, "Oh, yeah? What are you doing here?" "I live here," I replied. After a long pause a deflated voice came back, "You're not *the* Paul Newman, then?" Over the phone my "notice the close physical resemblance" line wouldn't work, so, with more pique than someone trying to get a donation should use, I said in measured tones, "I'm not any kind of Paul Newman. The name is New**lin**—Paul New**lin**." The line went dead. McCarthy was stiffed.

As Paul Newman became more and more famous, Paul Newlin became Paul Newman more and more often; even my college literature students, who, with no apparent sense of irony or even awareness that they were calling me by a name not mine, sometimes addressed me as "Professor Newman."

So it went, year after year. I got kind of used to being captive by mistake and the butt of good-natured ridicule; after all, how bad is it to be compared, even obliquely, to someone who was described by the movie critic Aljean Harmetz as "a strikingly handsome figure of animal high spirits and blue-eyed candor whose magnetism was almost impossible to resist." I decided to capitalize on Paul Newman, the iconic sex symbol and thief of my identity, and I wrote a short-short story, "Theory of Relativity," in which Newman plays an absolutely essential role.

I sent the story out and it came back—several times—which is frustrating in its own right, but Newman and I were aging, and if my story ever was to see print, a vibrant, blue-eyed, irreplaceable Paul Newman still had to be with us.

Alas, Paul Newman died at age 83 on September 26, 2008, and "Theory of Relativity" remained unpublished. I grant you that one has to be crass and self-absorbed to a monumental degree to feel a sense of cosmic injustice that his short story could not be published because Newman died. I plead guilty—and conflicted; but though I was really and truly sorry Paul Newman had died, I still wanted a chance to get my story published and thought maybe I could replace Newman in my story with another living idolized male sex-symbol-for-all-seasons. I tried Newman's younger compatriot in movies, Robert Redford, who also is cherished in the hearts of women of a certain age; I tried Sean Connery, the immortal James Bond character (the same age as I and with even less hair); I tried the whole panoply of living movie studs and renegades. None worked. None came close. My "Theory of Relativity" had to have Paul Newman.

Some weeks after Paul Newman's death, and resigned to my story's remaining stillborn, I reasoned that even though my story died with him, at least no longer would people confuse our names. Then, when picking up some tickets at a local theater box office I identified myself as Paul Newlin. "Paul Newman?" exclaimed the clerk, her smile spreading the plumpness of her fiftyish face. "He's dead, you know," I scolded. "Not for me he isn't," she replied, her smile stopping just short of a sigh.

And then there's my local small-town bank that, as part of its friendly customer relations agenda, has for the past many years sent me a birthday card. This year it came neatly addressed by hand to "Paul Newman."

So, here's to you Paul Newman! Clearly you still live. And so, just perhaps, my story still lives too. Here it is:

THEORY OF RELATIVITY

Their wine glasses touched and chimed in an unspoken toast, and the whole restaurant shone with romantic opulence. Yet one mistakenly could have taken them for an aging father and his thirtyish daughter.

"So let me pose this hypothetical—isn't that what lawyers call them, hypotheticals?" he said. "Suppose a relatively attractive man of ...say 62, not yet Social Security eligible...proposed having sex with you. He's a decent person, reasonably well fixed, discreet, good-humored. Would you consider it?"

Without a pause she replied, "Not a chance," and after sipping her wine added, "Too old."

"Too old?" he asked. "Flatout too old?"

Smiling, self-assured, she nodded.

"So how old are you?" he asked.

She sighed and played with her hair. "You never ask a woman her age, you know. But, what the hell—I'm 38, a long two years from 40."

"So that would make the difference 24 years, right?" he asked.

She shrugged, still smiling.

"Well, would you go to bed with Paul Newman?" he asked..

She sensed he had asked that question before. "Of course," she answered. "Is the Pope a Catholic?"

He held his wine up to the light before answering. "I'm sure he is. But for what it's worth, I'm also sure that the Pope and Newman must be near the same age. I mean, God, Newman has to be...what... eighty?"

She shrugged the same shrug and raised her glass to the light, as if searching for what he saw there. "So Paul Newman is eighty? Some things are relative, some things aren't. Like with wine—there are some wines I'd never taste. This, by the way, is very good," she said.

"Thank you. It is nice, isn't it? But let me get this straight. Doesn't the cliché go, 'All things are relative,'"? he asked.

"Puleese," she said in exaggerated condescension. "I do not cite clichés as my guide to who I have sex with."

"Whom," he corrected.

"Whatever," she responded, feigning indifference.

"Fine. New scenario then. Suppose you are 41, having aged three years, like fine wine, and the man, now 65, proposes sex and, shall we say, a life of semisplendor. The age difference is the same, except the woman is in her forties. And by now Paul Newman is— God knows!"

"And the Pope?" she asked.

He laughed quietly and saluted her with his glass. "You have great style! You know that? But, as for the Pope, well, he's not really in the equation."

She showed no sign of wanting to laugh, yet her serious manner was one that grew from pleasure—the setting, the wine, the repartee "The Pope doesn't count, huh? That's too bad. And Newman is somewhere beyond eighty? And I'm no longer in my thirties—I'm over 40? And the guy still wants to go to bed with me? Well, then it's got possibilities."

He looked at her carefully, trying to read her eyes, but she gazed over his head, off across the room. "Now let me be sure I have this right. If the man is 62 and you're 38, there is no chance. But if he is 65 and you're 41, then there is a possibility? That's a difference of only three years down the road, and the difference in age remains the same. What changes what?"

She smiled. "I can't explain it. But that's the way it works—at least for me."

"Some things are more relative than others?" he asked.

"Exactly," she said still smiling.

He shook his head, then asked, "Will I ever figure out which ones?"

"Maybe in three years—maybe not," she answered. Then, recognizing that her voice was coldly matter-of-fact, she reached across the table, patted his hand and said, "By the way, I like your style, too," and then added, "Do you think we can order now? I'm famished."

Although a Californian by birth, Paul Newlin from infancy was reared in rural and small-town Ohio. As an adult, he has lived in Columbus, Seattle, Ulm Germany, Los Angeles, Delaware and Long Island, NY. He is the author of the novel *It Had to Be A Woman* (Stein and Day), and the co-editor of the two-volume American Literature anthology *A Nation of Letters* (Wiley-Blackwell). Twice honored as an outstanding teacher, and now retired from academia, he lives with his wife Sue overlooking Penobscot Bay on Deer Isle, Maine.